Jonathan's Wings

Penny Jo Shoup

E-BookTime LLC
Montgomery Alabama

Jonathan's Wings

Library of Congress Control Number: 2004116244

ISBN: 1-932701-58-3

Published November 2004
E-BookTime, LLC
6598 Pumpkin Road
Montgomery, AL 36108
www.e-booktime.com

Contents

CHAPTER 1

Seventeen-year old Jonathan laughed and shouted. He spun in a circle with his arms raised toward the blue cloudless sky. The grass was vividly green and the birds sang louder than ever. Gone was the pain. Gone was the sorrow that he carried like a lead blanket. For the first time in months he felt alive and bursting with energy. He tossed off his shoes and unbuttoned his shirt letting it flap in the wind. He wanted to rid himself of any encumbrances. His gaze carried to the hill above the school. The trees at its crest were calling him. "Jonathan, come to us. We will help you fly. You can learn from the birds!"

Jonathan ran uninhibited through the schoolyard, up the hill toward the towering trees. His raven-black hair flowed in the breeze. Rocks cut his bare feet as the grass gave way to soil, gravel, and protruding chunks of limestone as he ascended the steep incline. He looked toward the tallest tree. "Only a hundred yards to go!" he thought as he ran. His breath was coming in big gulps, but he felt he was tireless and could run forever.

"Jonathan! Hurry! Climb quickly!" The tree sang to him through her branches. Jonathan climbed. The branches whipped his face and cut at his long arms. His heart beat wildly in his chest, begging him to slow down, but he felt he could do anything and the sense of power and freedom drove him higher. He reached the highest branches and looked across the view below. He could see the entire city! Orange, pink and blue colors filled the sky.

"Fly, Jonathan, fly! Just like the birds. You'll be free!" the tree called.

Jonathan spread his arms, arched his back and flew. He was gliding! Gone were the pain and sorrows, the worthlessness and inadequacies. He was free and soaring like a bird above the trees! Down below was the school and parking lot with buses lined up, ready to take their passengers' home. Home-where was that? Maybe others had homes, but he was a bird now and his home was in the tall tree with her singing branches.

Early in the morning, Britany picked up her hot chocolate and hurried to the conference room with a clipboard under her arm. She slid her slender body into an empty seat at the table. She wore a white dress and her brown curls were tucked snuggly into a bun at the nape of her neck. Toys were scattered about the room and bright murals decorated the walls.

"Britany! It's great to see you again!" exclaimed Carol. "I was pleased to see your name on the schedule. It's been awhile since you've been here in pediatrics!" She had been sitting at the table writing on the assignment sheet when Britany entered.

"It's great to be back," replied Britany. "I haven't worked much since little Andrew was born, but when I have it's been in the nursery or maternity. You must really need help today!"

"How is Andrew?" Carol asked. Her dimples made a distinct appearance as she smiled. Her uniform covered with teddy bears seemed to accent how young she was.

"Growing! He will be a year old in November," Britany answered. Her attention was drawn to two nurses entering the room, talking together. They slid into empty chairs at the table.

"Britany! Welcome back!" Sandra exclaimed and patted Britany on the back.

"Thanks," said Britany. "It's good to be back. Actually, I've been working for several months, but the nursery has been so busy I've spent all my time there. You guys must have a full house today."

"Actually," Carol started to say, but Laura interrupted with, "Britany, I do declare, no one would know you had a baby from looking at you. How did you get back in shape so fast?"

"Laura!" exclaimed Britany. "You're too flattering, but thanks for the compliment."

Britany looked around her. Each of the three nurses wore the same pattern of teddy bears as Carol. The only difference was that Sandra wore red uniform slacks and Laura had white.

"Actually," said Carol loudly. Everyone looked up, and she continued, "I was trying to say that we have a very special patient and that is why you are here."

Carol looked directly at Britany and Britany was very curious for her to continue.

"We have a young boy who tried to commit suicide, yesterday after school. When I saw your name I requested for you to come. You have a teenager and I was hoping you might be able to relate. The rest of us feel a little inexperienced in this area. We normally don't have too many teenagers."

Britany felt a twinge of anxiety. She wasn't sure how Carol thought she could possibly be qualified to handle a suicide attempt. She looked at the other nurses around her. None of them were married or had children yet. Britany realized she was the senior in the group by quite a few years. Carol must have read her thoughts from the look on her face.

"Britany, I know it sounds intense, but he needs one-on-one, and there are a lot of other children that need our attention. I wish we had more experience in this area, but we don't. Will you do it? We are kind of in a bind."

"Sure," answered Britany. She half listened as Carol went through the list of patients and explained their status. She was frightened to think of what she might find when she went to care for her patient.

"Room 302," Britany heard Carol say, and she was suddenly very attentive.

"Seventeen-year-old male, patient of Dr. Miller, admitted for multiple abrasions, fractured radius in left arm, and fractured femur in left leg. He was unconscious for twelve hours and is currently drifting in and out of consciousness. He is in traction until the muscle relaxes enough to allow the bone to be positioned and casted." Britany cringed. It had been a long time since she had taken care of a patient in traction.

"He was transferred to our unit at six this morning. He had been in the emergency room since he was admitted yesterday at two-thirty. The story so far is that several students reported seeing him run up the hill above the school. Then they saw him climb a tree and jump from the top."

"He's new to the school. No one knows who he is, and so far we have found no relatives. His driver's license says he is Jonathan Quarterman from Knoxville, Tennessee. But that doesn't explain what he is doing here. The school has a local address on him, but when the police went to the address listed no one knew who he was. We have a psyche consult out. Dr. Steward will be coming in this morning to go over the case. Jonathan hasn't been coherent enough to know his name or where he is, let alone to answer questions."

Britany couldn't write fast enough to keep up with the information that Carol was giving her.

"Jonathan has a ten-centimeter laceration above his left ear that is sutured. He needs neuro checks every half-hour until he regains full consciousness." Carol looked at Britany as she finished. Britany was writing furiously. She looked up at Carol with a distressed look on her face.

"How can you do this to me?" she asked.

Carol smiled. "You can do this, Britany. Don't underestimate yourself."

"Well, at least I don't have to worry about him making another suicide attempt immediately," Britany moaned. "It doesn't sound like he can move enough to try anything."

Laura patted Britany on the back. "We'll watch out for you," she assured her. Britany looked at Laura. She didn't look much older than her own daughter Crystal, who was nineteen and in her second year of college. Laura's long, dark hair was pulled back and caught in a barrette. Tiny ringlets framed her face and accented her blue eyes. To Britany it seemed strange having someone so young offer to help her. She seemed more in the position to be helping Laura, but she thought the offer was admirable.

Britany smiled. "Thanks, Laura," she laughed, "but you could help me out a whole lot more by taking my assignment."

"No, thanks," said Laura, shaking her head. "You heard what Carol gave me. I'm going to have my hands full!"

Britany collected her notes and walked to the end of the hall where room 302 was located. She knocked softly and entered. A still figure lay in the bed, covered with a thin sheet. Britany walked over to the bed and looked down at the pale face. Her heart went out to the boy who lay sleeping. The left side of his head, above his ear, was shaved, and she could see quite a few stitches. The rest of his black hair was covered in dried blood. Apparently he had needed so much attention that no one had been able to wash his hair. She looked down at the clipboard hanging beside his bed. His last neuro check had been at seven, and she noted on her watch that it would soon be time for another one. A nurse looked in through the open door. She motioned for Britany to come into the hall when Britany looked up.

"Are you new here?" the nurse asked.

"I've been on maternity leave, and I float. I mostly cover the nursery."

"Well, I thought you looked familiar," the nurse smiled, "but I wasn't sure. My name is Andrea and I just received Jonathan from the emergency room." Andrea looked at her notes and gave Britany the same information that Carol had just given her. Britany smiled and thanked her.

Britany returned to the room and obtained Jonathan's pulse, blood pressure and other vital information. He didn't stir as she held his wrist and moved his arm. She noted the observation on his chart. He didn't even flinch as she shined a flashlight in his eyes, but his pupils were equal and reactive. His eyes were dark and appeared almost black as she held open each eyelid. He flinched as she checked for a pain reflex. The bottom of his feet were cut and scratched. Britany checked the cast on his left arm. His arms were long, and although he didn't seem very large Britany determined that he must be fairly tall. She checked his fingers for circulation and they were fine. His hand looked rough, as if he had been used to working hard outside, although his fingers were long and slender like those of a pianist or a surgeon. When Britany had finished she sat quietly in a chair beside his bed.

The chart stated that he had gained consciousness twice during the night and that he was expected to fully awaken soon. He was still drowsy from the medication they had given him for pain when they put the pins in for traction.

"What in the world could have caused this teenage boy to try to commit suicide?" She thought as she watched him sleep peacefully. His face was long and slender like his body, with a strong nose and defined jaw. "His mother must be terribly worried about him. What kind of home does he have? Was it because his home life was bad, or was it simply due to a break-up with a girlfriend?

Britany rose and stood beside his bed. She reached down and clasped his free hand into both of hers. He didn't stir.

"Dear Jesus," she prayed, "I don't know what caused the pain in this child's life, but I know who can fix it. Please be with him and comfort him. Thank You for sparing his life. I pray that he would come to know You, and let You fill the emptiness inside. I pray that You would heal his body but most of all, his heart. I thank You for this opportunity to care for him, and I pray that You would guide me so that Jonathan might be able to see You through me. Amen," Britany finished and gently laid his hand back on the bed.

She looked at the ropes and pulleys attached to his leg and suspended at the foot of the bed. He had a metal pin protruding from each side of his left leg, just above his knee. She wanted to bathe him and change the sheets afterward, but she wasn't ready to deal with the traction yet. Well, at least I could bathe him and wash his hair. Later I could get someone from orthopedics to help me with the rest, she thought.

Britany gathered sheets and towels, drew warm water in a basin, and started to work. She remembered seeing a tray in the linen closet on another floor that was designed to wash a patient's hair while he was in bed. She didn't see one in the closet. She looked into the hall to see Carol standing several rooms away.

"Carol," Britany called as she saw Carol at the med. cart. "Could you keep an eye on Jonathan while I run down to the second floor and get something?"

"Sure," said Carol waving a med. cup at her. Carol's foot was propped on the side of the cart about a foot from the floor as she measured out medicine. "I don't really think he is going anywhere!"

"No! I don't think so. Thanks!"

Britany deposited the linens in the room and then hurried to the second floor, returning triumphantly with her tray.

It was quite a task working around the ropes and pulleys. Britany was careful and worked slow and steady, so she wouldn't bump or jar anything. She smiled as she washed Jonathan's face. He had the appearance of both a man and a boy at the same time. A few lingering traces of acne remained on his face, and she noted that he would need a shave shortly, but not so much that it wouldn't wait until the next day. His hair was going to be enough of a challenge for one day!

Britany drew clean water and prepared to wash his hair. She lifted his head carefully and placed the tray under it. She turned his face toward her so the sutures were facing the top. She washed the blood out of his heavy black eyebrows and removed traces of dried blood from his cheeks. She took a clean warm rag and continued tenderly to wash his face. His eyelids fluttered slightly.

"Jonathan, I am your nurse, Britany, and I am going to wash your hair," Britany said as she worked.

Jonathan felt caring hands brush his cheek and gently lift his head. He wanted to open his eyes and see who or what this person was. They wouldn't cooperate, so he relaxed into the mesmerizing spell of the soothing voice.

"I'm going to pour water on your hair, so don't be alarmed." Britany poured with one hand and moved his hair with the other. A river of reddish-brown flowed from his hair. "This is going to take a while, so please be patient. I need to get some more water."

Britany returned and started again. This time enough blood and dirt washed out that she could use the shampoo.

"Jonathan, don't be alarmed when you look into the mirror. You had a cut on the side of your head, and the doctor had to shave some of your hair to be able to get to it. You have very nice long hair, and if you want to keep it that way you could probably just comb it over the shaved part so it doesn't show too much." Britany continued talking, not sure whether Jonathan might be able to hear what she said.

The warm water pouring over his head felt good, and Jonathan once again tried to look out of his dark shell. This time he managed to open his eyes slightly and look into a beautiful face. His first impression had been right. He was looking at an angel. She even wore white! He closed his eyes and absorbed the tenderness. He hadn't felt warmth like this since he was a little child in his mother's arms. Even those times had been sparse, and the memory very dim. He smiled slightly.

Britany saw Jonathan's eyelids open, and she smiled at his large dark eyes. He closed them again and then she noticed a trace of a smile cross his lips. So faint was it that it could have been imagined. Britany quietly sang a song that she often sang to Andrew when she rocked him to sleep. He looked very peaceful and content, but didn't open his eyes again.

Britany finished and realized it was already time to do his neuro checks again. This time he stirred as she called his name and opened his eyes.

"Hi! I'm Britany," she repeated.

"Are you an angel?" he asked. He felt puzzled. If she was an angel why was he feeling pain? He groaned and tried to move. Britany quickly reached out and grabbed his shoulders.

"Easy Jonathan. You need to wake up more before you try to move. You could hurt yourself. Besides the stitches in your head, your left arm is in a cast, and your left leg is in traction."

"I don't understand. If you're an angel, where am I?" he asked in confusion.

"Jonathan, I am not an angel," Britany said firmly. "I am a nurse, and you are in the hospital."

"Was I in a wreck or something?" he asked.

"You don't remember?"

He started to shake his head no and then was stopped short by searing pain. He groaned and reached for his head with his free hand. Britany caught it by the wrist before he grabbed at the spot with the stitches.

"Jonathan, you are going to hurt yourself some more. Would you please just not move for a while and talk to me so you can realize what has happened," Britany commanded.

He sighed and looked up at her. She had a frustrated look. He relaxed and didn't try to move again, although the pain in his head was terrible. He could tell now that she was a nurse and not an angel, but she was still beautiful. He couldn't remember what had caused him to be in such bad shape.

"What happened to me?" he asked.

"You fell out of a tree," Britany said simply. He looked so young to be going through this, yet he had done it to himself. Her heart ached for him.

His dark eyes looked angry. "What in the world was I doing in a tree?" he asked demandingly.

"Jonathan, I don't know. You don't remember?" Britany asked calmly.

"No, that is so stupid! I hurt!" he moaned.

Britany reached up and pushed a button near his IV tubing. "Push this when the pain gets stronger. It won't take it away, but at least it will help some. It is automatically programmed so that however frequently you push the button, it won't overdose." She showed him how it worked.

Britany finished his bath. Jonathan seemed to relax as the pain medicine started to work.

CHAPTER 2

Jonathan drifted back to sleep, and Britany worked on cleaning the room from his bath. Jonathan could hear her working, but he kept his eyes closed. He needed to think. He vaguely remembered a tree, but nothing was clear. If the authorities realized his mother was dead they would put him in a facility. Or worse yet, send him back to his grandfather. His grandfather hated him, and he had made that very clear. That was why he and his mother had left Knoxville. Social Services had wanted to take him away from her. He had convinced his mother they needed to leave. What the authorities didn't realize was that he had been taking care of his mother since he was ten or eleven. She had been an alcoholic for as long as he could remember. She had needed him, and he couldn't leave her.

Things had never been good for them, but in recent years she had gotten hooked on drugs and hadn't been able to care for herself. She died shortly after they moved from Knoxville. He found her in the bedroom when he returned from work one Tuesday evening. It looked as if she had fallen asleep. He thought it was an overdose, but he had left as soon as he called 911. He didn't want anyone to find him. He had been doing yard work for people to support himself and was basically homeless, but that wasn't much different than before. Actually it was easier, because he didn't have his mother to care for. It was lonelier now though. How in the world am I going to hide the fact that I am homeless now that I am in the hospital? He drifted off to sleep and was awakened by a strange voice.

"Jonathan," Dr. Steward called. Jonathan opened his eyes and looked at the gentleman calling his name. He was a mild-looking man in his mid-forties, with graying hair at the temples. He stood taller than Britany, who stood at the bedside. There was something comforting about her presence, but there was nothing comforting about the man's! Jonathan panicked. They are going to find out who I am unless I do something quick. The trouble is I can't move!

Britany saw the panic in his eyes and moved closer. "It's all right Jonathan." She reached for his hand. "This is Dr. Steward. He wants to help you and try to find your parents! They must be worried sick about you!" She tried to comfort him, but she noticed he stiffened up as she spoke. She looked at the doctor. He took a step forward and tried.

"Jonathan, do you remember why you were in the tree?"

Jonathan looked at him in a daze. The tree! The tree with the singing branches, thought Jonathan. If I tell them that they will think I am crazy. He asked if I remember. That's it! I'll pretend I don't remember anything.

"No, sir. I don't remember a tree," he lied.

"Do you know where you are, Jonathan?" Dr. Steward asked.

"Yes, sir," he answered. "I am in the hospital. Britany told me that."

"Good!" Dr. Steward smiled. "I'm glad to see you've met Britany."

"Yes, sir. She's my angel!" said Jonathan with a steady face. Britany cringed and Dr. Steward looked at her with a startled look.

"Did Britany tell you she is an angel?" he asked.

"No, sir. She told me she was my nurse, but I know she is my angel."

"Well, Jonathan, can you tell me where you live?" Dr. Steward asked.

"I don't remember. I didn't even remember my name, but Britany kept saying Jonathan, so I figured it must be my name," Jonathan looked at Dr. Steward, who seemed to believe his story.

"Don't be alarmed. There may still be some swelling from the bump on the head you got when you fell. I'm sure your memory will start to return. We will continue to try and locate your mother and father. You rest some more now, and I will be back tomorrow," Dr. Steward said and turned to leave.

Britany had been watching Jonathan while he talked, and something seemed wrong. She noticed the panicked look he had and then the change in attitude as he talked with the doctor. Something was up. She wasn't convinced he couldn't remember anything. She followed the doctor into the hall. Dr. Stewart stood a foot taller than she, and she had to look up to talk to him.

"Well, I guess this delays our talking. Until he starts to remember why he was in the tree it will be hard to counsel him," Dr. Steward said opening Jonathan's chart. "I don't think we have an immediate concern that he will attempt suicide again. It would be hard with his physical condition."

"Have you found out anything this morning?" Britany asked. She wasn't ready to tell the doctor her suspicions. She wanted to find out more.

"Well, the boys we questioned yesterday said he just left the school, climbed the tree and jumped. We talked to a girl this morning, which said she saw him running and jumping crazily in the schoolyard before he took off for the woods. Then she said he ran wildly, like something was after him. It sounds rather strange. It seems the boys would have noticed behavior like that. You keep an eye on him, and if he remembers more, call me." Dr. Steward turned and left. Britany walked back into the room.

Jonathan's eyes were closed again. She wanted to question him, but instead she sat on the chair beside his bed. He appeared to be resting quietly. Carol came to the door and motioned for Britany to come.

Carol spoke quietly so not to disturb him. "I am going on to break. Do you need to leave for a while?"

"No," said Britany. "I am fine. I can take a breather now and just sit for a few minutes."

"Do you need anything from the cafeteria?"

"Yes," said Britany, reaching into the pocket of her scrub dress. "Bring back an apple. No, make it some grape juice. Apples are noisy. Here is some money," said Britany as she handed Carol some change.

"Someone from orthopedics will be coming this morning to check on the traction. They can help you change the bed."

"That would be most helpful. Those pulleys scare me," Britany said. "I'm afraid it is going to be a very painful ordeal for Jonathan." She cringed at the thought.

"The next several days will be the worst. Hang in there. I really appreciate your help." Carol patted Britany's shoulder and smiled her cheerful smile. "Be back in a half-hour," she called as she went down the hall.

Britany smiled and returned to the room. Shortly someone knocked at the door. A tall young man wearing white tennis shoes and teal scrubs energetically entered the room. He went straight to the traction and examined it.

"Hi!" said Britany, extending her hand. "I'm Britany.""Sorry." He shook her hand. "I'm Tony from orthopedics. I forgot my manners. Who's this young man?" he asked brightly, looking at Jonathan, who had opened his eyes when Britany spoke.

"I'm Jonathan, or so they tell me," Jonathan said in a subdued voice. He didn't trust the man who was standing at the foot of his bed. He didn't trust anyone, except maybe Britany. He hadn't decided whether to trust her or not.

"Jonathan, I am afraid I have some bad news," said Tony, walking around to the side of the bed where he could speak to Jonathan more easily. "We are going to have to move you. I am going to help Britany make your bed. It's going to be painful, and I apologize, but it needs to be done." He turned to Britany and said, "The more people you can get the better.

Britany turned and quickly left to find help. The only nurses left on the floor were Sandra and Laura. She found them in different patient rooms and asked for their assistance.

The three of them entered the room and took positions at the bedside. Britany looked beside her at the other two nurses. They were both small and probably weighed around a hundred pounds. Normally Britany was one of the smaller ones, but this time she was the larger one. Tony must have noticed also because he instructed her to stand in the middle.

He dictated orders confidently as he said, "I am going to handle Jonathan's leg and the weights. Britany you lift under his shoulders and hips." He pointed to Laura; "You work on replacing the sheets Laura. You help support across from Britany and help Laura," he said nodding toward Sandra. "Jonathan, you are going to have to help us. With your good arm grab the trapeze above your head and lift." Tony pointed to the bar that hung above Jonathan's head. From the look on Jonathan's face he apparently hadn't seen it before. "Now, he doesn't look heavy, but he is tall, and so it may be a bit awkward. Is everyone ready?" They nodded their heads in reply. Britany's heart raced. She knew it was going to be very painful for Jonathan, and she was worried something would go wrong. "OK, one...two...three...lift!"

Britany lifted, and his body moved easily. Jonathan grimaced in pain, but he didn't scream. She held tightly, one arm under his shoulders and one arm under his hips. Laura quickly stripped the sheets and expertly started to replace them with new ones. Britany felt Jonathan beginning to shake. Sweat formed on his brow, and his face twisted in pain. She could see that his teeth were clenched.

"Next time I'll try to find a bullet for you to bite," she said jokingly.

"Please hurry," Jonathan groaned.

"Laura is almost finished," assured Britany. She could feel her arms start to shake also. He wasn't very heavy, and she only had part of his weight, but after a while he was getting hard to hold.

"Done!" said Laura briskly. She was out of breath from working so fast and furious.

"Easy, just lower him slowly, together now," instructed Tony.

Jonathan was pale, and Britany was afraid he might pass out. She grabbed a clean washcloth from the bedside and gently wiped his soaked brow. She lifted his head and offered him a sip of water. He took a drink and sank back into the pillow with his eyes closed.

"It will be easier tomorrow," said Tony grasping, Britany's forearm and looking at her.

"I won't be here tomorrow," said Britany weakly.

Jonathan's eyes flew open. "Britany, you have to come back!" he pleaded.

Britany was shocked. "I...I can try," she stammered.

Jonathan's brown eyes closed again and he whispered, "You have to, you're my angel."

"You heard him," said Tony. "See you tomorrow, Angel!" He smiled and turned to walk out the door with a brisk spring to his step.

Laura giggled and turned to follow. Sandra bent down and grabbed an armload of discarded sheets.

"I'll get that," Britany said.

"Don't be silly. I'm going past the linen bin on the way out. I've got it," she said. She turned, and the linens caught on one on the ropes to the traction apparatus. The weights jerked and swayed.

"Owe!" Jonathan shrieked, and a string of profanity flew from his mouth.

Britany quickly stopped the weight from swinging and steadied Jonathan's leg.

"How could you be so stupid!" he yelled and raised himself up by grasping the trapeze bar, glaring at Sandra. He muttered another curse under his breath.

"I am so sorry. It was an accident. I should have been more careful," Sandra said. Her face looked close to tears.

"Its' all right," whispered Britany. "I'll calm him down. Thanks for your help." She put her arm around Sandra's shoulders and gave her a squeeze. Sandra took the laundry and left.

Britany quickly went to the head of the bed and pushed the button for the pain medication. She grabbed under Jonathan's shoulders and helped lower him to the bed. She pushed his shiny black hair back from his forehead. "Rest now, Jonathan. We will leave you alone for a while."

"Britany, don't leave. It hurts so bad. I can't stand it! Please make the pain go away!"

She held his hand and continued to smooth his hair.

"I wish I could," she sighed.

Tears welled up in his eyes, and he looked directly at her. "I didn't jump, Britany. I didn't, honest. The tree told me to fly, and I did. I was flying, and it was so beautiful!" He grasped her hand tightly. "Then I woke up in here, and I don't know what happened. Please say you believe me."

"Jonathan, I believe you," she whispered. "Rest now. The pain will get better."

"Promise me you won't tell anyone about the tree," he implored, his dark eyes pleading.

Britany's heart filled with compassion as she looked at his eyes. They seemed to reach deep into her soul.

"I won't," she said soothingly. "Rest now." Very softly she started singing the song she had sung earlier, and he started to relax. Soon his grasp relaxed on her hand, and his hand started to slip. She gently laid it on the bed and sang for a little longer. Then she resumed her seat on the chair. She took a deep breath and realized she was shaking. "What an ordeal!" she thought. "Lord this child has some serious needs and I'm not sure what to do. Please help me with this situation!"

Britany heard the food trays outside the door and went to see if Jonathan had a tray. Fortunately Carol had thought to order one, because Britany had forgotten. She took the tray and placed it on the bedside stand. Jonathan looked up as she did.

"Would you like to try and eat?" she asked.

He nodded his head, and Britany arranged the stand so she could reach the food and him more easily.

"In several days you will get this figured out, but for now I am going to help you," she said, placing a towel under his chin and across his chest. "Do you like mashed potatoes? They might be an easy thing to start with."

He nodded his head again. He eagerly ate, and his appetite surprised Britany. "We can send down for a shake in a little while if you would like," said Britany as he finished the last of his meal and she replaced the lid to the plate.

He smiled a large, full smile, and his eyes were warm. It was pleasing to see him smile, and Britany felt as if he had just given her a precious gift.

She smiled back. "I like your smile. I hope to see more of it. Do you want a chocolate, strawberry or vanilla shake?"

"Chocolate," he replied.

"That's my favorite, too. I need to get your vital signs again, and then I will go and order it."

"Britany," called Laura from the hall. "I am going to relieve you for lunch," she said as she entered the room with a springy step.

"Are you sure your patients will be all right?" Britany asked.

"I discharged several, the baby is sleeping, and Mary's mother is with her. They will be fine. Carol is watching them. They haven't called with any new admissions yet, so hurry while you have the chance!" she said cheerfully.

"Hi, Jonathan. We met earlier, but I hope to not put you in so much pain this time," Laura said, and went to stand beside the bed.

"Me, too," he replied.

Britany showed Laura the flow sheet containing his information. "I'll see you both shortly. Good-bye," said Britany and turned to leave. Jonathan nodded.

"Have a nice lunch," Laura called after her.

Britany went into the office. She needed to call Michael and tell him she wanted to work the next day. She also needed to check with the sitter and see if she could watch the kids. She pictured Andrew, and his chubby little smile. She hated to leave him two days in a row, but she really did feel she needed to help

Jonathan. Something about him and his situation seemed to call to her.

"Hi, Michael," Britany said into the telephone. "I'm working in pediatrics today, and I would like to work again tomorrow." She explained the situation as much as she could.

"Britany, I have an idea. The office is slow today, and I'll just take the day off tomorrow. I have some time, and it will be fun to spend the day with the kids!" Michael said.

"Oh, Michael, that would be great!" she said.

Britany was leaving the office when Carol saw her.

"Britany," she said as she came bustling up to her, "we are really in a bind!"

Britany put her hand on Carol's shoulder. "Don't worry, Carol," she said smiling. "I just made arrangements so I can work tomorrow."

"That's wonderful, but I already planned on that. Laura told me Tony and Jonathan already talked you into that. I need help tonight. Could you work over for four hours?"

"What!" Britany groaned. "Carol, how could you?"

"I'm sorry, Britany. We are getting four admissions, and Jonathan needs one-on-one. I wouldn't ask if we didn't need you!" Carol explained.

"OK, if the sitter can watch the children until Michael gets home," said Britany hesitantly.

Carol gave her a hug. "You're a lifesaver, Britany. Tell Michael I said thanks!"

Britany called Michael and the sitter, and then she went to get a quick lunch.

Britany was returning from lunch when Dr. Steward met her in the hall.

"Britany! I need to talk to you," he said urgently.

"What's up?" she asked puzzled.

"Come with me to the conference room," he said, starting in that direction.

"The conference room is also the playroom, remember? We had better talk in the office."

She led the way to the office, and they both took a seat.

"I went to the school and did some checking into the records. Jonathan's mother enrolled him into school in May. They had just moved from Knoxville, where he had finished his junior year of school. I did some further searching into hospital records and found that his mother, Bonnie Quartman, died several days after enrolling him in school. It was a drug overdose, but didn't look like suicide. She apparently had been on drugs for a long time. Jonathan just kind of fell through the cracks after she died. Apparently he has been living on his own, probably in the park or something since May."

"Wow," Britany replied. She sat for a minute to let the information sink in. "So what now?"

"I'm trying to find some relatives to take him in, but I doubt he has any, or someone would have already been looking for him. He will be in the hospital for several weeks, but when he leaves he won't be able to stay by himself, not to mention the fact that he is just seventeen. We will have to place him in a home or foster care. There will be a tutor coming from the school as soon as he feels well enough to do his work."

"Have you talked to him yet?" asked Britany.

"No, I was going to his room when I saw you in the hall," said Dr. Steward. "I don't know that I want to talk to him about this until his memory starts to return. I really don't want to tell him his mother has died when he doesn't remember who she is."

"That's probably a good idea to wait," said Britany as she got up from the chair and went to the door. She started to room 302 and then remembered to order the chocolate shake.

Jonathan was sleeping when she entered, and Laura smiled. "He's doing well. I'll get back to my patients now."

"Yes, Carol said you were getting four admissions."

"Yes, she came in and gave me report on one of them already. They are supposed to be coming up."

Jonathan was comforted to hear Britany's voice again. It seemed she was caring for him the way he had always felt a mother should, but his own mother had been too burdened down with problems to give him that nurturing. He wished his body would stop hurting. It seemed as if his entire body was one huge pain, and he wished it would go away.

"Britany, it hurts," he groaned. She came close and pushed the button again. "Jonathan, don't wait so long to push the button. It doesn't look as if you've even used it," she said. She took his hand in one of hers and smoothed his hair with the other.

He clung tightly to her hand, and she sang to him again until he relaxed into a quiet sleep.

Jonathan slept fitfully after Britany left for the evening. Suddenly the hospital seemed to him like an evil, scary place. What will they do with me when they find out I have no parents? He didn't want to go to a boy's home. He didn't want foster parents that he didn't know. Besides, who would ever want a seventeen-year-old boy! He wouldn't be able to work to earn money to care for himself until his leg healed. The world seemed dark and empty. It did before his fall, too, but then he had had hard work to keep his mind off the loneliness.

Britany was physically and mentally exhausted when she went home from work that night. Michael had gotten the children ready for bed, and they all sat together on the couch to talk. Amy, eight, told Britany every detail that had happened that day. Her dark curls bounced as she talked. Ben, eleven, was more reserved, but still managed to find time to tell his adventures. They were both very curious to hear about Jonathan and asked if it was painful for him. Britany cuddled Andrew on her lap as they talked and caressed his downy hair with her cheek. Michael put his arm around both of them, and Britany soon found her eyelids getting very heavy.

"OK, guys, let's say prayers, give Mom kisses, and then off to bed."

"Do you want something to eat, Britany?" Michael asked when the children were asleep.

"What did you have? I didn't have a chance to plan ahead," said Britany.

"I stopped and brought home hamburgers. I hope you don't mind," he said.

Britany laughed, "No, that's fine. We'll eat better tomorrow. I'm not hungry, but thank you." She paused for a while and then said, "The children start back to school in two weeks. I hate to see them go. I really enjoyed having them home this summer."

"At least they didn't start this week like the public school. They will probably be glad to see their friends again," said Michael.

"Yeah, I suppose so," she answered. She didn't think Michael understood how she felt about the children and school. She wasn't just making conversation. She would miss them very much. "It looks like Andrew is finished nursing. You need to go to bed. I'll put him in his bed and be right in," said Michael, gathering the sleeping infant in his arms.

CHAPTER 3

Crystal rushed through the crowded sidewalks and across the congested streets of the campus, glancing again and again at her watch. The air was still warm, and she felt her skin getting sticky. She was glad that her blonde hair was pulled back, or it would be full of tangles. She had to start getting up a little sooner. She was definitely late for class, and it wasn't the first time. It was not a very good start to the second week of classes. She reached the building and pulled open the heavy door. A surge of cool air greeted her. It felt wonderful. She rearranged her books and smoothed her hair and blouse. Then she walked down the quiet hall to room 106. The hall smelled of formaldehyde. She had loved biology her first year of college, but this year nothing seemed to interest her. The professor was just starting his lecture, and she sighed in relief. The girl she had slid next to when she sat down smiled. Crystal smiled back.

"You have got to start getting up sooner," Cortney whispered.

Crystal rolled her gray eyes. "I know," she sighed. The professor looked at her, and Crystal suddenly became very alert.

The lecture was soon over, and Cortney walked beside Crystal into the hall. "Crystal, you were never late last year," Cortney said. "What is happening?" she asked with concern.

"I wish I knew," said Crystal. She pushed out through the heavy door and went to sit under a spreading tree on the lush grass.

Cortney sat beside her. Her light red hair was as long as Crystal's and reached to the middle of her back. The warm air was soft on their skin, and the songs of birds filled the air.

"This is so nice," said Crystal, looking up into the top of the tree. She could see patches of blue sky through the green leaves. She leaned back against the tree. "I don't think I was ready for classes to start. I just can't seem to get back into the groove of school. My mom would be very upset if she knew I had been late to three classes already and it's only starting the second week of school."

Cortney opened her math book and laid it on the grass while she reached into her backpack for a notebook and pencil. "You cut it close, but you really didn't miss anything so I don't think you can count this class," said Cortney as she opened her book.

"I wasn't," said Crystal bluntly. Cortney looked at her in surprise. She made a rueful smile.

"Hi, girls."

Crystal was startled to see a boy standing at her feet. The brightness of the sky made it hard to see him, and she sat up. He was very cute, and she smiled. Cortney turned her head and looked over her shoulder to see where the voice had come from.

"It looks like you have a little break between classes," he said. "Do you mind if I share your tree?"

"That would be fine," said Crystal as she smiled up at him. He was very tall and looked as though he could be a member of the football team. His muscles bulged as he lowered himself to the ground.

"I'm Eric," he said, extending his hand. "Eric Wright."

Crystal shook his hand and said, "I'm Crystal Becker, and this is Cortney Pullum," as she pointed toward Cortney. This one time she wished Cortney wasn't so cute. The sun filtering through the trees seemed to bring out the red highlights in her hair, and her shorts and shirt were very flattering to her perfect figure. Crystal didn't realize that the sun was also very stunning on her blonde curls and her long bronze legs.

"So you are both in biology," commented Eric.

Crystal flipped her head slightly. "Yeah, it seemed so exciting last year, but I just can't seem to get into it this year. None of my classes seems too great, but if I want to graduate I need to get through."

"I know what you mean," said Eric. "If it weren't for football I don't know what I would do. One more year, and then I hope to get a contract from the pros. I could have possibly this year, but I only have this last year to finish, and I didn't want to give that up." He reached down and pulled a blade of grass and rolled it between his fingers. He wore a white shirt that had red lettering and a buckeye, the insignia for Ohio State.

He looked up at Crystal and grinned. "This group I belong to is having a party tonight. Would you like to come and be my guest?" he asked.

Crystal shrugged and looked at Cortney. Cortney gave her a warning look.

"You are both invited," Eric said quickly. "There will be a lot of people there. It is mainly for people on campus to get to know each other. It's a Youth for Christ party. We always have a fun time. It won't be late, either. I have an early curfew because of football. The coach is very strict."

"Come on, Cortney," coaxed Crystal. "It would be fun. We didn't do hardly anything fun last year. We spent our entire time studying."

Cortney looked up from her math problem. "I thought that was why we are in college, to study and learn." She waved her hand with the pencil in it for emphasis. "I'm sorry, but I don't think it is a very good idea."

Crystal looked at Eric. Cortney was right, but Eric was very cute. She thought about how it would be nice to go, but listened to Cortney.

"I guess she's right. I really do have work to get done," said Crystal with a disappointed frown on her face.

Eric sat up and grabbed his book. "I have to be getting to class. Why don't you take some time and see if you can get your work caught up? The party is in that house across the yard," he said pointing at an old Victorian-style yellow house with white trim. "If you change your mind feel free to come. Just tell them you are with Eric." He smiled and waved as he left.

Crystal watched as he walked away. He certainly did look like a football player. She was disappointed she had said no. She was eager to see him again and get to know him. She sighed and opened her book.

"Is it that bad?" asked Cortney.

"Yes, it is. I know I should be into school more, but it just doesn't seem interesting this semester. The party's more appealing," said Crystal.

"But we don't know anything about him," said Cortney. "I'm sure you will get to see him again around campus. He seemed just a little too nice."

"It's a Christian party," moaned Crystal.

"But you are already behind, and I have a lot to do tonight. Work hard, and we'll see what happens," said Cortney.

Crystal finished the rest of her classes for the day and went to her dorm room to study. She entered and took a pizza pocket, along with milk from the miniature refrigerator. She put the food into the microwave that sat directly above it. She gathered the bedspread that was wadded at the corner of her bunk and smoothed it so the Navajo print showed neatly. The coverlet accented the earth tones of her room. She picked up some stray clothes and put them in their place. The buzzer rang, and she grabbed one of the two plates on the shelf between two windows. She looked past the corkboard plastered with pictures to the clock. It said seven o'clock. She still had a lot of work to do, but nothing held her interest. She put down her book and hurried down the hall to Courtney's room.

Crystal knocked on the door and went in. The room was painted pink and adorned with floral prints by famous artists on every available space. Cortney looked up from were she was sitting cross-legged on the top bunk.

"How is your work coming?" she asked.

"Not bad. I'm almost done," Cortney said.

"Good," said Crystal enthusiastically. "Then we can go to the party. Hurry and get dressed."

"Crystal!" exclaimed Cortney. "I forgot about that party. I think you should, too."

"No, you didn't," said Crystal, and pulled her from the bed.

"Oh, all right," laughed Cortney. "You're right, I didn't forget. He was rather cute, and maybe there are more like him at the party."

"That's more like it. I promise we won't stay late. Now hurry," said Crystal throwing a pair of shorts at her.

When they got to the house there were students in yard and scattered around inside.

"We are here as guests of Eric," said Crystal as they entered the house and were greeted by several boys. All of them were handsome and seemed pleased to see them. Crystal looked at Cortney and gave her a smug look with her eyes.

"He will be here in a while. I'm Terry, this is Bill and Brian," said the young man who made introductions as he pointed to a person on each side. "I hope he forgets to come," Terry said with a chuckle.

"Terry, behave yourself." Crystal turned when she heard the voice behind her. "I'm glad you changed your mind," Eric said and put his arm around her shoulder. He smiled down at her. She was tall for a girl, but he towered over her. She smiled back.

There was a short devotional at the beginning of the party followed by plenty of food. The party ended early and Crystal turned to leave.

"Can I walk the two of you home?" asked Eric.

"Sure," said Crystal. He was pleasant to talk with and seemed very polite. Crystal was impressed with him and was pleased when he assured her that he would be around again. Crystal thought about her mother, Britany. She smiled. She was sure her mother would approve of Eric. He was nice and polite and was a Christian! She looked at the clock. It was only ten. Her mother was usually awake at ten, she thought as she reached for the phone and dialed.

"Hello," a sleepy voice on the other end answered.

"I'm sorry, Mom," said Crystal. "I thought you would still be up."

Britany reached for the light beside the bed and turned it on. "I usually am, but work was hectic and I went to bed early," Britany said quietly so she wouldn't wake Michael. "What's up that you are calling?"

"I just wanted to tell you about this guy I met. He's a football player. He's tall, probably about six-feet-four, with blond hair and blue eyes. He is very, very nice, and he invited me to a Christian party!"

Britany's heart froze as she listened to Crystal's description of Eric. His physical description and the fact that he was an athlete made him sound a lot like Crystal's father. Crystal had never met her father and had no idea what he was like. Britany had prayed in earnest that Crystal would not fall into the same trap she had at that early age. It was Britany's biggest fear. *I'm probably just a little too sensitive to the possibility and thinking things that are not there. I cannot stereotype all athletes,* she thought as she listened. Crystal sounded very excited and she didn't want to disappoint her, so she listened intently and tried to sound pleased.

"Did he ask you out again?" Britany asked. Michael stirred beside her and looked up. She reached over and patted his shoulder and smiled.

"Crystal, I'm really sorry," Britany said. "I am waking Michael and I think maybe I had better go for now."

"That's fine," said Crystal cheerfully. "I'll call back when you are awake. I just needed to tell you about Eric."

"Bye, honey," answered Britany. She put the telephone down and stared at the wall.

Michael had been watching her. "What's wrong? It sounded like Crystal is happy, but you look worried."

"Crystal met a new boy. She even said he is a Christian, but I just have this horrible gut feeling. He sounds too much like her father."

"Maybe it is just a coincidence," said Michael, putting his arm around Britany.

"Crystal is a smart girl."

Britany turned off the light and slipped under the thick quilt. "I know," she said softly. "I'm just being foolish." She curled up beside Michael, but it was long into the night before she fell asleep.

CHAPTER 4

Michael got up with Britany, and they had breakfast together.

"Britany, I would like to pray together before you go to work. From what you told me about Jonathan, I think God has you there for a reason and possibly you can reach out to him," said Michael from across the table.

"I would really appreciate that," said Britany as she reached for his outstretched hand and squeezed it. It was comforting having him support her. A year ago things had been different, and Britany thanked God for the change that had taken place in their marriage.

Jonathan had slept restlessly during the night. The uncertainty of his future and the pain had troubled him. He smiled and felt himself relax when he heard Britany's voice in the hall. She was the only one he trusted, and he wasn't sure if he should trust her. He had continued to pretend he didn't remember any of his past during the night. No one had questioned him.

Britany stopped at room 302 before she went to the conference room for report.

"Hi, Jonathan. How did you sleep?" she asked as she approached his bed.

"Not as well as the night before," he answered.

"Well, I hope not," she chuckled. "You were unconscious most of that first night! Seriously though, has the pain eased up any?" she asked with concern. He shook his head no.

"I'm sorry," she said, and lightly touched his cheek. He smiled faintly. "I need to go get report and be back in half an hour or so." She smiled and left.

Carol was waiting when Britany arrived.

"Did you stop in and see Jonathan?" she asked. Britany nodded. "They said he put in a pretty rough night," Carol told her.

"That's what he said," said Britany and took a sip of her hot chocolate. "I'm afraid he is going to be in pain for some time yet."

"I'm sure he is. The next time he'll probably make sure his suicide attempt works!" Carol said seriously.

"Oh, Carol, don't even think that!" exclaimed Britany. She almost spilled her hot chocolate.

"Face it, Britany, so far his situation hasn't changed. He's still a lonely child with no one to love him. It's a big, lonely world out there." Carol sounded so hopeless that it tore at Britany's heart. Carol wasn't a Christian, and Britany could only imagine how cold and lonely the world was without Christ.

"You're right, I guess," Britany said with a shrug of her shoulders. "Hopefully his situation won't seem so bleak once he is ready to leave here. Jesus can make this world a lot less lonely."

Laura entered, and Janice followed, laughing as always. Sandra had the day off and Janice was working in her place. Janice had light brown hair pulled back in a bun. She was the mother of a five and a seven-year-old. She was always full of laughter and happiness seemed to follow her. She was medium height and a little on the heavy side.

Britany looked up and said hi. Carol started quickly with report. Britany listened quietly and soon Carol came to Jonathan.

"He slept fitfully through the night, but he never pressed the button for the extra pain medicine. His nurse said he still has not regained his memory, and she doesn't think he understands about the button." Britany doubted that was correct, but she needed to do some research on her own before she said anything. Carol told the others, "Jonathan's mother died, and as far as we know he is on his own."

Britany gathered linens to take to the room as soon as report was over. She got to room 302 as the breakfast cart was coming down the hall. She took the linens into the room and deposited them on an extra chair.

"Oh, no," groaned Jonathan. "Don't tell me you have to change the bed again today!" His face mirrored his pain.

"I'm afraid so. I'll be right back. Your breakfast is in the hall." She helped pass trays and then hurried back to the room.

She took a seat beside him and helped him to eat.

"I'm glad to see your appetite is good," she laughed. He smiled, but didn't stop until everything was gone. "Maybe we can get some meat on those bones of yours," she said.

"I have plenty of meat on my bones," he said without smiling.

"Yeah, actually you seem quite muscular."

"I do yard work, but I'm afraid I will lose all my customers now that I can't work for them. They don't even know why I can't show up," he said with a dismal voice.

"We can get word to them," Britany suggested as she tidied up from breakfast. "Do you have their addresses?"

Jonathan looked hopeful for the first time since she had known him.

"I have them written in the little notebook in my jeans pocket," he said, and then his face went pale.

"It's all right, Jonathan," said Britany as she sat beside him. "Whatever is wrong, you can tell me. I don't have to tell anyone if you don't want me to, but you need someone on your side. I never really thought you couldn't remember anything, and I know about your mother."

Jonathan grimaced, and his face took on a determined appearance. Britany held his hand firmly. "It's fine, you don't have to tell me anything, and I won't tell anyone that you can remember your past, but maybe we had better get hold of those people."

Britany went to the closet and found a bag with his clothes. The jeans were torn and covered with blood, but there was no shirt or shoes. She thought it seemed strange, but she searched the pocket and found the book. That was the only thing in any of the pockets.

Britany dialed the numbers, and Jonathan talked to his clients. Many of them did not answer the telephone, but he left a message on the answering machines. Britany admired his determination. He didn't stop until he had finished the last one and his head fell into the pillow from exhaustion.

Britany reached into a bag that she had brought with her and pulled out a book.

"Why don't you just rest, and I will read to you," she suggested. He nodded gratefully. "I read this book several years ago. <u>Magnus</u> is about a teenage boy in 1312, in England. His mother had died several years earlier, and monks raised him. She had imprinted a mission into his mind, and as he matured he realized he had a job to do, although he didn't understand the impact. It is a mysterious story full of adventure. I thought you might enjoy it." She read for almost an hour, and he rested quietly.

"You are right," Jonathan said as she stopped reading. "It is a very good book. I love books."

"I'm glad you enjoyed it," she said, putting the book on the table. "I hate to tell you, but it is time for your bath. It won't be long before they bring lunch trays, and then Dr. Steward will be in."

"I don't like him," said Jonathan.

Britany got the water ready and took it to the bedside. "Why don't you like Dr. Steward?" she asked as she worked.

"I don't trust him," he said simply, and she could tell there was nothing else coming.

"It seems to me you don't trust anyone," Britany said as she continued to bathe. She turned him slightly with his help and cleaned and dried his back. Then she applied some lotion.

"Are you almost done? This is getting uncomfortable," he said.

"Sure," she said and helped him ease back. "Jonathan, people will let us down. There is nothing much we can do about that. I would like to promise that you can trust me, and you can, but there will always be times people will fail, because they are human. There is Someone Who will never fail you. That is Jesus. He loves you and always wants to be there for you."

"I don't know how you think I can trust Him when I've lived the life I have. Where was He when my Grandfather beat my mother?" he said angrily. "I depend on no one but myself."

Britany looked at Jonathan with warmth in her eyes. "I'm sorry. I'm sure life has not been easy for you."

"Why do you always make me say things I didn't intend to," he said.

"You need to talk to someone, Jonathan," she said softly. "Life won't be quite so lonely." Britany emptied the wash water and got some new. "If you think you can manage, I am going to give you some privacy to finish your bath. Call when you're done."

Jonathan smiled a lopsided smile. "Thanks, I appreciate that," he said.

She returned shortly and knocked before she entered. "One last thing," she said as he told her she could enter. "I noticed you could use a shave."

"That would be nice," he replied.

Britany prepared the supplies. "I'm glad you are awake today. You kind of needed a shave yesterday, but I was afraid I might cut you or something," she said as she finished.

"Man, is there no end to this embarrassment," he said and reached for the razor. "I've never done this one-handed before." Britany held a mirror so he could see. She was glad to have a reason to stay. She didn't want to tell him she had to stay because he was on suicide precautions. She watched as he shaved. Somehow she just couldn't imagine him committing suicide. He certainly had a hard life, but he seemed too much of a fighter to give up that easily. She also thought of what he had said about the singing tree. Something was not making sense, and she needed to look into it further.

"You need to rest again. We are going to need to change your sheets still, and then lunch will be here. After lunch Dr. Steward will be back," Britany instructed.

"If you are trying to cheer me up, you are doing a wonderful job," Jonathan said mockingly. Then he called out to her. "Britany."

"Yes," she answered and turned back to look at him. She had been going to empty the last of the water.

"You're wearing teddy bears instead of white," he commented.

"I knew I was working here today instead of elsewhere," she answered lightly.

"You are still my angel," he said with a smile.

"I wish I were, Jonathan, but I'm sure you have one here with you right now," she said softly.

"Britany, will you sing again?" he asked.

"Sure," she said and sat down and sang until he slept. Then she finished cleaning and did her charting.

She was still singing a half-hour later when Tony entered, followed by Carol and Laura. "So the angel sings," said Tony boisterously. "Very pretty, I might add." Britany blushed. Jonathan heard him and woke up.

"Oh, no," he groaned. "The execution team."

"Jonathan, press the button for the pain medication," ordered Britany. Jonathan reached up and pressed it. Carol looked at Britany with a surprised look. Britany shrugged her shoulders.

"Everyone in their places. Carol, you help Laura with the sheets," Tony called out. "Ready, one, two, three, lift."

Jonathan grimaced and beads of sweat dotted his forehead.

"I wish we didn't have to do this," said Carol as she worked furiously. "You are doing great."

"Please hurry," Jonathan said between clenched teeth.

"Just a little longer," assured Britany. He was shaking again, and Britany held him tightly, trying to support his weight as much as she could so he wouldn't have as much to lift.

"Done!" called Laura.

"Easy, now all together, let's ease him down," Tony instructed, and they lowered him down. Carol and Laura hurried to tuck in the sheets that they had left undone to speed up the procedure. "I think its time for a song again, Britany," said Tony. He patted her on the back. "See you tomorrow, same time," he said to Jonathan.

Jonathan was still in too much pain to respond. Tears threatened his eyes and he bit his lip to hold them back. Tony waved to him and left. Laura and Carol were finishing and gathering up the sheets.

"Be careful of the ropes," Laura warned.

"Thanks," said Carol. "Britany, I'll be in to relieve you shortly for lunch. Sorry, but we were too busy for a break today. None of us got one."

"I'm fine," said Britany. "Wait until the lunch trays have been passed. I'll help Jonathan with his meal first."

They left, and Britany turned back to Jonathan. She soothed his forehead with a wet cloth and sang to him again. She saw the tears in his eyes and wiped them away.

"I wish it didn't hurt so bad," he said brokenly.

"I do, too," she said.

"I didn't mean the leg," he said quietly. This time it was Britany who was close to tears. She squeezed his hand. "I think I'm going to try to trust you now, Britany. I haven't talked about my mother since she died. I was afraid to tell anyone. I'm not eighteen yet, and I wasn't sure what they would do." He held tightly to her hand, and his eyes looked at her pleadingly. "I have been living on my own since she died. I mow yards and do yard work for people. I live out of my truck. I bought it when we lived in Knoxville. I did yard work then, too, and I needed something to haul the mowers with. I had been taking care of my mother for a long time. She had a hard life, and she couldn't cope. She was an alcoholic and then got hooked on drugs. I was hoping we could make a new life here, but it didn't work, and she overdosed. I don't think it was on purpose." He paused and rested momentarily before he continued. "I lied about not remembering anything, because I was afraid of what would happen when they found out I had no family. I don't want to go back to my grandfather or be anywhere near him. I thought the lie would give me time to think of something else, but I can't think of anything else. I can't even eat by myself. What are they going to do with me?" he pleaded through tears.

"Jonathan, we'll think of something," Britany assured him. "I have no idea what will happen, but you will be in the hospital for at least two to three weeks in traction."

"I need to finish school!" he exclaimed.

"Dr. Steward already has arrangements for a tutor to come and help you. He just wanted to wait until you were feeling better. See, he's not all bad," she said.

"I have money saved to go to college. I want to make my life better."

Britany smoothed his hair again. "Thanks for telling me these things. It's always better to talk things over. You need to rest now," she said. "You look exhausted."

He nodded and closed his eyes. Soon he was sleeping peacefully. Carol came in while he was sleeping and relieved Britany for lunch.

Britany returned, hoping to find him still sleeping. He was very angry when she entered.

"Britany, Dr. Steward thinks I tried to commit suicide! I can't believe it! Did you think I tried to commit suicide, too?" he asked demandingly.

"Yesterday, yes, for a while, but it didn't seem to fit," she said. "You are too determined to give up that easily. Just relax a minute. The only reason Dr. Steward thinks that is because that's what was on your chart."

"But he didn't even give me a chance!" Jonathan explained. He grasped the trapeze tightly with his right hand.

"Jonathan, I believe you didn't commit suicide, but what did happen?" Britany asked. She touched the arm that grasped the trapeze.

"I don't know. I was talking to some boys in the parking lot of the school, and then I remember the tree calling to me. It was like a very vivid dream. The tree sang and told me I could fly like the birds. I thought I was flying. It was so beautiful. Then I woke up here! In this!" He pointed to the pulleys.

"Jonathan, please don't get angry, but I need to ask you this," said Britany sternly. "Were you high on drugs?"

"Britany, I thought you trusted me," moaned Jonathan.

"I have raised a teenager, Jonathan. I learned that you love them enough to make them own up to what is going on around them and not live in a lie. I trust you enough to expect you to tell the truth," she said.

"I don't do drugs," he said through clenched teeth. "That's what happened to my mother, and that is one thing she taught me that I am not going to follow. They mess your life up bad."

Britany pointed to the button on his IV tubing. "Is that why you won't push the button for pain medication?" she asked. He nodded. "I thought so. I just needed to be sure. Do you think someone could have given you drugs without your knowledge?"

"I don't think so," he said with a scowl.

"What about the boys you were talking to in the parking lot?" she asked. "Did they give you anything?"

"Britany, I don't remember. Some things are still a little foggy," he said. His forehead was wrinkled in thought.

"Well, you tell me if you remember anything. I think you had better rest for a while. I'll read to you some more," she said and sat on the chair. She reached for the book and started reading to him.

"Britany," he said when she had read for several pages.

"Yes, Jonathan," she said putting the book down.

"Are you going to be my nurse tomorrow?" he asked with sad eyes.

"No, I have a family I need to care for. My husband stayed home from work to care for them today."

"I was afraid you wouldn't," he said sadly.

"I was planning on coming to see you, though," she said. "Would you like to meet my children? Well, three of them. One is in college, and she's not at home now."

"You have four children!" he said in surprise. "And one of them is older than I am!"

Britany nodded.

"Man, you don't seem old enough to be the mother of four children," he said in amazement.

Britany laughed. "We have quite an assorted family. I was a single mother for eighteen years, and then I met my husband. He had a nine-year-old son, who is now eleven. My best friend passed away two years ago, and I adopted her daughter, who is now eight. Then Michael and I had a son, Andrew, who will be a year old in November."

"I really would like to meet them," Jonathan said.

"All right, we will come by tomorrow. I may even get here in time to help make your bed again," Britany said with a smile.

Jonathan groaned.

Britany went to Dr. Steward's office following shift change. He was in, and she knocked before she entered.

"Hi, Britany," he said. "I think I made a mess of things when I went to see your patient. I guess his memory is back."

"Yes, he is a little hazy on what happened before the fall," she said, taking a seat.

"He wouldn't say a word after I asked him about committing suicide," he said, shaking his head.

"He's not very trusting, and he felt angry that you would think he could do such a thing. He is a very determined young man," she said.

He nodded. "Yes, I gathered that. Did you learn anything?"

"That is why I am here. I would like you to look into the possibility of those two teenagers giving him drugs. He seemed to be hallucinating before the fall. He claims he never does drugs, and I believe him," she said. "He wants a clean record for college, and I think he deserves it. If we put on his record that he tried to commit suicide, or that he was on drugs, it wouldn't look too good. I think we need to seek out the truth, and right now I believe him. I also think he is ready to start a little tutoring."

"That is an interesting theory, and one worth checking into. I certainly blew my credibility with him. I am glad you are able to reach out to him," he said, shaking his head again.

Britany smiled. "Hang in there. You represent the establishment, which he is very much leery of at this point. Keep trying. Maybe if you can find out what will happen after he gets his cast on it will help."

"I would love to say foster care, but I can't think of a family who would be able to take on the challenge he will be with the extra care he will need. I will see what I can do," he said.

"I'll check back tomorrow," said Britany, "I'm going to bring the children in to see Jonathan. Good bye."

He waved and smiled as she walked out the door.

Britany went home and made supper, telling Michael about Jonathan as she worked.

"Britany, you are getting very attached. You had better be careful. You will be hurt when he leaves the hospital," warned Michael.

Britany shrugged, "I think it is already too late for that. I am going to take the children up to meet him tomorrow. I think it would be nice for all of them."

"I love you, Britany," said Michael. He went over beside her and gave her a warm embrace.

CHAPTER 5

Crystal found herself running across campus again. She looked at her watch. This time she was going to be more than just a little late. She slid in beside Cortney and opened her book. She tried not to breathe too loud while her heart rate returned to normal. She smoothed back some hair that had fallen from the barrette and was floating across her face. The professor looked at her and frowned. Crystal glared back at him. She didn't want to give him the satisfaction that he was intimidating her. She sat and listened to the lecture, but nothing seemed to make sense. She scribbled some quick notes and tried to stay awake for the short time that was left of class.

Cortney slammed her book closed and glared at Crystal. "Why did you even bother to come?" she asked. "Honestly, Crystal, no matter what the excuse, this is getting old."

"Who do you think you are, my mother?" Crystal asked with her hands on her hips.

"Someone needs to look out for you. You don't seem to be doing too well on your own." Cortney grabbed her books and turned to leave.

"Cortney, wait," called Crystal, rushing after her. "I know I'm goofing up. Just be my friend. I'll do better. I already have a mother. What I need is a friend."

Cortney smiled. "I'm sorry. I didn't mean to do that. Actually, if my mother talked to me that way I would probably do just the opposite, to spite her."

"Thanks," smiled Crystal.

Eric was waiting for them as they left the building. He smiled broadly and reached for Crystal's books as she came out.

"Hi!" he said. "It looks like another beautiful day."

Crystal nodded. "It certainly is. I need to start getting up earlier. I don't even have rain to use as an excuse," she laughed.

"It's so nice, how would you girls like to go for a ride?" he asked cheerfully.

Crystal's heart soared. "It sure sounds better than working on these horrid math problems!" she said.

"I have too much to do," Cortney said, shaking her head. "Crystal..." she started to warn her to get her work done, but she remembered her promise and said instead, "Have a good time. I'll pass this time."

Crystal smiled and gave her a hug. "Thanks," she whispered in her ear.

Eric led the way to a white Corvette parked at the curb.

"Wow!" said Crystal. "This is pretty flashy for a college student."

He walked over and opened the door for her to get in. "My parents are both lawyers, and I am the spoiled son," he said.

"I see," said Crystal.

"That was supposed to be a joke!" he said, acting hurt.

Crystal laughed. "So you're telling me you're not spoiled? I think I will just wait and see for myself. My mother is a nurse and was single up until two years ago. I have no car, and I work to help pay for my college. I don't feel too sympathetic for those getting a free ride."

"Get in and enjoy your own free ride!" Eric said and went to the driver's side. He lowered himself easily into the car, which was surprising to Crystal, considering his size.

He drove through the city and into the countryside. The breeze rushed through the car, and Crystal felt elated by the freeness that she felt.

"Isn't this better than studying?" asked Eric.

"I can't disagree with that," said Crystal. Before long he came to a wooded area and pulled to the side of the road.

"Nice day for a picnic. Don't you think?" he asked. Crystal nodded and opened her door. Eric reached into the back and produced a picnic basket. He had a very expensive array of luscious-looking foods inside. Crystal's eyes were wide in surprise.

"Looks very nice," she said. "Did you pack it?"

"No, I had it done," he said. "There is a nice creek just a little way into the woods. Crystal followed him while he found a nice spot and spread a blanket on the ground. She looked at him with amazement. He certainly had planned well. The picnic was beautiful, and Crystal forgot about the class that she was missing.

She looked at her watched and jumped to her feet. "We need to get back. I have a class in two minutes!" Crystal exclaimed.

"Just relax," said Eric, reaching for her hand. "It is a half hour drive to get back to campus, and then your class will be almost over. Enjoy the rest of the afternoon. Let's go for a walk."

Crystal looked at him hesitantly. He was right about missing class. How could she be so stupid!

"I guess you're right, but I have another class at three, so let's walk for a while and then get back," she said.

"That sounds good," said Eric. He reached out and started gathering the items on the blanket.

"Mom, do you think he will like me?" Amy asked. Her brown eyes were very serious.

Britany had just pulled into a parking space at the hospital. "I'm sure he will," said Britany. "Everyone loves you, Amy." Britany gave her a big hug for reassurance. "Remember what I told you about the traction. It looks scary, but it is all right. Just be careful not to bump the weights or pull on the strings." She went to the other side of the car and removed Andrew from his car seat. He smiled happily. She kissed his silky hair. She slung the diaper bag over her shoulder and grabbed Amy's hand. She led the way to the sidewalk.

"Does Jonathan like sports?" asked Ben.

"I guess you will have to ask him," Britany said as they entered the building.

Ben ran to the window of the gift store. "Mom, can we get him something?"

Britany smiled, "Sure," she said. She loved it when Ben and Amy called her Mom. They had called her Britany for a long time, but after Andrew was born they started to call her Mom. Andrew had just learned to say Mom. It was as if they wanted to call her Mom before he did.

"He likes chocolate," Britany said.

Amy ran and picked up a box of chocolates. "Like these?" she asked.

"I'm going to get him one of these baseball caps," said Ben.

"Those are both great presents," agreed Britany. Andrew was holding a teddy bear Britany had handed to him to look at.

"Andrew is going to get him a teddy bear," laughed Amy.

Ben frowned. "He's too old for a teddy bear."

"But Andrew's not, so maybe it would be nice," said Britany. They purchased the presents and went to the elevator. Ben jumped into the elevator and pushed the button for the third floor as soon as the door opened.

"I wanted to push the button!" whined Amy. She held the box of chocolates with a frown on her face.

"You push that button," said Ben, pointing to an orange button. "That will make the door close." Britany smiled at him with pleasure.

"Thanks," said Amy and quickly pushed the button. The door started to close as a gentleman entered. Britany quickly reached out and slammed the bumper on the door to get it to stop. The elderly man looked startled, but the door didn't hit him.

"I'm so sorry," Britany said.

The man smiled. "No harm done," he said.

After getting off on the third floor, they continued down the hall until they came to Jonathan's room. Britany didn't recognize the nurse who was caring for Jonathan when they entered. She introduced herself and told her she had been taking care of Jonathan the last two days. The nurse looked pleased and said she would take a break. Britany assured her it would be fine and that she would report into the nurses' station when she left.

Jonathan's eyes lit up when he saw them. She walked to the bedside with Andrew in her arms. "Hi! We are here like I promised. This is Amy," she said with her hand on Amy's head.

"Hi, Jonathan. I brought you something," Amy said boldly and walked up to place the chocolates beside him.

"For me?" he asked hesitantly, his eyebrows furrowed in question.

"Of course for you, silly," said Amy. "You are in the hospital, and we wanted to make you feel better."

His dark eyes gleamed with pleasure.

"I got you something, too," Ben said, handing him the baseball cap.

"Gee, thanks," Jonathan said. He placed it on his head and smiled.

"This is my son, Ben, and this is Andrew," said Britany, introducing them.

Jonathan reached up and touched Andrew's fingers.

"He has something for you, too," said Amy excitedly. She took the bear from Andrew's hands and gave it to Jonathan. "Like this, Andrew. Give the bear to Johnny."

Andrew squealed and clapped his hands. Britany thought Jonathan was about to cry, but he smiled and said thank you to Andrew.

Britany sat in the chair beside the bed and put Andrew on her lap. "How is today going so far?" she asked.

"You missed the fun part. They already changed my sheets," Jonathan said. He reached for the trapeze to move himself slightly.

"After I said I would come and help, I decided that might not be too wise with three little ones around."

"Yea, I think you were right. I thought they were going to drop me. That new nurse is a lot bigger than you, but not as strong," he said.

"Jonathan," said Ben, "do you like sports?"

"I do, but I never had a chance to play them," said Jonathan. "I guess right now that is a plus or I would be more discouraged than ever."

"I play baseball in the spring. I'm getting pretty good. Mom likes to play and helps me practice," bragged Ben. "Maybe when you are out of the hospital you can come to one of my games next spring."

"Maybe you could teach me to play," said Jonathan. He smiled at Ben. He liked Britany's children. They were very warm and attentive. He had never had brothers or sisters and watching them he realized he might have missed more than he had thought.

Britany let the children play and talk with Jonathan. He was the center of attention. When they slowed down talking Britany suggested that she read another chapter of Magnus. She had a very attentive audience.

"Mom, I really like that book," said Ben. "Why didn't you ever read it to us before?"

"I will someday, but I thought it was a little old for you now. Plus, it is a very long book," Britany said.

"I liked it," giggled Amy, "but it put Andrew to sleep." She pointed to Andrew, who was sleeping in Britany's arms. Britany smiled.

"Will you be able to come back tomorrow?" asked Jonathan.

"Please, Mom, can we please!" pleaded Ben.

"I don't see why not. We will come again tomorrow, and then I work Saturday. And now I guess we should go," said Britany. She gathered Andrew into her arms. His sleeping head lay on her shoulder, and his arms dangled like a rag doll. "See you tomorrow, Jonathan," she said, reaching out to squeeze his hand.

"They still don't believe me that I didn't commit suicide," said Jonathan quietly so that Ben and Amy couldn't hear him. His face looked sad.

"I'm sorry, Jonathan," said Britany. "I talked to Dr. Steward and told him you didn't."

"He told me, but he continued to ask me so many questions that I could tell he didn't believe you or me. I don't want that on my resume for college. I never told anyone, but I always wanted to be a doctor. I know I don't have much of a chance, but I would like to try. It's not true, and I don't want it held against me."

"We will find out what really happened, and then they will be convinced. Don't worry. We will get this mess straightened out," Britany said encouragingly. "See you tomorrow."

"Bye, Johnny!" called Amy.

"See you later," Ben said and waved as he went out the door.

Jonathan watched them as they left. They were a happy family. For a short time he had felt part of that family, and he liked the feeling. He hugged the teddy bear to him until the nurse came back in. He quickly put it on the nightstand when he heard the nurse at the door. He looked at it with pleasure. He had never had a stuffed animal. He could not remember receiving so many presents at one time!

The tutor came shortly after Britany left, and Jonathan was glad to get into his schoolwork. She started him with English and math. He tried hard to concentrate, but he tired easily and wasn't able to concentrate for very long. It was also difficult to write with one hand. The nurse brought him a clipboard to help hold the papers in place.

Ben and Amy attacked Michael with their excitement when Michael came home from work that evening.

"He was really neat," said Ben. "He has these two metal knobs sticking out of his leg. It looks painful, and we have to be careful not to bump things."

Amy sat on Michael's lap and said, "He really liked our presents. I thought he was going to cry when Andrew gave him the teddy bear. He loved the chocolates and even gave us some. They were good!"

Britany was surprised that Amy had been so observant, although she shouldn't have been. She knew Amy was very sensitive to others' feelings.

"Now you are not only attached to this boy, but the rest of my family is, too. Maybe I had better meet Jonathan. Maybe tomorrow we can go out to supper at the Chinese restaurant across from the hospital and then go to visit afterward."

"That sounds great!" exclaimed Ben.

"You'll like him, Dad," said Amy.

"Michael, that is a marvelous idea. I especially like the part about getting out of cooking. I'll call him so he won't be expecting us during the day. I'll ask him if he likes Chinese. If he does we can take him something to eat. The hospital food can get monotonous," said Britany.

"From what you've told me I'll bet he is grateful for a warm meal. I'll bet he is not choosy," said Michael.

Britany laughed. "He surely does eat like he's grateful. I've never seen anyone eat so fast. Not even Ben."

Michael laughed too. "That is fast!" he said.

"Dad!" exclaimed Ben and gave him a mean look.

CHAPTER 6

Thursday night Eric invited Crystal to a concert on campus and arraigned for Terry and Cortney to double with them. Cortney and Terry seemed to enjoy each other's company, and it made Crystal happy to see her have a good time.

Friday morning Crystal rose in time for her biology class and went to Cortney's room to walk with her to class.

"You look like you were having a good time last night," she said as they crossed the grass.

Cortney smiled. "Terry is very nice, and he seems very interested in the welfare of his friends. I like that. He is excited to see so many new students coming to the Campus Crusade meetings and hopes that they can reach others with the gospel of Christ."

Crystal squeezed Cortney's hand. Cortney stood only a little over five feet tall, and Crystal seemed to tower over her. They had met during their first year of college and had formed a very tight friendship. Cortney was studying pre-med, and Crystal had her sights set on becoming a psychologist.

"I've determined to make this next week a better week of school and get to all my classes on time, with my assignments ready," said Crystal with determination as they walked through the hall.

"That's the Crystal I know," said Cortney with a smile.

Eric was waiting for Crystal after class again. He wasn't smiling and Crystal was concerned. "What's wrong?" she asked.

"I just found out my mom and dad are filing for a divorce," he said. His shoulders slumped forward.

Crystal felt very deeply for him. She placed her hand on his shoulder and said, "I'm so sorry. Is there anything I can do?"

He took her hand and looked into her eyes. "Come with me for another ride. I really need someone to talk to."

Crystal glanced at Cortney. She stood behind Eric so he couldn't see her. She shook her head no. Crystal knew she was right, but she didn't know what else to do. She liked to help people with their problems, which was why she had chosen her field of study.

"Of course, but I need to be back for my one o'clock class this time. I don't need to miss it two times in a row," she said. Cortney shrugged her shoulders in the background, but Crystal knew she understood.

"I'll be sure you are back," he said without much emotion. He seemed different than Crystal had seen him before. They walked silently across campus while Cortney stood and watched them. She was concerned for Eric, but she felt apprehension and wished Crystal had not agreed to go. Crystal looked strong and capable as she walked across the yard, but Cortney was concerned about outside influences confusing her friend. She shook her head and headed to the library to study.

When she saw Terry she waved. He walked up to her and smiled. "Would you like to have some company while you study? I have some reading to catch up on," he said.

"Sure," she said with a shrug of her shoulders and they found a seat together at one of the tables.

"This is the first time I have seen you without Crystal," commented Terry.

Cortney sighed, "She should be here with me. Eric met us after biology and said he just found out his parents were getting a divorce. He looked pretty depressed. He wanted to talk to Crystal. She went with him."

"That's funny," said Terry. "I saw him as I was walking to the library. He didn't say anything."

Cortney grimaced, and she pushed her red curls from her face. "Do you know Eric very well?" she asked.

"Hey," said Terry, concern showing in his gray eyes, "don't worry. I really don't know Eric personally, but I have never heard anything bad about him. He has been coming to Campus Crusade for about a year now. He doesn't talk about God, and he avoids personal talk, but he seems like an all right guy. I think she will be safe enough."

Cortney twisted her pencil in her hand. Various other students were in the large room, but it seemed relatively quiet, and Cortney kept her voice low. "It's not that I'm worried about her safety. She is having a problem focusing on her studies this year. She doesn't need any more distractions. Eric seems to be a very big distraction."

Terry laughed softly. His deep voice still seemed to echo. "Cortney, I don't think you are going to be able to come in the way of romance." He smiled.

She smiled back. "I guess you are right. We had better get back to our studies."

Eric didn't talk while they drove. Crystal was at a loss as to what to say. She looked out the window. "You know, Eric," she began, and contemplated what to say. She used her arms in animation as she talked. "I am really having a hard time relating with you, because I grew up without a dad. I love my mother's husband, but they've only been married two years, so it's hard to put myself in your position. You're going to need to let me know how you feel."

He clenched the steering wheel, and his handsome face hardened. "I just feel as if they are deserting me. How can they be married for thirty years and then just decide it's over? I don't even know who to blame!"

"Are your parents Christians?" she asked.

"Yeah, they both go to church every Sunday, but I don't see what that has to do with anything," he said. He pulled the car into a park by the river and turned off the engine.

"Well, Jesus is the great healer, and I just wondered if they know Him," she explained.

"Sure. Let's just walk. I don't feel much like talking," he said and opened the door. Crystal didn't like his moodiness, and his attitude about Jesus worried her. They walked along the river in silence. It was a sunny day. The ducks swam through the water and hurried toward them looking for food.

"I wish we had some bread to give them," said Crystal. Her delicate lips curved into a pretty smile, and Eric felt drawn to her. He reached out and took her hand.

"You're making me feel much better already," he said and squeezed her hand. "I knew you would. That's why I went to find you as soon as I found out."

They walked farther, and Crystal looked at her watch. "I really need to be getting back to class," she said.

"Don't leave me yet," he pleaded. "Let's go to Tiffany's for lunch. That place always lifts my spirits."

Crystal pictured Tiffany's beautiful decorative lamps sparkling through the colored windows. She had always wanted to go there, but it was too expensive for her budget.

"You may need to watch your spending. Your parents may not be able to send you as much money," she said.

Eric stiffened, and his blue eyes glared. "I have my own money." As soon as he said that his eyes softened, and he continued. "Please, Miss Crystal, do me the honor of sharing a meal with me. You will not be disappointed," he said and gave her a bow.

Crystal giggled. "You are very theatrical! Maybe you should go into acting instead of playing football."

"But don't you know, there is a lot of acting in football. I act like I'm going one way and then go another," he said. He ran for a distance and then quickly changed direction. "See, like that!" he exclaimed. Crystal laughed and ran to catch up.

The restaurant was very nice, and Crystal wasn't disappointed. I hate to admit it, but I could get used to this, she thought to herself. She felt troubled because she had missed class, but she reasoned that she didn't want to turn down such an offer.

They returned in time for Crystal's next class.

"I have practice this afternoon, and we are going to Indiana for a game this week end. I won't be around until Monday. Thanks for taking the time and being with me. You cheered me up immensely," said Eric. He took her hand and held it as they stood beside his car.

She looked at him with her pretty smile. He bent down and kissed her. "Thanks," he said. "I'll see you Monday."

"Good luck at your game," she said and waved as he got into his car and drove away.

Michael accompanied Britany and the children to see Jonathan the following night. Britany clasped his hand and smiled at him warmly as they walked down the hall. "I don't think this is a typical evening out for families," she said. "But then I don't think we have a typical family anyway!"

He bent over and gave her a kiss. "Nothing is typical when you are involved," he said.

"I don't know if that is good or bad!" laughed Britany. They reached the door to Jonathan's room, and Britany knocked. Amy ran in before Jonathan could respond. Britany reached out to stop her but was too late. "Amy, it's impolite to enter before anyone answers," Britany said as she followed her.

"Jonny, what's wrong?" Amy asked with concern. Britany quickly handed Andrew to Michael and went to the bedside. Jonathan was thrashing in bed, and his eyes were glassy.

"Jonathan!" said Britany sternly. She clasped his arm with one hand and restrained his shoulder with the other to get him to stop moving. "Jonathan, it's me, Britany. What is wrong?"

"The tree is singing again," he moaned and continued to thrash. The weights on the traction started to swing because his legs were moving wildly. "Michael, stop the weights from swinging without taking pressure off!

Ben, go to the hall and get a nurse," Britany ordered.

Britany half lay across him to get him to stop thrashing. "Jonathan, it's all right, there are no trees here. You are in the hospital. You are safe. Please don't move!"

"The tree wants me to fly!" he said. His eyes were wild, and sweat covered his face.

"Relax, Jonathan, you are safe. Don't fly. Stay with us. Amy and Ben are here. They came to see you. Don't fly away! Jonathan!" Britany shouted. "Listen to me. Stop flying!"

He stopped thrashing and gazed into space. "Britany, is that you?" he asked.

"Yes, Jonathan, it's me. Can you hear me?" she asked and relaxed her hold on him.

"Of course, you are my angel again. You came to rescue me from the tree!" He was still staring into space with wild eyes.

A nurse came running into the room. Britany turned to look, and as she recognized her she quietly said, "Regina, get vital signs while I talk to him." She turned back to Jonathan.

"Jonathan, look at me," she said. "I need you to look at me. Don't listen to the tree. The tree isn't real." Slowly Jonathan's eyes moved toward Britany. His eyes started to focus and lost their glassy appearance.

"Jonathan, it's me, Britany. I brought Amy and Ben back to see you. I even brought my husband Michael."

"Britany, it's you! I thought you were an angel again." His entire body relaxed and his head fell back into the pillow. "I don't think I like you as an angel. You are better as a real person."

"I'm glad," she said and smiled. "Would you like a glass of water?" He nodded. She lifted his head and helped him to get a drink.

"His heart rate, respiratory rate, and blood pressure are up, but I would expect them to be after an incident like that!" Regina said.

Britany looked at Michael. "Did you get the weights calmed down?"

"Yeah, the ropes are a little twisted, though," he said.

The nurse untwisted the ropes. When she was finished she said, "I think I'll have someone from orthopedics check things out. Thanks for coming to the rescue. He was sleeping quietly, and I have other patients. I was just gone for a moment. We are really busy tonight. I'll call the doctor and tell him what happened."

"Call Dr. Steward, too," said Britany. "He needs to know. If he comes in tell him I want to speak to him."

Jonathan sighed and started to tremble. "It hurts," he moaned. He closed his eyes and his face grimaced in pain. He tossed his head back and forth. Britany reached for the pain medication button on his machine.

"You were thrashing around and pulling against the traction," she said softly. "Lie still for a while and it should get better." She held his hand and soothed his forehead.

Michael walked closer to Britany, carrying Andrew in his arms and holding Amy's hand. "Maybe I had better take the children for a walk and let him rest for awhile," he said.

Amy looked pale and Ben was very still. Andrew cuddled close to Michael's shoulder. "I think that would be a very good idea," said Britany. "He will be better in fifteen to twenty minutes, and hopefully ready for company." She stretched high and gave Michael a kiss on the cheek. "Thanks," she said. He smiled and led the children into the hall.

"Daddy, what happened?" Amy's concerned voice tore at his heart.

"I don't know, sweetheart," said Michael. "Mommy says that he will feel better in a little while, so I thought we could take a walk."

"He was in a lot of pain!" remarked Ben. "Those weights must have been pulling hard on his leg. I wish they would take them off and take that metal thing out of his leg." His face looked ashen as they walked.

"I'm sure those weights did pull on his leg, but I don't think he felt it at the time. He's feeling the effects now, though. They will need to keep all that stuff on for a week or two longer, and then they will put it in a cast for six to eight weeks," explained Michael.

"Where does he live, Daddy?" Amy asked.

"He doesn't have a home," said Michael.

"But he's not that old. Where are his mom and dad?" asked Ben.

Michael stopped in the hall and looked at them. "I didn't realize you didn't know. His mother died several months ago, and his father isn't around."

"But, Dad!" exclaimed Ben. "Where is he going to go when he leaves the hospital?" Michael shrugged his shoulders.

Amy lifted her head and straightened her shoulders. "He needs to come home and live with us!" she said firmly. "Mom is a nurse, and she can take care of him. I can be his sister. Andrew and Ben can be his brothers. You can be his dad, and then he will have a family."

"He is not some stray kitten we found on the street, Amy. We can't just take him home," Michael said with exasperation.

"You took me home when my mother died." Amy's face was solemn. Michael had no reply.

"Yeah, Dad," said Ben. "The only one belonging to our family who wasn't adopted is Andrew. Why can't we adopt Jonathan, too?"

Michael looked from child to child. Even Andrew seemed to wear a sorrowful face. How could I ever argue against the wisdom of children? He thought in frustration.

"You need to let me think about this one and talk it over with your mother," Michael said. After seeing how Britany interacted with Jonathan, he already knew what she would say. He needed to sort through what it would mean to the family financially as well as the extra work it would take while Jonathan was healing. He would talk to Britany later and see what she thought. They continued their walk until he felt they could return.

Jonathan smiled when they entered.

"Jonathan, this is my husband, Michael," said Britany.

Michael smiled and took Jonathan's hand in his and shook it firmly. "I'm glad to see you are feeling better. That must have been pretty rough," commented Michael.

Jonathan frowned. "You were here then?" he asked. Michael nodded. "Were the kids here, too?"

Michael wished he wouldn't have said anything about the episode. "Jonathan, we all go through tough times. That was just one of them. The children aren't going to think any less of you. In fact, they want to make you their brother," Michael said, and then wished he had waited. He didn't seem to be saying the right things, but there was something about the boy he liked. Maybe it was the way he didn't look away when Michael looked at him intently. He wasn't sure, but he felt that Jonathan was a good person inside and needed a better turn in life. Jesus was the great physician, and there was no doubt that Jonathan needed Jesus.

Britany looked at Michael with surprise. She had never heard him say anything as spontaneous as what he just said. Was this the same man she walked into the hospital with?

Amy squirmed her way between Britany and Michael so she could climb on Jonathan's bed, and sat beside him. "Are you feeling better?" she asked. He nodded with a smile. She kissed him on the cheek. His face beamed.

"We brought you some Chinese food," said Ben.

"That sounds great, but if you don't mind I would like to wait until later. I always get hungry just before bed," said Jonathan.

"I do, too, but Mom won't let me eat that late," said Ben.

They visited for a while, and then Amy and Ben begged Britany to read to them from the book.

"You'll love it, Dad!" exclaimed Ben. "It has knights and castles and fighting too. It's good."

Andrew whined to sit beside Amy. Michael cautiously lowered him to the bed. "Jonathan, if he wiggles too much let me know," said Michael.

"Hi, Andrew!" Jonathan said, and put his free arm around Andrew's tiny waist.

Britany handed the teddy bear to Andrew, and he played with it. She sat in the chair and started reading, while everyone listened intently. She looked up as she finished to see Andrew leaning against Jonathan. His sleepy eyes were drifting off to sleep. Britany looked at them and smiled. Jonathan looked much more peaceful than when they had arrived.

"I think maybe we should get these children home before they all fall asleep," she said. Jonathan leaned and kissed Andrew on the head. Britany reached down and gathered Andrew in her arms. He cuddled into her shoulder and closed his eyes.

"Come on, Amy," said Michael and reached to lift her off the bed. Before he grasped her, Amy put her arms around Jonathan's neck and gave him a kiss.

"See you tomorrow," Amy said to Jonathan. Jonathan's face beamed with pleasure.

"You won't be able to come tomorrow, Amy. I work tomorrow," said Britany.

"I'll see you Sunday, then," said Amy.

Britany smiled. "You always are scheming, aren't you, Amy?" she said.

Ben walked to the bed, and gave Jonathan a hug. "Bye, see you Sunday."

They walked out, and suddenly the room seemed very quiet. Jonathan had felt lonely in his life, but he couldn't remember feeling as lonely as he did when Britany's family left. For the two hours that they were at the hospital he had felt part of their family. He wondered what Michael had meant when he said the children wanted to make him their brother. He wondered if Michael and Britany would want him to be part of their family. The possibility was wonderful, yet he was afraid to even hope it would happen. He decided he would just focus on the next few days. They had promised that they would be back to visit him. The rest of his future was too uncertain to think about.

Michael talked with Britany as soon as the children were in bed for the night.

"Britany," he said crawling under the covers of the bed. "Ben and Amy were very serious about Jonathan living with us." Britany was already in bed, and she curled up around him while he talked. "The strange thing is I can't really think of a reason for him not to come. I don't think financially it will be that much of a difference, at least for the several months he will be unable to work. He has been supporting himself for a long time, and I am sure he doesn't expect a lot."

"Michael, I can't believe you are saying this," she said. She had been falling asleep when he crawled in bed, but suddenly she was awake and sitting up. "I mean, it is not something I ever expected you to suggest. He's had a hard life, and we really don't know that much about him."

He looked at her puzzled. "I figured you would want him to come stay with us," he said.

"With all my heart I want him to, but with my head I am concerned. He curses quite well when he is angry, and we have no idea what other negative influences he might have on the children. As far as I know he doesn't do drugs, he doesn't lie, and he doesn't steal. I know he's grown up to understand right from wrong, but I really don't know too much about him." Michael noticed the little wrinkle on Britany's forehead that always appeared when she worried.

"Britany, we don't have to ask him to stay with us. It was just a thought. Relax a little," he said and pulled her close. "You work tomorrow, and you need to get some sleep. You look as if you will be awake all night."

"It's just that I am frightened," Britany said, and her hands moved with expression as she talked. "Our house and family are dedicated to God, and everyone knows Jesus. Jonathan is angry with God, and I'm not sure what influence he will have on the children. I don't want Satan's influence on Andrew, Ben and Amy. Ben already has to face it when he goes with his mother. I want our home to be a haven, a place where they can feel God's love and protection. I don't want that balance to be destroyed." Britany was trying hard to explain, but she couldn't seem to find the right words to express the turmoil in her heart.

"Britany, I understand," Michael said, taking her hand. "I think we need to pray and put this into God's hands. If He wants Jonathan to come live with us, then He will provide. If not, then we don't want that to happen either, and your hesitancy might be a warning."

Britany covered Michael's hand with hers. "I would like that very much," she said.

"Dear Jesus," Michael began, "We bring this request to You. Amy and Ben have brought to our attention that we could possibly provide Jonathan a home and shelter from some of life's hardships he's had to face. Britany feels understandable anxiety about this. We have four lovely children that You have blessed us with and given us the responsibility to provide for. We do not, in any way, want to endanger them, either physically or spiritually. I ask that You guide us in this decision and give us both a peace about which way to turn. You have instructed us in Your Word to bring our requests to You, and that is what we are doing. We trust You to provide us with wisdom in this situation. Thank You, Jesus. Amen." Michael squeezed Britany's hand.

"Thank You, Jesus, for a loving, understanding husband. Amen," said Britany. She relaxed and fell into a peaceful sleep. She woke feeling rested, and she quickly prepared for work.

Jonathan was sleeping when she looked into his room. She got report and arranged her supplies for the morning.

She knocked softly and entered his room. He was still sleeping. He looked peaceful as he slept. She felt guilty as she watched him, remembering her response to Michael when he suggested they provide Jonathan with a home. He definitely needed them, and how could she be so selfish as to not provide it? "Lord, forgive me. You put Jonathan in my life for a reason. Now help me be open to Your leading," she prayed silently. Suddenly she felt the peace Michael had prayed about the night before, and she knew that they needed to take Jonathan in. "Ok, Lord, now You need to show me the way to make it happen!" she thought.

Jonathan stirred and opened his eyes. His thin lips curled into a smile as he sleepily looked at Britany.

"Good morning," she said. "Did you have anymore problems with the tree?" she asked.

"No," he said. "That was scary. It was like what I saw the day of the accident. What is happening to me, Britany?" he asked with concern.

She shrugged her shoulders. "I wish I knew," she said. "Do you remember any more about those two boys?"

"They were standing in the parking lot after school when I went to go to my truck. Hey, where is my truck? I never thought about it. Do you suppose it is still in the parking lot?" Jonathan looked disturbed.

"I don't know. I'll get your vital signs and then go call Dr. Steward. He can find out for us. I don't remember seeing any keys in your jeans pocket. Do you know where they might be?"

He suddenly looked alarmed. "They asked me for them!" Jonathan exclaimed and grabbed the trapeze overhead. He pulled his head up higher. "They were talking to me and offered me a candy bar. I ate it, and we talked for a while. Then I remember feeling very free and happy. They laughed and said we needed to take a ride. I offered my truck and got the keys out. Then I saw the tree and started dancing and running. I think I threw the keys on the ground!" He said with alarm.

Britany had been waiting to see if Jonathan remembered eating or drinking anything before the accident. She realized quickly that Jonathan just confirmed what she had been suspecting. "Jonathan, we will check into it. Don't worry about your truck. We will look for it. I need to talk to Dr. Steward right away." She picked up the phone and dialed his number.

He answered on the first ring. "Dr. Steward, you need to come to the hospital, to room 302, right away," said Britany.

"Can you at least give me an idea what is happening?" he asked. "It's Saturday morning!"

"I realize that," she said. "It involves Jonathan, and it's very important. Jonathan remembers some of the events leading up to the accident."

In half an hour Dr. Steward walked into the room. "Good morning, Jonathan," he said. Then he looked at Britany and said, "Hello Britany." She nodded and he looked back at Jonathan. "What are these events you are remembering?"

"I don't know why I should tell you," he said. "You won't believe me anyway!" Jonathan gave him a look of disdain.

Dr. Steward sat in the chair beside the bed. "Jonathan," he said. "I think you need to slow down a minute and think before you judge me too harshly. It seems to me that the first day we met I was ready to believe you, and you told me you didn't remember anything. I know you didn't trust me, but now you complain I don't trust you." He sighed and took a breath. He leaned back in his chair and waited. Jonathan looked uncomfortable.

"Well, I was afraid, and I didn't know what else to do," Jonathan said. "You can believe me now. That is, if I can trust you."

"We have a major obstacle here, don't we?" Dr. Steward asked.

Jonathan nodded his head.

"Let's start over. I will only tell you the truth, and I will promise to believe you, if you promise to believe me." Dr. Steward leaned forward and waited for a response.

Jonathan thought for a moment. "I guess that makes sense. I just don't want to be locked in some institution or something, and I really don't want a suicide attempt on my records. I have plans for college. I don't want anything to interfere. Suicide is not my style. I didn't try to kill myself. I have plans for my life. I'm not ready to give that up."

"Contrary to what you might think, I am here to help you. I want what is the best for you, too. You've convinced me that you didn't commit suicide, but we still have the mystery of how you got into that tree to begin with," Dr. Steward said.

"If you two would stop arguing, I think we could get to the bottom of this!" Britany said in exasperation with her hands at her side.

"Jonathan, tell Dr. Steward about the boys," she said sternly.

Jonathan told him the story, and Dr. Steward listened intently.

"Those sound like the two boys who talked to the police and told them you were depressed and had tried to commit suicide," commented Dr. Steward. "Your story sounds much more like that of the girl who came forward and talked to the police. We knew there was a discrepancy somewhere." He rose from his chair. "I have some telephone calls to make. I am going to have the police check those boys out a little more thoroughly. And I will find out about your truck. Don't worry, Jonathan. We will get to the bottom of this," said Dr. Steward. He reached out and firmly shook Jonathan's hand. Britany followed him to the door and into the hall.

She said quietly, so not to be overheard, "I think those boys gave Jonathan some type of hallucinogen in that candy."

"It certainly does appear so," he said, stroking his chin.

"Did you get the message that he had an episode last night?" she asked.

He looked surprised, "No. What happened?"

Britany quickly explained what Jonathan had experienced. "I think it was a residual reaction from the drugs they gave him."

"Wow, I will definitely check into the possibility," said Dr. Steward.

"Dr. Steward," said Britany. "I have one more thing to talk to you about."

"Yes?" he asked.

Britany stood tall and said firmly, "Michael and I would like to take Jonathan when he is released from the hospital and give him a home with us."

Dr. Steward laughed. "That would solve one of the biggest problems that boy has. I think it is a wonderful idea! I'll start the paperwork."

"I thought you would be surprised!" Britany said with a questioning look.

Dr. Steward put his hand on her shoulder, and for a fleeting moment she had the distinct feeling that he was going to pat her on the head. "You'll have to try harder than that to surprise me, Britany. His own mother wouldn't have stood up for that boy the way you have. I don't think Jonathan was hallucinating when he said you were his angel! I'll stop in later. Bye, Britany," he said and gave her a little wave.

She smiled. "Let us know as soon as you find Jonathan's truck."

Sunday night Britany couldn't sleep. She had woken up at two and couldn't get back to sleep. She quietly got up so she wouldn't wake Michael and went into the living room. She took the Bible off the shelf and curled up on the edge of the couch. She turned on the light and leafed through until she found a passage she was looking for. "Ask and it will be given to you; seek and you will find; knock and the door will be opened to you. For everyone who asks receives; he who seeks finds; and to him who knocks, the door will be opened." Matthew 7:7-8.

She walked out onto the deck. The night was warm, and the stars shined brightly. She looked up into the night and talked to God in prayer. He was her

Friend, her Counselor, and constant Guide, and she needed some insight into what was troubling her.

"Dear Lord," she said quietly, "I am having some very mixed emotions and I'm not sure where they are coming from. All summer I have dreaded this time when Amy and Ben are about to start school. I need to talk to Michael about the possibility of home schooling them. I have talked with You about this before, and I need Your guidance. I have this overwhelming desire to keep them home in this sanctuary You have provided for us. I'm not sure if this desire comes from You or from my own selfishness. I am going to talk to Michael about it tomorrow, and I pray for you to lead him. I feel more secure when he agrees with me. If this is what you want for our children, then make it clear in his heart, too. If not, then give me a peace as I send them to school. I don't know if having Jonathan come live with us is going to complicate the situation or help. You know, and in You is wisdom. You promised me in those verses that if we ask, You will give, and I am asking for wisdom. Thank You, Jesus. Amen."

Britany listened to the sounds of the night and felt the warm, moist air caress her face. God was wonderful, and she was thankful that she could take her cares to Him. She returned to bed and fell into a peaceful sleep.

CHAPTER 7

Crystal walked to the church on campus Sunday morning with Cortney beside her.

"You will be very pleased to know," she said with confidence, "that I finished all my work and am ready to start class Monday morning with all assignments completed."

Cortney looked at Crystal with pleasure. "Now that sounds like the Crystal I knew last year!" she said as they rounded the corner and started up the long flight of stairs to the brick church. The steeple rose to a sharp peak in the sky, and it made the church the tallest building around. The inside of the church was adorned with rich wood of intricate carvings that were softened by the sunlight filtering through the stained-glass windows. Crystal loved the church she had found her first year on campus. Many of the members were college students, but there were enough other members to keep it stable as the students came and went. There were also a good number of college professors, which surprised Crystal. It was a welcome reprieve from the pressures of college life.

"I looked for Eric as I watched the game yesterday," said Cortney.

"Did you see him?" asked Crystal. "I watched, too, but I was also doing my math, so I didn't watch too intently. I didn't see him. I was hoping to get to see him play."

Cortney shrugged her shoulders. "No, I was working on my humanities project during the game, but I didn't see him. It seemed rather strange."

They went to lunch following the service. Crystal spent the rest of the day reviewing for a test the next day and doing a few odds and ends. She was ready to go to bed when Tammy came bursting through the door. She and Brenda roomed several doors down in the dorm and were good friends with Crystal.

"Crystal, what you doing?" Tammy asked, her voice slightly slurred. She walked to the bed and plopped down on the empty bottom bunk that belonged to Tabitha, Crystal's roommate. Tabitha only made an appearance when her mother came to visit. The rest of the time she stayed in her boyfriend's apartment, but she didn't want her mother to know.

"Let's go to the movies!" Tammy said, a little too happy.

Crystal sat on the bed beside her. "Are you all right, Tammy?" she asked.

Tammy laughed and rolled onto her side. "Sure," she said. "Why would you think I'm not OK?"

Crystal frowned. Tammy was acting like she was drunk, but she didn't smell like it. "Have you been drinking?" she asked.

Tammy sat up and slapped Crystal on the back so hard that Crystal fell forward. "No, why would you say that? Let's go down the hall and see who we can find in the lounge."

Tammy stumbled to the hall as another girl burst through Crystal's door. "There you are!" she said. "We have been looking all over for you."

"Brenda, what is going on?" asked Crystal. Brenda and Tammy were very good students and not known for partying. It was out of character for Tammy to be drunk.

Brenda blew out through her teeth. "It beats me," she said. "This afternoon she went to the infirmary because she has been sick with a fever and sore throat, and now she won't stop talking!"

Tammy got up and started skipping down the hall. Brenda ran after her, and Crystal was quick to follow.

"Tammy, wait!" Brenda yelled. "You are in your pajamas, and there are boys in the lounge!"

"I know," Tammy giggled.

Brenda looked at Crystal and shrugged. Crystal rushed past and grasped Tammy's arm. "Tammy, let's go see what we can find for you to wear," she coaxed trying to lead her back to the room. "I'm sure I have something."

"OK," Tammy giggled again.

Crystal found her something to wear, and then she and Brenda followed her to the lounge. Tammy laughed and sang while everyone looked at her strangely. "Brenda, I think we need to do something," said Crystal. "Have you ever seen her like this before?"

"No," Brenda said and shook her head as she watched in disbelief. "Your mother is a nurse. What do you think we should do?"

"I think we should get her to the emergency room. Something is desperately wrong. No one slipped her some drugs, did they?" she asked.

"No. She has been in her room, except for when she went to the infirmary. She has been sleeping the entire afternoon until she woke up and started acting like this. I didn't know what to think of it, but now I definitely think you are right. Now, how do we convince her?" Brenda asked.

Crystal walked up to Tammy and took her arm again. "Let's go for a ride!" she said. She looked at Brenda and asked, "Do you have a car?"

Brenda shrugged her shoulders. "No," she said, "but Tammy does. We can take it!"

"Yeah!" exclaimed Tammy. "Where do you want to go? I'll take you where ever you want!" she laughed.

"We need to go back to your room and get the keys," suggested Crystal and Tammy agreed. She said a hearty good-bye to all the puzzled students in the lounge before they left.

Brenda had difficulty convincing Tammy to let her drive, but she finally agreed. They pulled up to the emergency entrance, and Tammy was ecstatic.

"Oh, great! A party!" She got out of the car and ran through the door. Crystal jumped out and ran after her. She got her to stop just inside the door. A dozen quizzical faces looked at them as they ran in. Tammy started dancing. She had an audience, and several children giggled and pointed. Brenda ran in after them as soon as she had the car parked. She went to the desk and explained what was happening. A male nurse came and helped coax Tammy to the exam room.

Soon a doctor came out to talk to Brenda and Crystal. "Tammy is having a reaction to the medication she was given this morning. She needs to stay in emergency for the night. We called her parents, and they will be here in a few hours."

He looked at them and smiled. "She has good friends to take care of her like you did. She will be fine in a day or two."

Brenda sighed, "Thank you so much, Doctor! We had no idea what was happening! I am glad she is going to be all right. Can we go see her now?"

"Sure," the doctor replied.

Brenda and Crystal hurried to the room. Tammy was still acting bizarre. The nurse was with her. "She'll calm down soon," the nurse said. Crystal and Brenda stayed with Tammy long into the night, until Tammy's parents came.

Crystal groaned when the alarm went off and she rolled back over. Two hours of sleep was definitely not what she had hoped for. She sleepily got up and showered for class. She arrived on time for biology, but not very alert.

"What happened to you?" asked Cortney when she arrived.

"Tammy had a reaction to her medication, and I spent the night in the emergency room until her parents could get there." Crystal sifted through her notes, looking for where she had left off after the last lecture. She looked up and continued, "I was all ready to start this week out right. Now I'm exhausted before it begins! I have a test this afternoon, too!" she groaned.

Crystal perked up some when she saw Eric waiting for them as they left the building. His arm was in a sling.

"What happened?" she asked in concern.

He reached over with his free arm and touched his shoulder. "I got tackled too hard in practice Friday night, and my shoulder muscles were torn. I wasn't able to play in the game. It looks like I may be out for most of the season," Eric said.

His blue eyes remained surprisingly calm. It was quite a contrast to the way he had reacted when he received the news his parents were getting a divorce.

"Oh, Eric!" exclaimed Crystal and grasped his free hand. "I know how much football means to you! I am so sorry!"

"That's why we didn't see you in the game!" Cortney exclaimed.

"Yeah," he answered. "I was there, but I didn't dress out, and I guess the cameramen aren't too interested in those of us who sit on the bench."

He walked with them and talked until it was time for the next class. Crystal was glad to see Eric, but she had wanted some time to look over her notes for the class. She had missed class twice the week before because of Eric, and she didn't feel very prepared. The test was very difficult, and she was discouraged as she walked out the door. Eric was waiting as she stepped outside the building, and he took her to lunch.

"I'm sure you did all right," he assured her as they ate. "How about going to a movie tonight? Maybe that will cheer you up."

"That sounds fun," she agreed, although she was tired and knew she should get to bed early.

She enjoyed the movie, and they went to a pizza place afterward.

The smell of pizza filled the air as they entered the pizzeria. Red and white checkered tablecloths covered the crowded tables. They found an empty table and sat down.

Crystal picked up the menu and then set it down. She looked up at Eric. "I am so tired," she said. "It was so scary when Tammy came into the room last night. I thought she was losing it, and I didn't know what to do!"

"It sounds to me like you did the right thing," he said and motioned for a waitress.

"We would like a large pizza with ham and onions," he said as she approached the table.

Crystal wrinkled her nose, "I don't like onions!"

Eric looked at her with question and then looked at the waitress. "Make that a large Pizza with half onions and ham, and half mushrooms and pepperoni."

"That will be ready in fifteen minutes," the waitress said as she gathered the menus.

"Eric, you are acting as tired as I feel," said Crystal as they were finishing their pizza.

"You haven't been listening to me." A group of guys came in as she was talking to him.

They looked at Eric but didn't speak, and he pretended not to see them, but Crystal saw him glance their way several times.

He turned back to her, but his mind seemed to remain on the group of young men.

"What did you say?" he asked.

She shook her head. "Maybe we should go," she said. "I'm very tired."

They left, and he seemed a little more relaxed as they walked through campus.

"Who were those guys at the pizza place?" she asked.

He looked behind them to be sure no one was following them. "I kind of stole one of the guy's girlfriends. It was unintentional, but they have had it out for me ever since. I really don't want to meet them in some dark alley."

"Wow," said Crystal and turned back to look. She saw no one.

"How is your arm feeling?" she asked as soon as she was sure no one was following them.

"I can't use it, but as long as I don't move it, it's not bad," he said and put his free arm around her and pulled her close. He was strong, and she felt secure. His closeness took away some of the insecurity she had felt since taking the test.

The time for school to start was getting closer, and Britany felt an urgency she couldn't explain. She had met a lady named Maria, in the spring whose son Randy was on Ben's baseball team. Their families had formed a close friendship throughout the numerous games. Maria home schooled her children, and the idea of home schooling seemed more and more appealing to Britany.

The year before it had been exciting getting Ben and Amy ready for the start of school, but this year she felt extreme anxiety every time she thought about new clothing or books. She wanted to learn all she could about home schooling and made an appointment with Maria to see her after she visited Jonathan on Monday.

Britany took the children with her to see Jonathan. He was in good spirits, but their visit was cut short when his tutor came. Britany was glad to leave early. It would give her more time to talk to Maria.

Maria welcomed her with a warm embrace as she entered. Maria's round face wore a perpetual smile. Her excitement about home schooling was contagious.

"Hi, Maria," said Britany. "I hope I'm not coming at a bad time."

"Of course not," said Maria. "We are always glad to see you." She led the way to the kitchen table and offered Britany some tea. Ben ran out the door to the backyard with Randy. Maria's youngest girl, Elizabeth, who was ten, took Amy by the hand and led her to the playroom.

Britany, wearing white cotton slacks and a cool blue blouse, sat at the table and placed Andrew on the floor with several of his favorite toys. He looked around and crawled toward a big, fluffy black and white cat.

"Be careful!" called Maria from the kitchen. "That cat bites sometimes."

Britany whisked up Andrew and steered him in another direction. The cat ran off to another room. "Thanks for the warning," said Britany. "Andrew loves cats."

Maria brought the tea to the table and took a seat. Her dark hair was in a bob and waved neatly around her face. Britany took a sip and looked up. "I was hoping I could ask you some more questions about curriculum," she said.

"So has Michael agreed to home schooling?" Maria asked, her eyes gleaming with excitement.

Britany gave a guilty smile. "I haven't talked to him yet. I really haven't decided for sure myself, but I want to get everything organized in case we decide to. I plan on telling him tonight."

Maria beamed. "I am just so excited. We could do some activities together. Ben and Randy are the same age, and Amy and Elizabeth are close enough to really have a good learning experience. I have a good friend, Connie Franklin, who has two boys that are our boy's ages also. She has an older girl that would probably help with Andrew when we go places."

Britany laughed. "Maybe I should have you ask Michael if we can home school! You make it sound so wonderful. I wanted to look through your books to see what materials I would need."

"Sure," said Maria as she went to get a pile of books and pamphlets. They spent an hour looking at prices and writing things down. Britany told Maria about Jonathan and how he might be coming to live with them.

"I guess he will still have tutors, at least until he is able to get around enough to go back to school," Britany said as she looked through booklets.

Andrew was sitting in Britany's lap and starting to look very tired. Britany watched his face and said, "I guess I had better get the children home. It will soon be time to start supper." She looked at Maria and smiled. "Thank you so much. You have been very helpful."

"There are two good bookstores in Nashville," said Maria. "If you both agree to go for it, I will be glad to drive up with you some day. You can probably get most of the items you were interested in. At least it would give you books to get started with until the rest can all be shipped. Most things take two weeks to a month to arrive. I still need science and history books for my two."

"Thanks. That would be great!" Britany said with excitement. She called for Amy and Ben, who were not ready to leave yet, and walked to the car. She placed Andrew in his car seat and turned to say goodbye to Maria. She gave her a big hug. "Thanks again. I work tomorrow. I'll call you from work if it's not too busy, or call you tomorrow night to let you know how things are going." Maria smiled and waved as they left.

"Mom, I really want to home school, like Randy does," said Ben with excitement, as he strapped himself into the front seat.

"Me, too!" added Amy from the back.

"You both know you will still have to work. It will just be different than at school. It won't be all playing during the day," said Britany sternly.

Ben was very animated as he said, "Oh, I know. Randy said he does a lot more work around the house to help his mother, but he really likes learning at home. They get to do a lot of neat things and go on a lot of field trips."

They were almost home as Britany turned the corner and said, "I am going to talk to your dad tonight. Let me talk to him first and then you both can talk to him about it. I'm sorry to say I should have said something a lot sooner, but I just kind of put off making the decision until now it's less than two weeks until school starts."

Britany was preparing supper when Michael got home. Andrew was still taking his nap. Amy and Ben came running when he came in the door. He gave them each a big hug and then walked over to where Britany was working at the counter and gave her a warm embrace. She kissed him and smiled.

"I went to see Maria Crockett after we visited Jonathan at the hospital today," she said as she cut tomatoes for tacos.

"How was Jonathan today?" he asked as he took a carrot she had laid on the table.

"He is having a lot less pain and looked in good spirits. I haven't said anything to him about coming to live with us. I'm waiting on Dr. Stewart to see if it will work." Britany wiped her hands and went to the table to sit beside Michael.

"I went to Maria's because I have been thinking a lot about home schooling the children," said Britany. She prayed silently as she spoke.

Michael smiled. "I thought maybe you had. What exactly do you think?"

"Well, I'm not sure if it is a selfish desire on my part or Gods' gentle urging, but I really want to try teaching Amy and Ben," she said.

"I don't see how having three children to care for all day and all night is a selfish desire," said Michael. "I have been thinking about it, too. I like their school, but there are some things I don't care for. I just would never ask you to do it unless you want to. I can help some, but for the most part it would be up to you."

"I realize that," said Britany, looking down at the table and then back up at him. "When you put it the way you do, it makes me sound crazy!"

Michael laughed. "Yes, it does, but God often seems to ask us to do things that seem a bit different than the rest of the world. If you want to attempt it, I'm all for it."

Britany gave him a hug and hurried to the stove to keep the meat from burning. She told him about all the information she had gotten from Maria and how excited her friend had been.

"One thing I do hope you have considered," said Michael. "I don't see how you can continue to work and take on this enormous task, especially if Jonathan comes to live with us."

Britany carried food to the table and called for Ben to place the dishes and silverware in their positions.

"You're right," she said. "I can ask for a leave of absence until we see how it is going to work."

Ben walked beside Britany and whispered, "Does that mean we get to home school?" Britany nodded.

Ben yelled and hurried to get Amy. The rest of the evening was filled with happy talk and telling Michael the different things they could do. Britany called Maria and told her the news. The two women decided to go to the bookstore together on Thursday.

CHAPTER 8

Jonathan had been disappointed when his tutor came, causing Britany and the children to leave early. He looked forward to seeing them everyday, and it didn't seem fair to have the time cut short. He wanted to keep up with his studies, but he wished they could time it differently. Britany had said she would be back the next day, but that seemed a long time away. The days in the hospital seemed endless. He was going to find out who those two boys were who gave him the drugs and make them pay. He needed to make careful plans, because if he got caught it would ruin his future chances for med. school. He didn't dare tell Britany he wanted revenge. He knew she would not approve. She talked to him often about God and Jesus. But if there really is a God and He cares so much, then why do I have such a hard life?

His mother had never once mentioned who his father was, so as far as he knew it could have been a passerby, a one-night stand that meant nothing to his mother or father. Why had he come to be as a result? How could God care about him when no one else had seemed to? His mother Patsy seemed to have cared about him, but she had been too weak to ever get over her own problems. She never seemed to have enough left for him. Patsy had always lived with her father, Jim Quarterman. Patsy's mother had died in childbirth and Jim always seemed to blame Patsy. It seemed ironic to Jonathan now that she had stayed with her father up until the time Jonathan had persuaded her to move, and then she had died shortly afterward. Jonathan could never understand the attachment his mother seemed to have to the old man. Maybe she thought Jim was right and that she was the reason her mother had died.

Jonathan had always wanted to get even for the way Jim had yelled at his mother and hit her when things didn't go his way. Now he had two other people to get even with. Darn it anyway, why did he have to be so helpless in the hospital like he was? He didn't even have his truck. Since as early as he could remember he had been finding odd jobs to do and saving his money for the truck. When he turned sixteen he had had enough money for an old truck, and then as he worked mowing yards he had earned enough money to buy a nicer one.

Jonathan wished the slow night would hurry. He didn't like thinking of all the things he couldn't do while he was in the hospital. He must have drifted off to sleep, for the sun was just filtering through the window when he heard Britany's voice in the hall. She opened the door a crack, and he smiled.

"Good morning, Jonathan," she said cheerfully. "How did you sleep last night?" The room that had been so plain when he first arrived was covered with paintings and drawings Amy and Ben had made for him. A vase of fresh flowers that Michael had sent from the florist shop, sat on the nightstand.

"Not too well," he said honestly.

"I'm sorry to hear that," Britany said. "I will be back to check on you as soon as report is over." He nodded, and she was gone.

It wasn't long before she returned. She was joyful, and it cheered him to see her smiling face.

"I didn't like it when the tutor came shortly after you got here yesterday," Jonathan said before she had time to stick the thermometer in his mouth.

Britany shook her head. "Yeah, the kids were pretty unhappy about that too. Does she always come at the same time?"

"No, it seems like she could have some kind of schedule. I know I'm not going anywhere, but I would like to know when she is coming," he said.

Britany put the thermometer in his mouth. "Sorry, I don't mean to silence you, but you convinced everyone that you didn't try to commit suicide. I don't need to watch you constantly, so now you are not my only patient. I need to get your vitals quickly and check on a little baby I am caring for." She reached for his wrist to check his pulse. "It actually worked out well that we left early yesterday. I stopped at a friend's house and got some information on home schooling. Have you ever heard of that?" she asked.

He shook his head no, so she continued, "Well, Michael and I are going to be teaching Amy and Ben at home instead of their going to school." Jonathan gave her a puzzled look.

"I know," she said and reached for his arm to get his blood pressure. "It sounds very strange, but actually it's not much different than what you are doing until you heal enough to go back to school." He shrugged, and she took the thermometer from his mouth.

"I'll be back in about half an hour to help you with breakfast. I need to check on my other patient. Later I hope to go up to Dr. Steward's office to check on your truck," Britany said as she finished his vitals.

"I hope they found it," he said. A worried frown crossed his brow.

She patted his arm and said, "I do, too."

For some reason life seemed brighter when Britany was around, and Jonathan was glad when she returned.

"I talked to Dr. Steward," she said as she entered his room carrying the tray of food. I hope you don't mind I'm a little late, but I have good news." She arranged the tray beside the bed so he could reach some and she could help with the rest.

"I don't mind one bit if you have news about my truck," Jonathan said and pulled himself up slightly with the trapeze.

She smiled brightly. "It is," she said. "They found it parked in the driveway of one of the boys."

Jonathan's face darkened with anger. "How could they be so bold as to park my truck in their driveway like it was theirs!" he exclaimed.

"My thoughts exactly!" exclaimed Britany. "They told the police you gave it to them before you tried to commit suicide."

"What!" Jonathan exclaimed, and Britany thought he was going to come out of the bed.

She quickly reached out and grasped his shoulders to hold him down.

"Jonathan, stop! You are going to hurt yourself. Just calm down and let me finish what I was going to say," she said sternly.

He lay back, but anger raged in his eyes.

"Your truck is in perfect shape, and the police are going to park it in our garage for safe keeping, if that is all right with you. You just need to call the station and tell them. The police have already arrested the boys for possession of drugs and the theft of your truck. They are in plenty of trouble, and you don't need to worry about getting them. They will be punished," Britany explained.

"They won't be punished severely enough to satisfy me," Jonathan said between clenched teeth.

Britany looked at him sternly. "Have you ever heard, "Vengeance is mine, I will repay says the Lord?"

"But, Britany, you aren't in traction, unable to move and not sure you will ever be able to walk the same again," Jonathan said and met her stare.

She sighed. "You're right. I'm not, and it's a lot easier for me to say." Her look softened, and she touched his cheek. "But anger and hate are more destructive for the person who is angry than for the person who receives the anger. Jesus loves you, and I hope that someday you will realize just how much. Then you might look at things with a different perspective."

She turned toward his tray and put a straw in the milk. "Eat, Jonathan," she said when he hesitated. "Be happy your truck is safe."

Jonathan knew Britany didn't understand how he felt about the boys, and how angry he became when he was alone and had nothing else to think about. She probably never felt anger like he was feeling.

He obeyed her and ate his breakfast. She remained quiet while she helped him eat. He was sorry he had become so angry. She didn't deserve his anger. He took a bite of his eggs and suddenly remembered what she had said about his truck.

"You were serious when you said I could keep my truck in your garage?" he asked.

She nodded.

"And I need to call the police and tell them to take the truck there?"

"Yes, they will come to the hospital and have you sign a release and then drive it to our house," she explained.

He looked at her in amazement. "I can't believe you would do that for me."

She smiled, "We have room in the garage. That isn't a big thing. You might get your cast on next week and then be able to get out of the hospital. You can see your truck then. Of course it will be some time before you will be able to drive."

Jonathan reached for her hand and squeezed it. "Thank you. Can I call the police station now?"

"Sure," she said and helped him with the telephone. "I need to check on my other patient, and then we will get your bath started. I'll be back in about an hour. Put your light on if you need anything sooner," she said and left.

Jonathan felt amazement when Britany left. Life was starting to look a little more hopeful. His truck was in good shape and would be taken care of until he was released from the hospital. Suddenly his momentary good mood fell. When I am released from the hospital! The thought hit him hard. His truck would be fine, but what would he do? He wouldn't be in traction, but with a cast on both his arm and leg it was going to be very difficult to get along. Where will they send me! He felt panic again. He was very distraught when Britany entered again, and she noticed.

"Jonathan, you were so happy, and now you look very worried," she said. "What happened?" She stood beside the bed and looked at him. A small crease appeared between her eyes.

"I don't know what is going to happen to me when I get out of traction. I don't like this contraption, but I don't know what to expect when it's gone!" he complained with frustration.

Britany went and got the warm water for his bath. She got the towels and toiletries ready as she spoke. The way she talked seemed very ordinary, but what she said next was extremely surprising to Jonathan.

"Michael, Amy, Ben, Andrew and I would like it very much if you would come and stay with us," she said as she worked. He looked at her, speechless. "I spoke with Dr. Steward, and he says it should be fine. He will work on the paperwork if you want to live with us. The children will be around since we are home schooling, so it won't be the most peaceful place to recuperate. We have a room downstairs until you are able to maneuver stairs. Then I guess you can use Crystal's room until she comes to visit, and then you can share with Ben. I hate to throw her out of her room since she had it first, but I'm sure she will be happy to share when she's not home," Britany said.

Jonathan stared at her with a blank look. She had to stop what she was doing and wait for him, because he seemed to be frozen. She noticed a tear slowly forming in the corner of his eye. He still didn't speak and she waited patiently.

Jonathan was overwhelmed with emotion. For his entire life he had felt unwanted. His grandfather certainly had made it clear that he didn't want him around. His mother may have wanted him, but he had always been a little more of a burden than she could bear. His father had thought so little of him he had never made himself known. How could this family possibly want me? I wouldn't even be able to take care of myself, let alone help them in any way. He felt a tear coming to his eye, and he knew that if he tried to speak more would follow. He was afraid it was a dream and he might wakeup if he tried to talk. Britany waited patiently beside his bed. He knew he should respond in some way. Finally he took a breath and chanced breaking the spell of an impossible dream by saying, "Britany, how could you possibly want to take me in? You know how hard it is to care for me?"

"It's not just me. Remember, Michael and the children want you, too. It was their idea," she said with a smile.

"But why would they want me?" he asked brokenly.

"They love you Jonathan. We are not a conventional family. All of the children have been adopted in someway except for Andrew. They know what it's like to love and make someone else part of the family. Don't question love. Just accept it and give it in return," she said softly.

He tried again to speak, but tears came instead. Britany reached out to wipe them from his cheek. He grasped her arm with his good hand and pulled her close. He clung to her tightly and cried hard.

"It's all right Jonathan," Britany said quietly into his ear. She felt his body tremble as he cried. She patted his back until he relaxed a little, then she kissed his cheek and pulled back from his embrace.

"I'm sorry," Jonathan stammered.

"Don't be," Britany said patting his shoulder. "I just hope someday you can come to accept the deep love Jesus has for you, the same as you are accepting the love we have for you. He is the author of love."

Jonathan didn't understand what Britany was talking about, but he determined to be very careful not to talk badly about God from now on in her presence. He knew that God meant a great deal to her, and the last thing he wanted to do was to hurt her.

"Britany, I just can't believe your family would do this for me," he said in amazement.

She smiled and laughed, "Believe it! The children are coming up tomorrow, and they will probably be all over you with excitement. Ben says he always wanted an older brother. Amy is a little concerned that the boys will outnumber the girls, but she likes you so well that she feels you will help her out and be on her side sometimes."

Jonathan smiled his big smile, and his black eyes shone with pleasure.

CHAPTER 9

Crystal couldn't believe it when she got her paper on Wednesday. She knew the test had been difficult, but she had never made anything less than a B. Seventy-five percent would hurt her average very badly, and she needed sociology class for her major. She didn't want to tell Cortney, but Cortney knew what had happened as soon as she saw her.

Cortney put her arm around Crystal's shoulder and said, "I'm sorry, Crystal. That wasn't completely your fault. It's hard to do well when you don't go to class, but you were very tired from the night before. I'm sure you can raise your grade."

Crystal looked downcast. "I certainly hope so. This is one grade my mother is not going to find out about unless I don't get it raised by the end of the semester." They walked together toward the library. Eric saw them and came running to them before they reached the building.

He reached an arm around Crystal's waist. "So, why the long face?" he asked.

"I practically flunked my sociology class," Crystal moaned.

"I've got just the solution for you," he said. He grasped her hand and pulled her across campus lawn so that she almost had to run to keep up. She glanced back over her shoulder to see Cortney staring at them with a look on her face of puzzlement and disapproval.

He took her to his car and opened the door. She stood beside it and looked at him. "I have a class at three. I still need to do some reading. I don't have time to go anywhere," she moaned.

"You won't get any studying done until you cheer up. Lighten up. You'll like it, I promise," he coaxed and closed the door as she got in. He ran to the other side and lightly jumped over the door onto the seat and slid under the steering wheel.

He drove downtown to a coffee shop. He jumped out and went around to open her door. He helped her out and led her into the cafe. Inside he found a booth and sat her down at it. A waitress came to take their order. Crystal just looked at Eric. "What are you doing? I need to get to class?"

Eric looked at the waitress. "We'll order in a minute." As she left he pulled a box out of his pocket and opened it. Crystal stared in amazement as he placed a gold bracelet on her wrist.

"What are you doing?" she asked in wonder. "We are not even dating!" she exclaimed.

"How about if we change that status right now?" His blue eyes twinkled.

Cortney was livid when she heard what had happened.

"Lighten up, Cortney," Crystal said.

"But he made you miss another class! Don't you care about school anymore?" she asked. Her green eyes shone with concern and anger at the same time.

"I really like him." Crystal tossed her head, and her hair flipped over her shoulder. "He's fun, and maybe college just isn't for me anyway. I like being with him a lot more than going to class. He seems very rich. If I marry him I won't need to work." She walked down the hall to her dorm room and spoke behind her as she went. "He's at practice now. He said that he still needs to go and help even though he can't practice. He is coming in an hour to take me to dinner, and I need to get dressed. I think I need to get some nicer dresses. Maybe Brenda has something nice I could borrow."

Cortney fumed and followed her down the hall. "You don't even know him, and already you are talking of marrying him! I didn't think you were one of the girls who came to college to find a husband!" she fumed. "You don't even know if he is a Christian."

"For crying out loud, Cortney! He invited us to a Youth for Christ party for our first date!" Crystal shot back as she stopped and turned to face Cortney.

"That doesn't mean he's a Christian, and you know it!" Cortney exclaimed with clenched fists. Her tiny frame didn't back down.

Crystal stared back. She knew deep inside that Cortney was right. She realized that if she would stop and take a look at Eric she would have to agree, but she pushed the thoughts from her mind.

Crystal opened the door to her room. "Come in. I don't want to finish this conversation in the hall."

Cortney entered, and they both sat at the desk. "Look, Cortney, I watched my mother work hard to have enough money to raise me. She didn't even look at guys because she was so intent on raising me. Now she is happily married, but she spent all those years alone working hard. Eric is wonderful, and I think I love him. Maybe education isn't what I really need right now. I can always go back and finish. He isn't the only reason I am not doing well. School was a drag before he came along. I don't want to lose him because I am too narrow-minded."

Cortney sighed. "I think you are making a big mistake!"

"Maybe so," said Crystal with a smile. "But it's my life, and my mistake to make!" She gave Crystal a hug and went down the hall to see Brenda.

Brenda had an elegant dress that Crystal loved. She tired it on and turned in the mirror. Crystal had to admit to herself that it was very short, but she was surprised at how good she looked in it. Maybe it was time to try something a little more daring. An hour later she met Eric at the curb below her dorm.

"Wow," said Eric with a whistle. "You are a real knockout."

"Thanks," Crystal said, beaming with pleasure. The thought crossed her mind that her mother would not be very pleased, but it left quickly when she looked into Eric's blue eyes.

The evening was beautiful. Eric continued to show up every time Crystal turned around, and she spent most of the next two days with him. She managed to attend some classes. She wondered how he was able to keep his grades up. Eric claimed he had football obligations to keep when the weekend came, so Crystal worked frantically to make up with work she had neglected during the week. Even though she had told Cortney she didn't care about school, she still didn't want to totally give up on it yet. She had the scholarship to worry about. If her grades fell, so would the money!

The warm sun embraced him. Jonathan marveled at how wonderful the slight breeze felt on his face. He breathed deeply as Michael pushed the wheelchair to the car. Amy walked beside them, chatting constantly. Ben walked on the other side. Jonathan wanted them to slow down so he could bask in the wonderful feeling of being outside. He had lived outside for the entire summer, and the last two weeks in the hospital had seemed an eternity. The x-ray they had taken on Wednesday showed that the bone was in good alignment, and on Thursday they had taken him downstairs to take out the pins and apply the casts. They had dismissed him from the hospital the day after the cast was put on, but he would be going to the hospital daily until he was able to use his crutches successfully. Britany had told him he would learn fast, and he hoped so. He hated to make her drive him to the hospital. He knew she was very busy with the children.

He looked around him in amazement. The brightness of the sunlight hurt his eyes, but he didn't want to miss any of the beauty around him. He took Amy's hand. "Look at the blue bird," he said to Amy. She stopped talking and pointed so the rest of them could see the bird.

"Look, Andrew, see the pretty bird!" she exclaimed. Andrew looked but didn't see it until it flew. Then he squealed with delight. Jonathan smiled. It was fun having someone with whom to share little pleasures.

Michael wheeled him to the van door. Jonathan felt awkward as he tried to move from the wheelchair to the van.

"Use the pivot turn," Britany reminded him when he was standing. Michael helped him when he seemed to be struggling.

"We made it!" Jonathan said triumphantly when he was securely in his seat. "I hope everything isn't as awkward as this."

"It will get easier," said Britany. She secured Andrew in the car seat beside him. "But don't expect too much. You were pretty broken up. You are doing sensational compared to a little less than two weeks ago!"

"Yea, when you put it that way it does seem pretty good," Jonathan said in agreement. "At least I get to leave!" Jonathan watched closely as the city streets turned into country roads. They passed a golf course and then green pastures dotted with cows and horses grazing on the lush hillsides.

"Our house is just around the corner!" exclaimed Amy.

The van pulled into a drive, and Jonathan was amazed. Their house looked like a castle compared to what he was used to and the landscape surrounding it was beautiful. The steep drive rose to the house that was surrounded by a splendid view of the valley below. Horses were grazing on the side of the hill, and a stream flowed down the back of the property through a small wooded area.

They helped him up the stairs onto a porch that overlooked the valley. A bench swing hung on one side, along with wicker furniture. He would have liked to sit and enjoy the view, but Ben was eager to show him where his room was.

Once he was in the house they helped lower him back into the wheelchair to show him the lower level.

"I think you will need to wait a while before tackling the stairs to see the upper level," said Michael as he pushed him through each room.

"We converted this room into a bedroom temporarily," Ben explained. "You might have to listen to Amy practice the piano. I hope it's not too painful. Maybe you can leave when it is time for her to practice."

"Ben!" Amy yelled. "I'm just learning, and I can play some songs really good."

"I will love to listen to you play," said Jonathan. Ben laughed, and Michael sent him a stern glance.

Jonathan saw the piano in the room and wished he could play. He loved music of all kinds, but had never learned to play an instrument. They moved on to the living room and then the kitchen. The house was more elaborate than anything he had ever been in. It was warm and inviting even though he felt a little hesitant to touch anything. He cringed to think what damage he might do trying to get around, but Britany and Michael didn't seem concerned.

"Do you want to see my pony?" Amy asked as they went out onto the deck.

Jonathan looked at her pleading face. He didn't want to hurt her feelings, but he was extremely tired.

Britany touched Amy's hair and knelt down beside her. "I think we should let Jonathan lie down and rest for a bit. Maybe he can see the horses after lunch. He is going to be here a long time, and there is no hurry."

Jonathan gave Britany a grateful look. She wheeled him back to his room. She moved the wheelchair beside the bed and helped him move into it. He practically dropped into the bed. It was lower than the hospital bed, and he hadn't expected it.

"It will get better," said Britany as she helped him get comfortable. "You get some rest. Let me know when you are getting tired, and don't let Amy and Ben make you push yourself too much."

Jonathan quickly fell asleep with the words, "He will be here for a long time," gently caressing his thoughts.

Jonathan slept into the afternoon and then kept his promise to see Amy's pony. It was a struggle, but they were able to get the wheelchair to the barn. Andrew sat on Jonathan's lap for the ride.

"I kind of like having a third person to carry Andrew," Britany said as they walked along.

Being helpful was a very satisfying feeling. Jonathan smiled despite being jarred from side to side on the uneven path.

Ben put the halter on Trigger and led him next to Jonathan. "Have you ever ridden?" Ben asked.

Jonathan stroked the long, powerful neck. "No. I have always lived in the city."

"Would you like to? Mom can teach you! She taught me, and I ride real well!" Ben said with excitement.

Jonathan laughed and said, "I think it will be a while, but I would love to."

Amy brought her pony Sissy up to see Jonathan, too. Andrew reached up and begged to be put on her back. Britany took him and set him on top of the pony.

"Sissy likes Andrew. She is really good with little kids. My mom got her for me when I was three years old, after my father died. Trigger was her horse, too. My mother loved to jump, and Trigger can jump a four-foot jump with ease. I am jumping Sissy a little. Someday we will jump higher."

Jonathan realized that she wasn't talking about Britany when she had said her mother. He had never asked what had happened to Amy's mother. He just knew that Michael and Britany had adopted her when they married two years ago.

Ben pushed him up to the stall where Britany's horse Misty was kept. Misty reached her nose out the door and sniffed his hair. She almost touched his hair, but not quite. Then she lowered her head so he could stoke her forehead. She had a white star just above her eyes, and a silky golden mane. He liked the soft velvety feel of her muzzle.

"She likes you," said Amy. Misty nudged him slightly with her nose.

Britany handed him a carrot. "Give her one of these and she will love you forever. She is a very cuddly horse."

It was Friday, and Michael had taken the day off to be with the family when they brought Jonathan home. "Well, I guess it's back to work for both you and me on Monday," he said to Jonathan at the dinner table.

"Yeah, the tutor said she would be here Monday morning," said Jonathan. "I hope she can't find the place. It seemed kind of far out in the country."

Britany laughed, "You wish. She will find it. I gave her directions, and it's really not so far out. You have just never been in this direction before. Don't feel too bad. All three of you will be having school on Monday. Ben and Amy are going to start, too."

Britany got up early Monday morning to prepare for the day before the children got up. She nervously went to the kitchen and heated water for tea. Then she took her Bible and, when the tea was finished, sat at the table to read. She turned to the passage that she had been clinging to for the last several days, Joshua 1:6-9

Be strong and courageous, because you will lead these people to inherit the land I swore to their forefathers to give them. Be strong and very courageous. Be careful to obey all the law my servant Moses gave you; do not turn from it to the right or to the left, that you may be successful wherever you go. Do not let this Book of the Law depart from your mouth; meditate on it day and night, so that you may be careful to do everything written in it. Then you will be prosperous and successful. Have I not commanded you? Be strong and courageous. Do not be terrified; do not be discouraged, for the Lord your God will be with you wherever you go.

"Dear Lord," prayed Britany with her head bowed. The warm scent of orange spice tea filtered up to her from the steaming cup. "You have given me a command and a promise. I am scared to death to embark on this journey with the grave responsibility that comes with it, but I prayed about it and feel strongly that You have given me this call. Help me to be strong and courageous to lead these children into a deeper and stronger relationship with You and to grow in knowledge and wisdom of the world You've created."

Britany felt her anxiety ease as she hurried to start some laundry. Then she went to the barn and gave grain to the horses. The sun was making a grand entrance in the sky above her. It promised to be another beautiful day. She let Misty out of her stall and mucked it out. When she was finished she went to the house to shower and change her clothes. She was tempted to wear what Amy called her teacher's dress, but decided it might be easier to handle the day in a pair of Jean shorts and a T-shirt. Michael was up and in the kitchen when she finished. He had gotten Andrew from his bed, and Andrew was in his high chair, beside Michael. They both smiled when she entered the kitchen.

"How's my little teacher?" asked Michael and gave her a kiss as she leaned over him.

"Scared to death," she admitted.

"I see you were reassuring yourself again with your verse of encouragement," he said, pointing to the Bible. She grinned and nodded.

"I think I hear Jonathan." She caressed Michael's wavy hair with her cheek. "I will go help him while you are still here to watch Andrew," she said. He nodded, and she went to the next room.

"Good morning," she said as she knocked gently and entered the guestroom.

Jonathan gave her a happy, contented smile that she had never seen before, and it made her heart melt. "Did you sleep all right?" she asked.

"Better than I ever remember," he said, and it was the truth. He felt a warmth and security in their house that he had lacked, and he had slept very peacefully.

"Michael has Andrew, but he will be leaving soon, so I am going to help you get up and dressed," said Britany as she got his things. When they were finished she pushed him in his wheelchair to the kitchen. Andrew made delightful noises as they entered.

Michael was snapping his briefcase closed as they entered. "You're looking rested this morning," said Michael to Jonathan as he entered. "Well, I'm afraid I am going to have to leave." He rose from the table and patted Andrew's head. "You be good for Mom today," he said. Then he kissed Britany and reached down to shake Jonathan's hand.

Britany got some cereal and hot chocolate ready for Jonathan. She placed them in front of him at the table. "If you are able to eat by yourself I am going to put the clothes in the dryer and get Amy and Ben up," she said to Jonathan as she took Andrew from his high chair. She washed Andrew's face and hands while he objected.

"I'll be fine," Jonathan assured her.

Amy woke happy and excited to start the day as Britany entered the room. Ben tried to roll back over and go to sleep.

"No, you don't!" laughed Britany. "Summer vacation is over."

"But I thought sleeping in was one of the advantages of home schooling," he said sleepily.

"It is, silly," she said. "You got to sleep until eight instead of getting up at seven." He groaned and stumbled out of bed.

She went to get Andrew dressed as the other two went to the kitchen to get breakfast.

"Amy," said Britany, "you clear off the table and counters and put the dishes in the dishwasher as soon as you are done eating. Ben, you fold the load of clothes that are in the dryer. They should be dry soon. Both of you make your beds, and we will meet back here at nine to start Bible." Britany put Andrew on the floor and reached for the broom.

"Doesn't Jonathan have a job to do! It's not fair that he doesn't work. He's part of the family, too," complained Ben.

"He's right," said Jonathan. "I do need to help out." Ben smiled in triumph.

"I love to cook," said Jonathan. "If Amy and Ben help me, I can get lunch when it is time."

Britany smiled and started to sweep. "That would be wonderful. Ben, when you fold the load of clothes in the dryer, put the clothes from the washer into the dryer and turn it on. Don't forget to empty the lint trap!" she called after him as he left.

Britany glanced at the clock and noticed that it was ten minutes until nine. She hurried to make her bed, and then went to make up Jonathan's. She called for everyone to come to the table. She had decided to read a psalm each morning and chose to start reading Genesis for their Bible time. Jonathan was scheduled for physical therapy at two that afternoon, and his tutor was coming at ten. It was going to be a very busy day.

"Amy, would you please start us off by reading Psalm 1?" Britany asked. She looked around and realized no one had a Bible. "Ben, go to the shelf and bring the Bibles. You and Amy each have your own, and Jonathan can use Michael's." Jonathan gave her a strange look.

"Jonathan, I don't want to force you read the Bible, but we like to start the day by reading and memorizing the Bible. Then we have a time of prayer. I was hoping you would join us so we could do it together. We will be done in the mornings before your tutor gets here." Britany couldn't determine what the look on his face meant and she felt her heart beat faster as she waited for him to respond. He simply took the Bible that Ben offered to him. Ben helped him find Psalm 1 while Britany helped Amy. Britany prayed silently and urgently for wisdom in how to proceed.

"I guess you can read now, Amy," she said in what she hoped was a normal voice. Andrew crawled up to her chair and raised his arms for her to pick him up. He nestled into her lap as Amy read. Amy struggled with a few of the words, and it was slow, but they were in no hurry.

"I think that would be a very good passage for our memory work for the next few weeks," said Britany as Amy finished. "Let's repeat the first verse together several times and see if we can remember it."

"Blessed are those who do not walk in the counsel of the wicked or sit in the seat of mockers or stand in the way of sinners," they all said in unison. Andrew jabbered right along with them, and Britany noticed that Jonathan said it, too. She said a silent thank you to Jesus, and they continued.

"Let's turn to Genesis, and, Ben, you start reading for us. It is the very first book of the Bible," said Britany. Britany noticed Jonathan's eyes cloud over when Ben read about God creating the heavens and the earth. He had probably only been taught evolution. She knew that when it was time God would open his eyes and help him to see the truth.

"Jonathan, I think Ben could use a break. Would you please finish the chapter?" Britany asked. He didn't look up but started reading very fluently. His voice was clear and pleasant to listen to. When he finished it was time for prayer.

Britany asked Ben to pray for Michael and Amy to pray for Jonathan. They each prayed, and Britany finished by asking for guidance and wisdom as she taught and that each of them would learn and glorify God. She looked up and noticed that Jonathan had a trace of a tear in his eye.

"Ben, I have a book on Egypt here. You and Amy look through the pictures and then you start to read it aloud to Amy if I am not back yet. Amy, you put the Bibles back on the shelf. I am going to help Jonathan get set up in the living room for when the tutor comes. She should be here shortly."

Britany was relieved when Andrew went down for an early nap. She hadn't been looking forward to taking Jonathan to therapy with a grumpy baby. The tutor brought Jonathan into the kitchen before she left.

"Well, what would you like to eat?" he asked Ben and Amy.

Amy looked at him with serious brown eyes and said, "I like macaroni and cheese. Would that be hard to make?"

Jonathan smiled and patted her head. "It's my specialty. Do you know where the cooking pans are?"

She reached for them, and Ben went to get the box of macaroni and cheese out of the cupboard. They cooperated, and the task went quite well. Britany suggested that they add carrots and apples to the menu. She smiled as she watched them work together. I guess if they didn't learn anything else today, they are learning how to work together, she thought.

Britany took Amy and Ben's reading lessons with them to the hospital to work on during Jonathan's therapy. They hadn't been reading long when the door opened and Jonathan came out with a big smile on his face. There was no one pushing him, and Britany was amazed.

He wheeled down the hall, then wheeled around and came back.

"How did you do that with one hand?" yelled Ben in astonishment.

"They gave me a new wheelchair. The wheels are connected to each other, and I can control them with one hand," he said with pleasure. "That was all I did. They want me to come back Thursday and they will have special crutches for me to use, also. They want me to practice with them before they will let me use them. Then I will be done with therapy until the casts are removed."

Britany was relieved. It sounded like a lot fewer trips to the hospital than she had planned. It wasn't an easy task to load them all up.

Jonathan showed off in his new chair when Michael came home. Everyone attacked Michael, trying to talk at once during supper. They were very excited about their first day of school.

"How did you feel about the first day of school?" Michael asked Britany as they prepared for bed.

"I was extremely pleased, but it was a very full day. It is going to be next to impossible to keep up with things."

The rest of the week went well, but the second week of school didn't flow as smoothly. It seemed like they spent too much time sitting, reading and writing. She had hoped to have more hands-on learning opportunities. She called Jonathan's tutor and made arrangements for her to come early on Thursday. Then she announced to the family that they were going to the Nashville zoo on Thursday as soon as Jonathan was finished.

Thursday, while the tutor was with Jonathan, Britany was able to get the children dressed and the house straightened. She realized it would be too difficult to do school work plus go to the zoo. They used the time during the drive to do Bible. The day was warm and sunny, for which Britany was grateful.

Britany helped Jonathan from the van to his chair when they arrived. Amy and Ben were excited and started to run for the gate.

"Ben! Amy! Don't run through the parking lot! You are both old enough to know better!" Britany yelled. They stopped and walked sheepishly back to the van.

"I'm sorry, Mom. I wasn't thinking," said Amy.

"Race you to the gate," Jonathan challenged Ben. Britany gave him a mean look. "Got ya!" he laughed. Britany shook her head and frowned. Getting everyone ready for the outing and the long drive had made her tense.

"Hand Andrew to me," Jonathan offered. "If Ben will push for a while Andrew can ride with me."

Andrew was pleased to be on Jonathan's lap.

"Can I put Andrew's bag on the handle to your chair?" Britany asked. "Then I won't have to carry it, and we won't need the stroller." She looped it over the handle. She took a deep breath of the fresh air and started to relax as they walked through open fields where gazelle and deer grazed.

Jonathan was thrilled to see the animals. "This is great. It looks like we are in the jungle with them," he said as they went through the area where the mountain lions were kept. "I have never been to the zoo before."

Amy pointed at a cub that was below the bridge where they stood. "Look, Andrew, a baby cub! Isn't he cute? He is playing with his mother's tail!"

The animals were hard to see at times through the lush vegetation. The smell of leaves and trees filled the air. Various birds flew from bushes.

Ben and Jonathan looked down the ravine at the white tiger. Britany and Amy wondered across the walk to see the mother on the other side.

"I think it's wonderful how God made so many different animals, each with its own characteristics," said Ben. Jonathan didn't say anything. Ben looked at him. "You know, there was a time I didn't believe in God. Oh, I believed in Him, but I didn't want to admit it. I didn't realize how much He loved me and wanted me to be part of His family."

"Really?" asked Jonathan. He was surprised. "I just thought your family always believed in God."

"Amy has," said Ben. "She is one of the few people who has had a relationship with Jesus from the time she was little. My dad wasn't a very strong

Christian when I was little, and my other mother doesn't believe in God at all. She told me that even if there was a God, I was so bad He would never want me."

"What changed your mind?" asked Jonathan.

Ben smiled at Britany, whose back was to him. Her arm was around Amy as they watched another tiger. Andrew was balanced on her hip.

"Britany did. She never preached to me, but I could see that there was something different about her life than my own mother's. I gave her a really hard time for a while after she and Dad got married, but she always seemed to love me, really love me. I began to realize that if she could love me as horrible as I had been, then Jesus could love me, too. One day in church I asked Jesus to forgive me of my sins and come into my heart. He did, too. I could feel a difference. Life was much less lonely after that and not nearly as scary. You don't have to believe in Jesus or pretend to. Britany will love you anyway, and so will we," said Ben.

Jonathan smiled a faint smile. "Thanks, Ben," he said. "I appreciate that."

Jonathan wheeled his chair around and started down the path. Ben's comments made him think, and he began looking at the animals in a different way. He watched closely as the sleek cougar moved silently between the trees. It was built to perfection for its task in life. He gazed at the beauty of the numerous parrots and wondered at the awkward, but practical design of the anteater. Each creature was wonderful and unique. He had never considered the possibility that God created each life. He had always thought they had evolved, but as he watched them he wondered. A new realization dawned. If God did create everything, then each was designed for a purpose, which they certainly seemed to have. He started to think that if God cared enough to create each animal with a vast variety of features, that maybe God could care for him. Ben was right about Britany and the rest of the family. There was something there that he had never experienced before.

Britany and Amy crossed back to where Jonathan and Ben waited and Britany placed Andrew on Jonathan's lap. He held Andrew close and was almost glad that he had fallen from that tree so many days ago.

They ate lunch at the snack bar on the far side of the zoo and watched the peacocks as they sauntered around looking for dropped crumbs. They carried themselves proudly and occasionally bobbed to whisk a morsel off the ground.

"When we get to the other side across the pond we will have seen the entire park," said Britany as they finished.

"Do you think we can come back again sometime?" asked Ben.

"Sure," said Britany with a smile. "This is how I envisioned home schooling to be!"

CHAPTER 10

Eric walked Cortney and Crystal to the Campus Life meeting. It was hard for Crystal to believe that she had only known him for a month. Her days and many evenings were spent with him. On weekends he had football obligations he had to keep even though he couldn't practice. His arm seemed to be doing well. He always wore it in a sling, but it never seemed to bother him. He had his other arm around her as they walked.

They came to the yellow house that was full of activity.

"Hi, Cortney," said Terry as he came down the steps to greet them. "Hi, Eric and Crystal. How is your shoulder doing? We could have used your running skills in the game Saturday. They came real close to losing that game."

"Yeah," said Eric. "They had me worried. I was on the edge of my seat until that final buzzer sounded. More games like that and we won't go to the Rose Bowl for sure."

Terry laughed and patted him on the back. "Come on in. We are ready to get started," he said.

Cortney had been asked to prepare a devotional for the evening and Crystal could feel her start to panic as she grasped her arm to say something to her.

"You will do fine," Crystal said and squeezed her arm.

"Say a prayer for me," Cortney whispered in Crystal's ear. Crystal smiled and nodded her head. She started to say a silent prayer for Cortney, but the words just wouldn't seem to come to her. Just be with her. Amen, was what she finally managed.

People kept coming, and Cortney enjoyed talking with others. Terry came over and told Cortney it was time to get started. "Don't be nervous. I will introduce you when we finish singing. Relax and have fun. You'll do fine!" he said encouragingly. Cortney smiled up at him.

They were in the middle of singing "My God is an Awesome God," when Britany saw three young men enter amidst a slight commotion. When Eric saw them he looked troubled. He excused himself and went to meet them at the door. They went outside, and he soon returned.

He walked to where Crystal was seated and said quietly, "I need to go. A friend of mine needs some help. He was in an accident and is in the emergency room. I'll see you tomorrow."

Crystal quickly got up. "I'll go with you!" she exclaimed. The singing stopped, and everyone looked at them.

Eric looked around and addressed the crowd. "It's all right. I just need to leave. See you guys later." Then he said more quietly to Crystal, "Your friend needs you here. I will be fine. Just enjoy the meeting and I will see you tomorrow after class." He turned quickly and left before Crystal could say more.

She looked around and realized that she was the center of attention. She smiled and sat down. They sang a few more songs, and then Cortney gave her devotional. Her thoughts were inspiring, but they made Crystal aware of how little time she had been spending reading her Bible or praying. She was letting studies and Eric push her time with God away, and she wasn't too proud of it. When Terry closed in prayer, Crystal prayed silently and asked God to forgive her. She promised Him that she would try harder.

Crystal went to the kitchen and got herself a cola as soon as the meeting was finished. Terry and Cortney came up to her. "You did wonderful!" exclaimed Crystal and threw her arms around Cortney.

"Thanks," said Cortney letting out a big breath. "I certainly was nervous. Thanks for praying for me."

Crystal felt herself blush when she remembered the lousy prayer she had prayed.

"Where did Eric go?" Terry asked.

"He said his friend was in an accident, and he needed to go to the emergency room. I offered to go with him, but he wanted me to stay so I could hear Cortney. I felt bad, but I am glad I got to hear her."

Terry looked around. "When this place clears out I need to clean up, but then if you like I can take you to the hospital to see how his friend is doing," Terry said.

Crystal looked pleased. "Thank you. I would like that very much. I'll help so it goes faster." She wanted to be with Eric. If his friend was hurt badly he might need some emotional support.

"I'll help too, and, go along," said Cortney cheerfully. Crystal knew Cortney was pleased with how well the devotional had gone and relieved that it was over.

They cleaned up and were soon on their way. Britany didn't see Eric's car in the parking lot. "He must have come with one of his friends," she said as they looked around. "I don't see his car."

The waiting room was full, but they didn't see Eric or any of the young men that had came to get him.

"I guess they must have gone already," Crystal said puzzled.

"With as many people as there are here it seems like it would have been a long wait. I hope nothing really serious happened," said Terry. Crystal cringed. She wanted to find Eric even more when she thought about the possibility that his friend may have died. They didn't know where else to look. Crystal had never been to his apartment. She had no idea where he lived except that it wasn't on campus. He never talked about his home other than his parent's house, and as she thought about it she realized that she didn't know where they lived either.

Cortney put her hand on Crystal's shoulder. "Please don't think the worst. They may have gotten here and realized he didn't need to be seen, or they may have already released him by the time Eric arrived. We don't know how long it took his friends to find him at the meeting."

"Yeah, I'll take you girls back to the dorm and don't worry. You've done all you can do," said Terry.

Crystal smiled a half-smile. "I really appreciate your bringing us here even if we didn't find him. Thank you," she said.

Crystal ran to Eric as soon as she saw him Wednesday morning. "Eric! How is your friend? We went to the emergency room, but we couldn't find you, and I didn't know your friends name to ask anyone," Crystal said.

Eric's smile turned to a look of disapproval. "What were you doing? Checking on me?" he asked defensively.

"No! I was worried about you!" exclaimed Crystal.

Eric smiled again. "I'm sorry. I just didn't get much sleep last night. It turned out that my friend was in jail, not the emergency room. He's out now. I'm sorry we had you worried. I would have called, but it was late, and I wanted you to get some sleep."

She smiled as they walked. It was getting cooler outside so they went to the library to study for the next class. Eric walked her to the next class and promised to take her to supper. Crystal was alarmed when she got her test results back for sociology. It was a C. She wanted to get an A or B for the class, and she groaned.

She told Eric at dinner. He grinned and said, "Do you want a ring this time to cheer you up?"

Crystal lifted her eyebrows. "No," she said. "I just want a better grade! You don't have to buy me presents every time something bad happens. I think I am going to have to stop seeing you as much and go to class more."

Eric smiled. "That is cheaper than a ring. I will be more careful to not monopolize your time. That will be very hard, though."

September turned into October. The weather was cool enough to require a coat, and it seemed to rain everyday. Crystal hurried to class. She was with Eric as much as before, and now sociology was not the only class she was having trouble in. She didn't like the way her life was heading, but she seemed drawn to Eric by an unexplainable attraction. He seemed to coax her into doing things she wouldn't normally do. He had never made sexual advances on her, and although Crystal was a little curious as to why he had never asked her to his apartment she was also glad. She knew the effect he seemed to have on her was a little scary.

She sighed and walked on. She wished she could talk to her mother about Eric, but she really hadn't told her much other than she had met him and they were going out some. She didn't tell her that her grades were falling because she wasn't going to class enough or that she wasn't spending time studying. Crystal didn't want her mother to be disappointed in her, yet she was the one person who could help her see her way out of the dilemma. Cortney tried to coax Crystal into not seeing Eric. Crystal just wouldn't listen. She wanted to date Eric and still do well in school. Others dated and did well, but then, she thought, not all guys were as demanding as Eric!

Britany awoke at dawn and began preparing for church. She hurried to feed the horses and then went to the kitchen to clean potatoes. She took a roast from the refrigerator, washed it, and placed it in the large pot, adding onions and herbs. She arranged potatoes around it, added some water, and set the oven to cook for three hours, to be finished when they arrived home from church. Andrew was waking by the time she finished, and she relaxed while she nursed him and then fed him some breakfast. When he had finished, she went to wake Jonathan. He looked at her sleepily and closed his eyes to sleep some more.

"Oh, no, you don't," she laughed. "Look, I got you some new slacks and a shirt for church. I even cut the leg already for you to get them on."

Jonathan sat up and looked at them. "They look really nice! When did you do that?" he asked. He looked wide-awake.

"I wanted to surprise you," she said. "I thought you were probably getting tired of wearing the same things."

Jonathan laughed. "I've worn the same things all my life and really hadn't thought about it, but this is great. Thanks!"

"I hope I don't have to get you something every Sunday to get you out of bed. I left some cereal and milk on the table so you can eat as soon as you are ready. I am going to try and get Ben out of bed now. He is harder than you are!" she said and turned toward the stairs with Andrew on her hip.

"If I could get up the stairs I would get him up for you," said Jonathan.

Britany turned back. "Before you know it that cast will be off, and you will be running up those stairs. You will be dancing again by Christmas," she said.

Britany felt full of hope as she dressed Amy and Andrew. They seemed to sense her exuberant mood and laughed and chattered as they dressed. Michael peeked into Amy's room to see what all the chatter was about.

"We're just getting ready for church," said Britany. "It has the promise of being a wonderful day."

"This is the day that the Lord has made. I will rejoice and be glad in it!" exclaimed Michael.

"Exactly!" agreed Britany.

Amy started singing the song that goes with the verse, and soon they were all singing. Jonathan could hear them from where he sat in the kitchen. It felt secure to be included into their warm, loving family.

Britany sat in church and wished Crystal could be with them. Crystal hadn't been calling as much lately, and when she did she wasn't her usually talkative self. Britany sensed things were not going well at school, but Crystal wouldn't admit to anything being wrong when Britany asked. She prayed for her, as always, during the service.

Britany looked at her family as they sat in the pew. Her heart filled with love, and she thanked God for all He had done in her life. The pastor taught about God's saving grace and His great love. Britany noticed that Jonathan struggled to find the passages as the scriptures were read, but he found every one and followed intently what was being said. Britany prayed for him that he would believe the words that were spoken and ask Jesus to forgive him and become his personal Savior.

When they entered the house following the service, the smell of pot roast filled the kitchen. Britany hustled about to change and prepare the meal. Ben set the dishes on the table. Amy filled water glasses, and Jonathan entertained Andrew.

Soon the meal was ready, and they bowed their heads in prayer. Before

Michael started praying Jonathan cleared his throat. Michael looked up at him. "Is there something you want to say before I pray?" he asked.

Jonathan took a deep breath. "Actually, there is," he said. He looked a little embarrassed. He hesitated and then looked at Ben. Ben smiled at him encouragingly, and he continued. "Today when the pastor asked if anyone wanted to know Jesus as their Savior to pray with him as he prayed, well, I thought about it and about how much Jesus means to all of you. I prayed the prayer with the pastor, and I really could tell Jesus listened and came into my life. It was remarkable." He looked at Britany. "I started to feel that love that you have been talking about," he said and smiled.

Tears sprung up in Britany's eyes. She got up from the table and went over to Jonathan. "Jonathan, that's wonderful," she said and wrapped her arms around him. "Thank You, Jesus," she said softly and kissed the top of his head.

Britany thought to herself, I can never replace his earthly mother, but now I can be his spiritual mother. She laid her cheek on his silky black hair and smiled.

Amy jumped up from her seat, too, and ran up to Jonathan. She threw her little arms around him and reached up to kiss his cheek. He bent over so she could reach it. When they were finished Michael reached out and shook his hand. His face beamed.

"Congratulations, son," he said. His voice was rough and choked with emotion.

Ben sat in his chair and grinned.

"You knew, didn't you, Ben!" Britany exclaimed.

Jonathan looked at her. "I told him after church," he said. "We talked at the zoo and had a little understanding. I wanted to let him know what had happened. He told me to tell the rest of you right before we prayed for dinner, but I hope I didn't spoil anything. I think the food is getting cold."

"Oh, it didn't spoil anything," said Britany. "We are just so happy for you."

"I couldn't tell," said Jonathan, and everyone laughed.

Michael helped Britany clean up following dinner. "All of you can take some time off and enjoy yourselves," announced Britany. "Dad and I will take care of the dishes."

"Yea!" yelled Ben. "Come in Amy, and Jonathan. Let's go do something." Jonathan took Andrew into the living room, and the four of them played with Ben's Legos.

"I just can't believe it," Britany sighed as she washed another pan.

Michael reached for it and dried it. He laughed. "Didn't you think God was able to save him?"

"No--I mean yes--I mean, I knew God could save him," she stammered. "I'm just surprised that it happened so soon!"

Michael wrapped his arms around her and raised her into the air. "You are so cute when you're flustered. I love you Mrs. Kaiser," he said and kissed her deeply.

"I love you too," said Britany with a giggle when she was able to talk again.

Britany, Amy and Ben rode horses in the arena during the afternoon while Jonathan and Michael watched.

"I really would like to learn to ride a horse," said Jonathan dreamily.

Michael smiled, "Ben was right about the fact that Britany is a very good teacher. She will have you riding in no time once the doctors say everything is healed."

Later in the afternoon, Britany sneaked into the kitchen and made a cake while the others were watching a movie.

"Since today is Jonathan's spiritual birthday, I thought it was only right that we should celebrate by having birthday cake," she announced as she came into the room with the cake in her hands. It had one candle burning on the top, along with Jonathan's name and some flowers.

Amy started singing "Happy Birthday" as she entered. Michael and Ben joined in.

Jonathan blew out the candle, and they all clapped. "Thank you," he said, and his dark eyes sparkled.

CHAPTER 11

Crystal cringed as she looked at her midterm paper that was due in two hours. She had been up all night, and it looked as if she had barely started. Tears filled her eyes and threatened to spill onto her paper. Her head dropped to her desk and rested on her arms.

"Crystal, wake up!" Cortney said and shook her shoulder.

"What!" exclaimed Crystal as she woke with a start. "Oh, no! I must have fallen asleep."

"Well, we need to go," said Cortney, tossing her a sweater to put on. "If we don't get to class to take the midterm test the paper won't do you much good anyway."

Crystal dressed quickly and grabbed her paper. "At least it's finished. I just don't like it at all. I wish I wouldn't have waited so long to start it."

They hurried across campus to biology class. A cold breeze blew rain into their faces. Crystal held her coat tightly around her and turned her face so it wasn't directly facing the rain. As cold as it was, she was almost glad for the rain, because it would cover the fact that she had not taken time to put on make-up and fix her hair. Her coat was waterproof, but by the time they reached the building she was getting wet.

"I am so cold," she muttered between chattering teeth.

"Me, too," agreed Cortney. "I think he should give us extra credit for coming out in this weather." She took off her hood and her red hair cascaded around her shoulders.

Crystal didn't feel comfortable with the test and was convinced that if she got a C she would be lucky. It wouldn't do too well for her grade point average. But the next class, sociology, she was afraid would be even worse. It was the class that she seemed to continually miss for various reasons, all centering around Eric. She wasn't sure why he chose that time of day to show up, but he frequently did and seemed very good at convincing her that whatever he had to do was more urgent than going to class.

He wasn't at the door as they left biology.

"Maybe the weather is so bad that Eric will actually let you go to class and take the midterm," said Cortney sarcastically.

Crystal's blue eyes looked at Cortney. She wanted to be angry, but she knew Cortney was right and justified in the remark she made. Crystal had just been thinking the same thing. She smiled faintly.

"I guess I have an hour to study and cram what information in I can."

Terry was in the library waiting for Cortney when they entered. He smiled a warm smile and took Cortney's books.

"It looks like you had a rough night, Crystal," said Terry with concern in his voice.

Crystal tried to smooth her hair a little and smiled. "I was hoping it didn't show. The rain didn't help much."

When they took the test Crystal realized that the hour she had spent studying had done little to compensate for the hours she hadn't. She knew she would be very lucky to pass the class with a D. She was disappointed as she and Cortney walked back to the dorm. She took a short nap. Eric was taking her to supper following her next class.

"Hi!" Eric said cheerfully as she answered the knock at her door. "Are you going to invite me in?" He was entering as he asked. A sly look was on his face.

"Hi," said Crystal wearing her blue silk blouse and short skirt. She took a step back as he walked into the room.

"It looks like you were working furiously," he said motioning to the pile of books and scattered papers on her desk.

"To no avail, I'm afraid," she sighed.

He stepped forward and took her in his arms. "Let me see if I can make you feel better," he whispered in her ear. He kissed her.

It was comforting to have his strong arms around her. The entire day Crystal had felt like a failure. It was nice to have someone care. She was confused about how she felt toward Eric. It wasn't a "can't live without you" type of love, but she did feel very warmly toward him. Was it love? She wasn't sure, and since she had never been in love she had nothing to compare it to.

He looked down at her. "We've been dating for two months now," he said.

She smiled. "Yes, we have. The second week of school you walked up to where we were sitting beside the tree."

"And I haven't pressured you in any way," he continued.

"I do remember you convincing me not to go to class," she reminded and tilted her head to the side as she smiled up at him.

He gently massaged her back with his hands and drew her close. "That's not what I meant. We have been dating long enough. Don't you think it's time we get a little more intimate? I know your roommate is never around. It seems we have no reason not to!" He kissed her again.

Crystal was starting to agree with him. Suddenly there was a knock, and the door flew open. "Crystal," began Cortney. "Oh, I am so sorry," she apologized. Her hand was still on the doorknob, and she started to back out, pulling the door closed as she went. "I'll come back another time. I just wanted to see how you were doing after the tests," she said and quickly finished closing the door. Eric walked over and locked the door.

"There," he said with finality. "Now that won't happen again. Now where were we?" he said as he came back to Crystal.

Crystal put her hand up against his chest to stop him and backed up. She shook her head. "I don't think we should do this," she said.

"You seemed more than willing a few moments ago," Eric said with a look of anger.

Crystal grabbed her coat that lay across the bed. "Let's just go to dinner. I am really hungry."

"Yeah, you're right," he said, and his face mellowed. "I am hungry, too.

Where should we eat?"

He held the door for her, and then they walked to the car. "Tiffany's?" Crystal asked hopefully with a lift of her eyebrows.

"If you promise to be a good girl when we get back," he whispered in her ear.

Crystal laughed. "I promise to be a good girl, but it's not a good girl you want me to be!"

Eric moaned and opened the car door. "Well, I guess Tiffany's it is!"

The meal was lovely, but Crystal had the feeling they were being watched. "Eric," she said quietly. "Do you know those men?" she asked, looking toward a table with two men in suits. Eric looked toward the table. He shrugged his shoulders.

"No, I've never seen them. Why, do they look familiar?" he asked.

Crystal looked toward them again. "No, they just seem to be watching us. They are giving me the willies," she said and shivered.

"Don't worry. Just ignore them and enjoy your meal," he said taking a bite of his salad.

Crystal tried, but she couldn't keep from looking at the men.

"You look lovely tonight, Crystal," said Eric.

Crystal grinned. "You are just trying to get my mind off of those two men."

"You're right, but you really do look lovely. That blouse brings out the blue in your eyes," he said and grasped her hand.

"Thank you," she said.

Crystal was hoping the two men would finish their meal and leave, but they were still there as Eric stood up and put down the tip.

"I am really glad to get out of the sight of those two," Crystal said and breathed a sigh of relief as they left the restaurant. They walked up the dark street, Crystal's arm looped around Eric's. When they got to the car he took her in his arms and kissed her. Then he pleasantly opened her door and went to the other side. He smiled at her as he got in and put the key into the ignition.

Suddenly policemen surrounded the car. Crystal gasped as she turned and looked into the barrel of a gun.

"Get out of the car with your hands up!" a loud voice sounded.

"Eric, what is happening?" Crystal screamed. Her alarm immediately changed to anger. "They can't do this to us!" she exclaimed.

Eric's shoulders slumped as he shook his head. "I'm sorry, Crystal. Just do as they say," he said. He turned to open the door and get out with his arms raised high.

"Eric, what are you talking about?" she asked and looked at him in astonishment. "Eric, your arm! You have it raised above your head! I thought it was hurt!" she cried.

"Come out of the car, Miss," the voice said again. Crystal turned to see the gun still pointed at her head. She opened the door.

"What are you doing? What gives you the right to come after us with guns and make us get out of the car?" she yelled angrily. She held her hands up high as she got out, but the anger was getting stronger and she brought them to her side with her fists clenched tightly. "Eric, tell them to leave us alone. They can't do this to us!" she screamed and turned toward Eric. He didn't look at her. He hung his head and tried to look away.

"Ma'am, we have a warrant for his arrest and since you have been seen with him frequently you are under arrest too until you are cleared," said a man in a blue suit.

"It's you!" gasped Crystal. "I knew you were watching us at the restaurant. Eric, it's the man who was watching us!" Eric didn't respond, and she looked to see him get into the police car parked beside the curb. Suddenly she was alone with several policemen around her, and the man in the blue suit was talking to her. "You have the right to remain silent," Crystal heard him say. She couldn't believe this was happening. What in the world was she going to do! They placed handcuffs on her and helped her into the police car. She was scared and started to shake. She squirmed and tried to get her skirt to cover more of her legs. She had no success and turned to face the window as familiar signs went by. The ride seemed to last forever.

When they got to the police station the officer opened the door and grasped her elbow to help her out of the car. She looked from one stone cold face to the other. They escorted her into the building with her hands still cuffed behind her back. She stumbled as she tripped on the step. The policeman grasped her arm and kept her from falling. He was polite but very formal. She felt humiliated and wanted to scream in defiance. Instead she stood quietly and lifted her chin, trying to look proud.

"You can use the telephone here on the desk to make your one call," the officer said. Crystal looked at the telephone as if it were a foreign object. Who was she going to call? I need to reason this out, she thought. Cortney is in the dorm, but she will be as alarmed as I am if I call and won't know what to do. She really wanted to call her mother, but she didn't know how she could help her from five hundred miles away. Her uncle lived in the city. She tried his number, but no one was home. She decided to go ahead and call her mother. She was the only one Crystal really wanted to talk to anyway. She needed to hear her soothing voice.

Britany was preparing for bed when the telephone rang. She was pleasantly surprised to hear Crystal's voice. "Crystal," she said as she recognized her. Suddenly all she heard were sobs coming over the telephone. "Honey, what is wrong? Are you hurt?" she asked. Michael was in the bathroom and came into the bedroom when he heard Britany's alarmed voice. He looked at her and she returned a puzzled look. The sobs continued, but Britany could make out a faint "no."

"Take a deep breath and try again, Crystal. I am here and listening. Did something happen between you and Eric?" she asked. She heard another faint "no."

"Well, kind of," Crystal said as she started to regain her composure. "I'm in jail, Mom!"

"What!" exclaimed Britany. "Were you in a wreck?" she asked. She looked at Michael and said while she covered the receiver, "She's in jail!" Michael looked alarmed.

"No, Mom, I wasn't in a wreck or anything. Eric and I went out to supper.

There were two men watching us. They followed us when we left, and when we got into the car we were suddenly surrounded by police officers. They said that they had a warrant for Eric's arrest, and since I was with him they brought me here, too."

"You don't even know why?" exclaimed Britany in astonishment. "I will be there as soon as I can. I will see if I can get a flight, and if not, I will drive. Don't worry. I will be there soon."

"Mom, please don't drive all night. Don't do that to yourself. It's my problem, and I don't want you to suffer for it."

"Don't worry, Crystal," said Britany. "I will be all right. I will be there as soon as I can. I am going to go now so I can call the airport. Please don't get discouraged. We will get you out, don't worry."

Britany put the phone down and looked up at Michael.

"I'm going with you!" he said sternly.

Britany took a deep breath, and her shoulders drooped as she released it. "I wish you could," she sighed. "But we can't just pack up six people and fly out of here in a moment's notice. You stay with Jonathan, Ben and Amy. I will have to take Andrew because he is still nursing." She thought for a moment and then continued. "If I can't get a flight, maybe my mother could drive to Columbus and see if she can help Crystal until we get there. Then we can all go. If I fly and find that I need help, then you can drive and bring the others later."

Michael frowned, and his brown eyes showed concern. Britany reached up and smoothed a strand of stray hair from his forehead. She kissed his cheek.

"I guess that does make sense," he said in resignation. "I will call the airport to see if there are any flights tonight. You start packing."

Britany tried not to picture Crystal in a cold jail cell, but the thought wouldn't leave her mind. She worked quickly.

"They have a flight that leaves in ninety minutes. I told them to hold a ticket for you. We will almost have to fly ourselves to make it," Michael said, shaking his head as he looked at her.

"We can make it. I have just a few more things to pack for Andrew, and then I am ready," answered Britany. Anxiety made her work vigorously as she tossed items into a bag and tried to concentrate on toiletries they might need for what she hoped would be a short trip. Michael went and explained to Jonathan where they were going. Ben and Amy were in their rooms, but they hadn't gone to sleep yet.

They came running down the stairs, their eyes wide with excitement. Amy ran to Britany.

"Is Crystal all right?" she asked with fear in her eyes.

"Yes," said Britany, drawing Amy into her arms. "I need to go and be with her. You be good for Jonathan tomorrow."

Amy shook her head solemnly. "I will help him fix lunch and supper. Won't we, Ben?" she asked as she looked at him seriously.

Ben nodded. His eyes wore a serious expression. Britany left with apprehension.

The officer led Crystal through steel doors and down a long cement corridor with several cells on each side. A dingy-looking young man with long, straggly hair came to the door of his cell as they approached. "Hi," he said. Crystal cast a hesitant glance toward him and quickly looked away as he eyed her lustfully. He whistled as they went past, and Crystal shuddered. Several other inmates tried to talk to her, but she ignored them and walked as close to the officer as possible, trying to hide behind him. They went through some more steel doors, and she realized they were in the women's part of the prison. This can't be happening, she thought as he opened the door and motioned for her to enter. He remained silent and shut the door as soon as she was inside. She stood alone in the middle of her prison cell and looked at the simple surroundings, realizing that she could be viewed from all sides of the cell except for one. She looked at the commode and single sink and cringed. She walked to the door of her cell and touched one of the steel bars. She felt the coldness of it on her warm skin. She quickly withdrew her hand as if the bar had carried an electrical current. She could see one other person, a middle-aged lady lying on a bed, down the corridor. She could hear some noises from the male part of the prison, but other than that, it was very quiet. She backed up from the door and went to sit on the bed. She looked at her watch. She was glad they hadn't taken it as they had her purse. It said nine o'clock. Even if her mother could get a flight it would hours before she could get there. Crystal looked down at her lap. She felt embarrassed by the amount of leg exposed by her dress moving up when she sat down. She reached for a blanket and covered her legs. She realized that no one was looking at her, but she still felt exposed.

She couldn't help wondering what in the world she was doing in jail. What had Eric done that could possibly get them both in jail? She felt ominously alone. She wished she could call Cortney and talk with her just to listen to the sound of another voice, but even if they did allow her to call they wouldn't allow her to visit with Cortney.

Britany gave Michael a warm embrace, and then she boarded the airplane. Soon it was moving down the runway and lifting lightly into the air. Britany tried to relax, but she felt as if every fiber of her being were on edge. It was comforting to have Andrew with her as he slept quietly in her arms. A tear slipped down her cheek. She wished she could hold her oldest child just as she was cradling her youngest. She didn't know what had happened or what she was going to do, but she knew Crystal needed help.

Britany had been concerned about her since she had started back to school at the end of summer. She suspected that her classes were not going well. The fact that Crystal never commented on her classes seemed to confirm her suspicions. Britany had not liked what she heard of Eric the first time Crystal had spoken of him, and now she was more worried than ever. What had he done to get her daughter thrown into jail? There was also the possibility that Crystal was not telling Britany the entire story and that she had done something herself to be arrested. Britany didn't even want to think of her biggest concern about Eric. She had prayed every night that Crystal would say no to any advances he might make, but Britany realized that it depended on Crystal. Had she been firm enough in her convictions? Britany sighed and tried focusing her thoughts on what needed to be done to get Crystal out of jail. It would do neither of them any good if she were emotionally distraught when she arrived. Britany closed her eyes and tried to let sleep come.

The lights of the jailhouse went off, and Crystal jumped off her bed where she had been sitting. She was startled and tried to see. There were lights over the exit signs, and as her eyes adjusted she realized she could make out her bed and the other objects in her cell. She sat back down. She never remembered feeling so alone. The odor of the institution even seemed harsh and impersonal. What was going to happen to her? What could Eric have done to get her into so much trouble? What if she had to spend time in prison? What effect would this have on her schooling? Crystal thought back to the first week of school. She had taken her education for granted. She had been so excited to go to college the first year, but recently she had forgotten what a privilege it was. She had been foolishly bored and tired of it.

She tried to blame what was happening on Eric, but she realized that if she had put more emphasis on schoolwork she would have been in the dorm studying for the next day's test, instead of going out to eat. She had taken advantage of Eric's money and was very much enjoying some of the finer things in life, which she didn't have the funds to get for herself. She had thought that since she had never been able to experience life in that way that she deserved it for a while. How foolish could she get?

She realized that it was getting close to midnight and that she was getting very cold. She found another blanket and wrapped it around her. She was feeling the need to relieve herself. It was dark, and she was glad she couldn't be seen, but the thought of using the commode in the open was still distasteful to her. She didn't feel like lying down, but she did take off her shoes and put her feet on the bed and wrap her arms around her legs. It seemed to warm her and make her feel a little safer. She knew it was silly to feel afraid when no one could get in and she couldn't get out, but afraid is exactly how she felt.

"Oh, Lord," she prayed and then couldn't go on. She had no right to be praying to God when she had neglected Him for three months. She had hardly gone to church since she had gotten to campus, and she couldn't remember the last time she had opened her Bible. She had been going to Campus Life, but that was just because Eric went, and it seemed to ease her guilty conscious. But she knew it wasn't sincere, and God knew the difference. How could she pray to God when she had neglected Him so? She buried her head on her knees, and despair filled her. She wanted to cry, but didn't feel she deserved the privilege. What was she going to tell her mother? Now she wasn't sure she even wanted her to come. What would she tell her if she stayed for a while and started asking about her classes? She didn't want to tell her that she was only making passing grades in one class.

Crystal's future looked grim, and she started to realize what she had been doing by going her own selfish way. She wanted to pray, but the words did not come. The tears did come, though, and they threatened to never stop. Her body convulsed, and she trembled. She seemed out of control, and it scared her even more. From somewhere out of the darkness some verses that she had memorized as an adolescent came to her mind.

If I say, "Surely the darkness will hide me and the light become night around me," even the darkness will not be dark to you; the night will shine like the day, for darkness is as light to you.

For you created my inmost being; you knit me together in my mother's womb.

(Psalm 139:11-13)

Crystal's convulsing slowed, and she was able to take a deep breath. She blew it out slowly. Then she knelt beside the bed. The floor was cold and hard, but she didn't care. There was something more important on her mind.

"Dear Lord," she prayed. "If it is true, if You really do see through the darkness, then I pray that You hear me and come to my aid. I have done wrong. I know better. I have no excuse. I don't feel like I deserve Your forgiveness, but I plead with all my heart for exactly that. Please forgive me and bring me out of the darkness into Your loving light. I'm sorry for putting my own selfishness in front of You. I'm sorry for putting Eric in front of You. I'm sorry for having a relationship with someone and leaving You out of it when You should be the center of it." Her knees ached, and she shivered with cold, but Crystal was filling with a different type of warmth, and she continued in earnest. "I have no excuse for the things I have done. I was raised to put You in the center of my life and all I have done is put me in the center of my life. If You can see through my sin to forgive me, I pray that You would."

Crystal was filled with a warmth and joy that she couldn't explain. She knew Jesus was with her in her jail cell, and suddenly it lost its harsh indifference. She got up from her knees and curled up on the bed, tucking the covers around her.

CHAPTER 12

Britany watched the lights of the runway as the plane descended. It was shortly after eleven her time, but was after midnight in Columbus. Andrew stirred as they entered the cold night air outside the airport. A taxi was parked at the curb. Except for the other passengers from her flight the airport seemed deserted. She had fit all her belongings into one bag that she now flung over her shoulder.

"I need to go to the police station where someone arrested near campus would be taken," Britany said briskly to the taxi driver. He gave her a puzzled look. Britany realized that it was a little strange for a woman with a baby to ask to be taken to the police station after midnight from the airport.

The police station was busy, and Britany was very careful to keep away from most of the people there. She didn't want to seem snobby, but she felt a strong urge to protect Andrew and herself. Crystal needed her. She made her way across the room and tried to talk to someone at the desk. No one seemed to care. She saw an officer standing a few feet away and went to him. She glanced at his name badge.

"Officer, Carlton, my daughter was arrested this evening, and I have come to get her out of jail," said Britany when she had his attention.

"I'm sorry, ma'am. We just changed shifts, and I'm afraid I don't know who that would be. Do you know what she was arrested for?" he asked politely.

"She called me around seven—no, eight-thirty your time--and said that a man in a blue suit had been following her and her boyfriend Eric. When they went to get into the car the police arrested her and Eric."

His eyes lit up with recognition. "Oh, yes. That was Captain Major's arrest. They have been trying to get that boy for a long time now. Anyone involved in that group is bound to be in trouble." Britany's heart sank, and for the first time she felt deep fear for Crystal's future.

"I've got to talk to her!" Britany pleaded.

The policeman looked at her kindly. "The cells are almost empty. I can take you back to see her."

"That would be wonderful," said Britany. "Could I make a phone call first?" He nodded and handed her the telephone. Britany called the lawyer who had helped her with Amy's custody case. He answered on the third ring with a thick, sleepy voice.

"Mr. Fitzpatrick, this is Britany Kaiser. I hate to wake you, but my daughter Crystal is in jail, and I have no idea why. I know you are two hours away. I am in the police station in Columbus, but I don't know who else to call," said Britany.

"Britany, hi! I'm sorry to hear that!" His voice came through sounding awake. "I don't understand how they can arrest her without giving the reason. Give me the number there. I will see what I can do. Call me back in an hour, and we can talk after I find out what is going on. We'll see what can be done to get her out as soon as possible."

Britany felt a brief tinge of relief. "Thank you so much. I do hope you can do something. They are going to let me in to see Crystal now, and then I will call you back."

Britany handed the telephone back to Officer Carlton. He moved it into position, and then, taking his keys from his pocket, he led the way through the corridor. Britany walked close behind him as he led her through the dimly lit walkway. Britany could sense the presence of prisoners on both sides of her more than she could see them. Chills went through her and she thought of how Crystal must have felt walking the same path. She prayed that Crystal hadn't done anything to deserve being in this place, but she realized the possibility existed. At least she was going to get the chance to talk to Crystal first-hand.

Crystal woke with a start as she heard steps approaching. She almost jumped off the bed at the loud sound of the door slamming shut. She could make out the shapes of two people coming near.

"Crystal, I brought you a visitor," said Officer Carlton as he put the key in the lock.

"Mom!" exclaimed Crystal in amazement. She ran to her mother and grasped her tightly.

"Oh, Crystal!" said Britany smoothing her silky hair as Crystal clung to her. Her body trembled as she cried. Andrew stirred slightly on Britany's shoulder.

"Come, sit down," said Britany, grasping Crystal's arm and walking toward the bed. She sat and pulled Crystal down beside her. Crystal cried while Britany held her close.

Britany wished for more light so she could see. "Are you alright?" she asked.

Crystal nodded yes.

"I talked to our lawyer and he is going to call as see if he can find out more. Have they told you why you are in here yet?" Britany asked.

"No," said Crystal faintly. "I have been trying to be brave, but I'm afraid I lost it when I saw you." Crystal wiped at her tears and Britany reached for a tissue from her bag.

"Has it been frightful in this place?" Britany asked.

Crystal wiped her face. "It was really scary when they turned off the lights. Some of the male prisoners where disgusting. I hope I can leave soon, like right away. It just seems so unfair to be forced to go through this."

Britany sighed. "Our government is supposed to protect us, not confine us without cause. You need to be perfectly honest with me, Crystal. I will fight for all I am worth to get you out of here, but I need to know the entire truth." She looked at Crystal. Because of the dimness she couldn't see the look in her eyes, and that bothered her for now she would need to rely on her other instincts to be sure Crystal was telling the truth.

Crystal paused. She knew her mother was looking at her, but she couldn't look up. "Mom, you've got to believe me. I have done nothing to go to jail for, but I haven't been honest with you. I have spent much of my time with Eric the past two months, and I am not doing well in school."

"How bad is not well?" asked Britany. She tried to keep her voice calm and not to act surprised.

"I'm passing one class. Other than that it is iffy," Crystal said with remorse.

Britany readjusted Andrew as he slept. Her arm was getting very weak. She wasn't sure what to say and waited to see if Crystal would continue. She didn't like what she was hearing, but it seemed a relief to finally find out what was happening in Crystal's life. She had known things were not right since Crystal had gone back to school, but she had never been quite sure what was going on. Now she was finding out. The silence continued for a long time.

Britany tried to see into Crystal's face. "Crystal, this is not easy, but I really need to ask. Have you slept with Eric?"

Crystal stiffened and gave Britany an ugly glare. "Mom!" she exclaimed. "How can you even ask that? Don't you trust me?"

Britany sighed. "Crystal, no one is above doing the wrong thing in the wrong situation and it seems to me that you have gotten yourself into exactly that." She reached out and grasped Crystal's hand.

"Sit back down and relax a little," urged Britany. Crystal sat down and started to cry again.

"Mom, what am I going to do?" Crystal shook her head slowly. "I'm in jail. I am failing school, and I'm sure you are not the only one who thinks I've been sleeping with Eric. My future is ruined, along with my reputation."

Britany was starting to feel the effects of no sleep. Her back ached from the burden of Andrew. She leaned against the wall as much as she could to give herself some support.

"Crystal, I know this will seem like a lecture, but I'm sorry it is the only thing that comes to mind. Proverbs three, verses five and six, says, 'In all your ways acknowledge Him, and He will make your paths straight.' Once again Britany reached out for Crystal's hand. "Seek God, ask His forgiveness, and trust Him to help you find the answers."

Crystal squeezed her mother's hand, "You are right Mom. I was doing a lot of thinking before you got here. I realized that is exactly what I needed to do. I asked God for forgiveness and I really want to start following Him again."

Britany kissed her cheek. "I hate to see you have to go through all this, but if it has helped you to recognize the need to put Jesus first in your life, then I am glad it happened." She paused and tried to see down the hall. "I think I hear the guard coming. He will probably tell me I need to leave."

Crystal grabbed Britany's arm, and Andrew woke with a start. He looked around with a terrified look, and Britany quickly cradled his head and tried to comfort him before he started to cry out.

Keys sounded in the lock, and Officer Carlton opened the door.

"You are free to go, Crystal. Follow me." He held the door and waited for them to go through it.

"What happened?" exclaimed Crystal turning to Britany. Britany was gathering Andrew in her arms.

"I don't know," she said. "But would you carry this bag for me? Don't question the officer. Let's just get out of here!"

"I guess we will go back to my dorm," said Crystal as they left the building.

"I'll give you both a ride," said Officer Carlton. Britany jumped when she heard the voice come from behind her. She didn't realize anyone had followed them out of the building.

"That would be wonderful!" she exclaimed gratefully.

"You both look very tired, and it might be a long wait this time of night for a taxi," said Officer Carlton.

He opened the door to his squad car, and they both got in.

"I'm confused as to why they let Crystal out in the middle of the night without bond," said Britany as they drove across campus.

He smiled. "I'm not at liberty to say, but you called the right person. Call your lawyer back later this morning, and he can go into detail. Good luck to you, Crystal," he said as they came to her dorm. "And please stay away from the likes of Eric. He's trouble, and you are too nice of a girl to get wrapped up in that!"

Crystal was puzzled by what the officer said. She stared at him as he pulled away. She was going to do some investigating of her own and find out just exactly what was going on with Eric.

"Crystal," said Britany to get her attention. "Where do we go? I don't remember the way, and I'm exhausted."

Crystal looked at her mother blankly. "Oh! Yeah! I'm sorry. It's up this way," she said and led the way up a flight of stairs and down a hall.

Crystal fixed the bed for her mother to sleep on the bottom bunk, and she slept on the top. Britany gratefully took off her shoes and snuggled under the covers, tucking Andrew in beside her. He looked at her with a smile and then went back to sleep.

The telephone rang, and Britany woke with a start. She looked around a minute trying to determine where she was. Andrew woke and looked just as confused. He cried when she tried to get up to answer the phone.

"I've got it, Mom," said Crystal from above her. Britany saw her arm reach down toward the desk and grab the receiver.

"Oh, hi, Dad!" said her sleepy voice. "Yeah, Mom is right here," she handed the phone to Britany and went back to sleep. Andrew continued to cry as Britany took the receiver.

"Michael, I am so sorry not to call you last night. We were so tired that we simply came back to the dorm and went to sleep."

Britany sat up and tried to soothe Andrew. She knew he was hungry and probably soaking wet. She reached for the diaper bag and withdrew it from the duffel bag lying on the floor beside the bed where Crystal had let it fall. She found a jar of apple juice and gave it to him while she changed his diaper. She held the phone cradled on her shoulder.

"I had no idea where you would be, and I was very worried, so I just thought I would try Crystal's room on the chance that you would spend the night there," Michael was saying as Britany worked with Andrew. "I left the two children with Jonathan and came to work, but I can leave and bring them up there if you need me."

"I need to call Mr. Fitzpatrick, the lawyer this morning. I really have no idea what is going on. The officer simply said we were free to go and let us leave. He said I would need to talk to my lawyer to find out more."

"Eight forty-five!" Crystal exclaimed. She had turned over and looked at the clock as she slowly started to wake. "I need to get to class!" At the same time Cortney came into the room. She looked surprised to see Britany and Andrew in Crystal's room.

"Where were you last night?" she asked Crystal. "I was worried sick! You need to hurry. The professor is going over the material for tomorrow's midterm!"

Crystal had jumped out of bed and was throwing clothes around. "I will explain everything that I understand on the way to class," Crystal said to Cortney, and then, turning to Britany, she said, "I will come back as soon as class is over. There might be some milk and cereal. If not, there is a store on the corner. See you later!" She kissed Britany on the cheek, gave Andrew a hug, and was out the door in a hurry.

"What was that?" asked Michael.

"I'm not sure if it was Crystal or a whirlwind. I think she is making a good recovery," laughed Britany. "This time I will call you when I find out anything. I promise, but I don't think you will need to come, at least not today. I hope Jonathan can handle the children from a wheelchair."

"He will do fine. I don't think there is much that boy can't do," laughed Michael. They said goodbye, and Britany replaced the telephone. When she had freshened up and fed Andrew she called her lawyer.

"Good morning, Mr. Fitzpatrick," said Britany. "What strings did you pull last night? They let Crystal out in less than an hour after I called you. Thank you so much. I didn't want her in that place a minute more. She was pretty distraught."

"As I did some investigating I found out that they really had no reason to arrest Crystal in the first place," said the lawyer. Britany had to stretch the phone cord to reach for Andrew, who had found a pencil on the floor. She took it away from him and gave him a Tupperware bowl of Crystal's to play with. His brown eyes lit up when he saw it.

"They had a warrant to arrest Eric. He is suspected of being the ring leader in a fencing operation." Britany gasped as she heard what he said.

Keith continued. "They expected to find stolen goods in his car or on his person, but they didn't. If they had Crystal would have been arrested for stealing also, but since they found nothing, there was really nothing they could charge her with."

Britany was alarmed. "Crystal got herself involved with someone really corrupt!"

"If the charges are correct, I'm afraid so," he said. "Remember, he is considered innocent until proven guilty."

"Does this mean Crystal is cleared?" asked Britany.

"I wish it did," he said. He took a sip of the coffee his secretary had brought to him. "I am going to leave in half an hour to drive over there. I want to check things out for myself in case something develops that we need to be concerned about. Can I meet you and Crystal for lunch?"

"Sure," said Britany. "I am not sure of Crystal's class schedule, but I will be there." She looked out the window and gave him the address in front of the dorm. Then she hung up and called Michael to tell him what was happening.

Crystal came back to the dorm just in time to go with them for lunch.

Britany and Crystal were seated a short time before Keith arrived at the restaurant. He was exited and talkative, but Crystal was horrified when she heard what Mr. Fitzpatrick had to say.

"How could I be so blind?" she asked, her blue eyes deeply troubled.

Keith Fitzpatrick reached over and patted her shoulder. "Don't blame yourself. If the charges are true, he is an expert. Tell me everything you know. I am going to do some research and get back with you this evening. I have a room at the Town Center. We can have supper at Tiffany's and talk."

"No," groaned Crystal and buried her head in her hands.

"That is where she was arrested," explained Britany. The lawyer looked sympathetic.

"I'm sorry. How about O'Charley's?" he asked.

Britany nodded. "That will be fine." They finished their meal. Britany and Crystal went back to the dorm. Britany called Michael and then lay with Andrew and sang him to sleep. She then fell asleep herself as she sang. Crystal tried to study for her last midterm, scheduled for the next day, but gave up and napped also.

Mr. Fitzpatrick met them at the dorm and was excited that he had found out some news. He drove them to the restaurant and talked almost nonstop.

Crystal found it hard to share in his excitement. She was relieved to be out of jail, but Eric was still in jail, and she wanted to see him. But Keith Fitzpatrick had strictly forbidden it. She looked at the menu but found nothing that looked appealing.

"Crystal, are you not hungry?" asked Britany. Crystal shook her head no. The last time she had gone to supper was disastrous, and being in a restaurant was bringing back memories.

"Why don't you just have a bowl of soup?" asked Britany.

Crystal agreed. She listened half-heartedly as Mr. Fitzpatrick spoke until he started to talk about Eric.

"It seems," he said, "that Eric started school two years ago, and then quit after the first year."

"Eric wasn't taking classes?" Crystal asked. She looked perplexed. "Then what was he doing on the campus?" She continued shaking her head. She laid her spoon down and sat back in her chair.

"They think he was using the college campus to sell his goods. He had attended school there and played football for a year, so it was easy for him to look as if he belonged." Keith cut the steak with a knife as he spoke and then took a bite.

Britany noticed that he ate heartily for someone so slim.

"If he wasn't in school, then how could he be on the football team?" Crystal asked in defiance. She felt the need to defend Eric. The police must be wrong, she thought.

Britany fed Andrew some of her potatoes and then looked at Crystal softly. "Crystal, did you ever see him play football or watch any of his practices?"

"No, he injured his arm soon after we met." Crystal thought of the sling and how easily Eric had lifted his arm when the police arrested them, but she refrained from mentioning it. She put down the spoon and sat in silence.

"He lives in an apartment with two other guys who are also under arrest for stealing and selling stolen items," Keith continued.

Crystal heard what he said, but she didn't like what she heard. She sat staring at her dish. Britany watched her but didn't comment. She knew her daughter was hurting on the inside.

"The car checked out to be his. The police were sure it was stolen also," Mr. Fitzpatrick said between bites. "It's good for Crystal's sake it wasn't, or she would be in much more trouble than she is."

"Stop it!" Crystal yelled. "Just stop it! I don't have to listen to all these lies about Eric." She pushed herself from the table and glared at Keith. He stopped eating and looked at her in amazement.

"Eric's parents are rich! That's how he has the car and is able to afford so much! They are going through a divorce, and it is tearing him up inside. Now he is in jail! He is already hurting! Can't you just leave him alone!" Crystal remained seated, but was ready to walk out at the slightest provocation.

Mr. Fitzpatrick wiped his face with his napkin. A slight bald spot on the top of his head reflected the light from above as he moved. "I'm sorry, Crystal," he said gently. "Please sit back to the table. I didn't mean to disturb you."

Crystal wanted to run from the room, but the possibility that what he was saying might be true kept her glued to her chair. She had suspicions about Eric from the time that she met him, but she wasn't ready to believe what the lawyer was saying. Curiosity made her listen. She needed to know what the police thought if she was going to help Eric.

"I'm sorry," continued Mr. Fitzpatrick, "but not for Eric. I'm sorry he involved you in this," he said sternly.

"He didn't harm me in any way!" protested Crystal. "He was always the gentleman and treated me like a queen!" She tilted her shoulders and cocked her head. "I just wish he were here to defend himself."

Britany tried to reason with her daughter. "Crystal, your grades are falling because of him. You can't sit here and say he didn't harm you!"

Crystal glared at Britany in a way that Britany hadn't seen since Crystal was thirteen. She knew Crystal was hurting, but it wasn't a pretty sight.

"My grades fell because I was stupid and my classes are too hard. Eric didn't make me fail my classes," Crystal retorted.

"Crystal, Eric's parents got a divorce ten years ago," Keith said.

Crystal threw down her napkin and jumped up. She grabbed her jacket and left with a flourish. Britany's heart pounded as she watched her go. Andrew started pounding his high chair tray, and Britany jumped. She turned to look at him. Tears stung her eyes. Andrew looked at her as if he understood what was happening.

"Where will she go?" Britany asked without realizing she was saying anything.

"Probably to see Eric," said Keith quietly.

Britany looked at him in alarm. "But you told her not to do that!"

He took a deep, deliberate breath and let it out. "The police will tape the conversation. It might be to our benefit. It will show that Crystal has no idea what kind of a person Eric is."

"Could you take me back to Crystal's dorm now?" Britany asked with a despairing look on her face. "I think I will wait for her to return."

Britany got to Crystal's room and sat on the bed with Andrew beside her. She reached for the telephone and called Michael. He answered it almost immediately.

"I think maybe you had better come now," she said weakly.

"It's that bad?" he asked softly.

"Yes. The lawyer told us some terrible things about Eric. It seems he has been lying to Crystal from the time they met. She doesn't want to believe it. She got mad and left. We think she went to see Eric."

"I'll get the children's things together and take off," said Michael. "We should be there by early morning."

Britany gasped, "No, Michael! I didn't mean right now! Tomorrow will be fine. There is nothing you can do right away. There is probably nothing you can do tomorrow, except give me emotional support."

"Are you sure?" he asked.

"Yes, I'm sure," said Britany. "I will call my mother. I think it would be better to leave Jonathan, Amy, and Ben with her. I'm sure she would be glad to watch them for a few days."

"Do you think she will mind looking after Jonathan?"

"She will love him as much as we do," Britany said mildly. It was comforting to Britany to picture Ben and Amy. It helped to think of the other children and get her mind off of Crystal. It was hard to imagine how Crystal could be so mixed up and confused.

CHAPTER 13

Crystal walked for what seemed like hours, but in reality was only one. She was angry and frustrated. Surely those things can't be true, she thought. She turned toward the police station. She needed to find out for herself what was happening to Eric. When she arrived she walked up the stairs and stared at the door. She started to go through and froze. She couldn't make herself step inside. Crystal turned and walked away, back toward the dorm. She walked a block and stopped. She stomped her foot and looked toward the dark sky. What was she doing? She needed to talk to Eric and hear his side of the story. She spun around and walked with determination toward the cold structure. When she got near the door she took a deep breath and barged through before she could have second thoughts. She looked around and immediately started to shake.

She whirled around and was ready to bolt out when she heard a voice say, "May I help you?" A lady officer addressed her, and she turned to look.

"I'm here to see a prisoner," she said faintly.

"There are just fifteen more minutes until visiting hours are over. Can I ask who you wish to see?" she asked. The lady seemed very polite, and Crystal started to relax a little.

"Eric, Eric Wright," she mumbled.

"He is under tight security, but you can see him for ten minutes." She led the way. They walked through a metal detector. The door slammed shut as they passed, and Crystal jumped. She fought the urge to turn and run out, and soon found herself seated at a counter, not really knowing how she got there. Soon Eric came out from behind a steel door. Seeing him in handcuffs tore at Crystal's heart. He smiled. She tried to smile back, but her lips started to quiver.

He reached his fingers through the small opening and grasped Crystal's hand. "I'm glad they let you out."

"But you are still in this horrible place," Crystal said with dismay.

"They will drop the charges and let me out soon. Don't you worry," he smiled confidently.

"They are saying some awful things about you," Crystal said.

He shrugged his shoulders. "Let them talk. They won't find anything and I will be out of here in no time." His blond hair was perfectly in place. Crystal wondered how he was able to maintain his immaculate appearance even in jail.

"My lawyer said your parents divorced ten years ago and that you are not even in school," Crystal said.

"Lawyers lie more than anyone I know," said Eric. Crystal felt him press something into the sleeve of her blouse, but she kept her eyes on his. "They will tell you a bunch of lies so you won't come to see me. I'm glad you came anyway. That is the worst thing about this place is, not getting to see you. You go get some rest. See you later." He blew her a kiss through the glass.

Crystal looked hesitantly toward the lady officer who had been watching her. She was careful not to reach for whatever it was that Eric had shoved into her sleeve. She hoped it didn't fall out as they walked. Thinking about Eric kept her mind off the cold steel doors they passed.

When Crystal was far from the prison she slipped the paper from her sleeve. In it was a man's name and address. It also contained instructions to the man to get Eric out on bail. Crystal's heart soared. He was going to be free, and she could talk to him again, outside of those terrible walls.

Crystal stopped under a streetlight and tried again to read the address written on the paper. She didn't recognize the name of the street. She walked to the nearest service station where she found a telephone to call for a taxi. The air was cool, and she began to shiver as she waited for the cab. Headlights came and went as she looked expectantly at each one. Crystal could see the sign on the top of the car as it turned the corner, and she stepped toward the curb.

"Ma'am, the name's Melvin, and I guess you are the one who called for a ride," the driver said as he doffed his ball cap that sported a Cincinnati Reds emblem. His tight jeans were worn with a tear in the knee, but clean.

"Yes, I'm the one who called. I need to go to this address, and I have no idea where it is. I was hoping you would know." She held the paper toward him, and he reached out his hand to take it from her. His fingers grazed hers, and she quickly drew her hand away. He looked up and gave her a questioning glance.

"Ma'am, I beg your pardon, but I don't think you need to be going to that part of town. Let me take you home." Crystal realized he wasn't much older than she was, and she resented his acting like a parent with her.

"Look, it's your job to take me where I need to go," Crystal said as she slipped into the back seat. "I won't take long. I just need to deliver a message. I would appreciate it if you would even wait for me to come back to the cab, and then you can take me back to campus."

Crystal's confidence started to wane as they drove into a dark, dilapidated part of town. She sat tensely as they drove away from the familiar streets of campus. She was beginning to think she should have waited until morning. The taxi driver stopped in the driveway of a white house. It looked out of place in the midst of the others. Crystal felt a bit relieved. She got out and went to the door. A man in his late forties answered the door.

"Hello!" he said brightly. "What brings a beautiful lady like your self to my doorstep?" he asked as he appraised her with his eyes. Crystal cringed.

"Are you Mister Krenshaw?" she asked.

"Yes, I am," he nodded as he answered.

Crystal looked at the paper in her hand as she handed him the note and said, "I have this from Eric. Do you know his parents?" she asked hesitantly. "I'm not sure why he wanted me to give this to you instead of calling his parents." She stood on the porch at the door as they spoke. He hadn't asked her in, and she was more than content to stay on the porch. The man was nice enough, but there was something about him she didn't care for.

He looked at her with what was beginning to seem like an ever-present smile; a little too present, in Crystal's mind. "Eric's parents are vacationing, and I am taking care of their business. I can handle this just fine." He looked at the note and chuckled. "So it looks like Eric has himself in a bit of trouble. I'll take care of things. Eric will be out shortly. Thank you for delivering this." He reached into his pocket and pulled out a wad of cash. "You take this for the cab expenses," he said and handed her two twenty-dollar bills. "Eric may even be out in time to take you out to dinner and dancing tomorrow. You go get some rest now." He put the money in Crystal's hand and sent her back to the taxi.

Crystal glanced behind her at the house as she walked away. Her mind was not eased by the man she had just met.

"Take my advice and stay away from the likes of anyone that would bring you back to that part of town," said the cab driver as he drove to the dorm.

Crystal felt very confused. She sat quietly as he talked. Maybe the taxi driver was right. What was Eric doing being involved with someone like the man she had just met?

Crystal determined to not tell her mother what had happened as she walked into the dorm.

Britany looked up as Crystal entered her room. "I was worried," said Britany. Andrew lay curled up at the foot of the bed. Britany had been reading.

"I know," said Crystal with a sigh as she sat at the desk. "I needed to get away for a while and think things through."

"How was Eric?" Britany asked and Crystal looked at her startled.

"How did you know?" she asked.

Britany looked at her daughter with compassion. "Mr. Fitzpatrick told me you would go there."

Crystal threw an angry look to the ceiling, and clenched her fist. "I hate that man!" she exclaimed.

"He is trying to help!" pleaded Britany. Crystal jumped from her chair and went to stare out the window.

"He hates Eric! I can't understand why he keeps making up all these lies about him!" She wouldn't turn to look at Britany as she spoke. Britany got up from the bed and went to stand beside her. She put her arm around Crystal's shoulder.

"He's only trying to help," she said.

Crystal turned and glared at her. "He lies Mom. You haven't even met Eric and you take Mr. Fitzpatrick's side. I can't believe you are doing this. You usually stand up for others."

Britany threw up her hands in exasperation. "What am I supposed to do, Crystal! I get a call saying you are in jail. Your boyfriend is arrested for robbery. Keith finds out that not only is he not in college, but he is thought to be the leader of a fencing operation! You expect me to think the best of him! Right now I am so angry that he put you into the middle of the whole thing that I could punch him a good one, and you wonder why! Wake up, Crystal!" Britany grasped her shoulders. "No one is lying to you except for Eric, and you need to see that!"

Crystal shook Britany's hands from her shoulders. "I'm tired now, and I want to go to bed."

Britany sighed. "That sounds like a good idea. Things tend to look brighter in the morning." She curled up beside Andrew and fell into a troubled sleep.

Crystal slept peacefully as Britany and Andrew woke and got around in the morning. Britany didn't know if Crystal had class or not, but she hated to wake her. Soon she woke on her own and dressed for class.

"Mom," Crystal said as she combed her blonde hair, "there is a possibility Eric may get out of jail today. Would you meet him and at least see what he is like before you judge him?"

Britany felt resentment build up in her. She wanted to lash out in anger. Instead she paused and took a deep breath. She finally said, "I would like that very much."

Crystal gave her mother a hug. "Thanks, Mom. I know you will like him and see that everything they have charged him with is lies." She grabbed her books and hurried to class.

Britany took Andrew to a nearby park that was quiet and almost deserted except for a few scattered joggers.

"Dear Lord," she prayed as they walked. "This seems like a mess, but I know you are in control throughout. Please help me keep an open mind as I meet Eric and help Crystal see the truth, whatever that might be."

Crystal walked to her class. Eric was waiting for her when she came out. She ran to him and threw her arms around him. He had showered and put on clean clothes.

"Your friend helped you!" she exclaimed.

Eric smiled. "He always comes through."

Crystal took his arm and walked beside him. "My mother came and I would like for you to meet her. She is staying in my dorm. Would that be all right?" she asked. "Maybe she will take us to lunch."

"I would like that, but I can't believe she would want to meet me after you ended up in jail," he responded.

"It did take some convincing," Crystal admitted. "She's pretty cool though."

They walked to the dorm and Crystal took Eric up the stairs to the room. Britany had just gotten back from taking Andrew to the park.

"Hi, Mom!" exclaimed Crystal. "This is Eric."

Britany suppressed a gasp as she looked up into Eric's face. It was alarming to see how much Eric resembled Crystal's own father at the same age. Even his charming smile was the same learned response. It seemed that men with his looks learned early how to charm with a smile. She hesitantly reached out her hand, and he promptly grasped it.

"Hello," he said. "I'm pleased to meet you."

Britany stiffened as he leaned forward, and it looked as if he were going to give her a hug. He didn't, and she relaxed slightly.

"I was hoping we could go to lunch!" Crystal said brightly.

Britany looked to Crystal. "I guess that would be all right. It won't be too long until Andrew will need a nap though. Tired babies are disasters in restaurants, but he should be fine for a while." She didn't want to spend any more time with Eric than she had to, but for Crystal's sake she would go to lunch and try not to compare him to Crystal's father.

The lunch convinced Britany that Eric was definitely lying to Crystal, and she wasn't sure why Crystal couldn't see it. She ate slowly and analyzed what he said as they talked. Twice she found that he contradicted himself. To Britany he seemed very egotistical and determined to get his way. She found herself hoping that he would be convicted and sent to jail to get him out of Crystal's life.

"I think we need to go," said Britany as she asked for the check. "Andrew has been very good, but I don't want to ask too much of him. He really needs a nap."

They returned to the dorm, and Crystal left for her next class. Britany rocked Andrew to sleep. An hour later there was a knock at the door. She fell into Michael's arms as she opened the door and saw him standing there. He held her tight and she felt comforted by his strength. She drew back and offered him a seat. They sat at the desk as Britany explained what had happened.

Michael shook his head. "I guess it's hard to see things clearly when you are young. I'm like you. I wish Eric were still in jail. It's a little scary to think of what he might do next. Do you think I should talk to her?"

"You could try," said Britany. "But if her reaction is anything like it was to Keith, I don't think you'll like it." Britany reached out and took his hand. "Did you get the children settled at my mother's?" she asked.

He smiled and said, "She even promised to do their schooling with them." He shook his head again. "She will definitely be busy. Hopefully we won't have to stay here too long." Britany nodded in agreement.

Crystal was surprised to find Michael when she got back to the dorm. "I didn't realize you were coming," she said.

"I'm sorry, Crystal. I forgot to tell you when you were so upset," explained Britany.

"So you brought someone else to tell me how wrong I am," Crystal said angrily and crossed her arms in front of her.

"Crystal, I have never heard you talk to your mother that way," Michael said sternly. "I don't ever want to hear it again. You need to apologize."

Crystal thrust her finger toward her mother. "She needs to apologize for coming here and accusing Eric of all those horrible things!"

Michael stood in front of Crystal. "It seems to me that Keith said the police accused Eric, not your mother."

"And she believes them," Crystal said coolly.

"I think we are no longer needed or wanted here, Britany. It's time for us to go," Michael said.

Britany was angry and said, "You're right. We will be at Grandma Liz's if you change your mind and decide to listen to someone besides Eric."

Britany gathered her and Andrew's things. He was awake and looking around in trepidation. Britany took him into her arms, and Michael took her bag. Britany kissed Crystal's cheek and left.

Michael put his arm around Britany as they walked to the car. He could feel her shake and pulled her close. "She will realize the truth eventually. There is not much we can do in the meantime."

"As much as I hate the thought, you are right," admitted Britany. "I just pray nothing awful happens before she sees the truth."

Crystal thought she would be relieved to have her mother gone, but suddenly she felt very lonely. She tried to concentrate on her schoolwork. After her last class she was anxious to see Eric again, but he never showed up.

She went up to Cortney's room when he didn't call by eleven that evening.

"Doesn't it seem a little odd that you never know how to get hold of him when you need to? He just always seems to show up." Cortney asked as they talked.

"Don't take my mother's side," Crystal said harshly.

"I just made a statement!" Cortney exclaimed. "You don't know how to call him, or even where he lives now, do you?"

"He's very busy with studies and football," Crystal tried to defend him.

"You think!" Cortney corrected.

Crystal jumped to her feet. "I can't believe this. Now my best friend is turning against me!" she exclaimed and started for the door. Cortney stepped in front of her.

"Not against you, just Eric. You need to step back and think about him. There are some very curious things about his lifestyle. Your parents were just trying to help you. They came to protect you, and all you can do is defend Eric, who, by the way is quite capable of defending himself," Cortney said as she stood facing Crystal.

Crystal turned and went out the door to her room. She wanted to go with Eric. Where is Eric? She wondered. She went back to her room and tried to study some more. At midnight someone knocked on her door.

"Eric, where have you been?" asked Crystal as she opened the door. "I wanted to see you tonight, but I didn't know how to find you," she said.

"I've been making plans. I want to leave and go to another state," he said. Crystal noticed that he seemed agitated.

"But what about school and football?" she asked.

"Do you thing they are going to let me stay on the team with my police record? Get real, Crystal. They will kick me out of school, too. My parents live in Florida, and I want to go there. Then I won't have all these lies going around about me. I can't stand it!" He paced across the small area of her room as he talked.

"But what will you do?" she asked and sat on her bed.

"My parents have a business. I can work with them," he answered.

"What about their divorce? Won't that complicate things?" she asked with a sweep of her hand.

"Gosh, Crystal, didn't I tell you they are getting back together?" Eric said with agitation in his voice. "You ask too many questions. I just have to get out of here."

"What about your bail? I didn't think you were allowed to go across state lines when you are on bail." she pointed out.

"Sure you can, but listen. I want you to go with me." He knelt beside her and took her hands.

"What?" exclaimed Crystal. "I have my classes. What can you possibly be talking about?"

"You can stay with me and my parents. I want you to go with me. I love you, Crystal. Don't you love me?" he asked urgently.

Crystal stared at him in disbelief. "I...I...don't know!" she pleaded.

"Please, Crystal. I need you. You are the only one who understands me. Everyone else is against me. I need someone to believe me and be on my side!" He kissed her hand and looked deep into her eyes.

Crystal took his face in her hands. She thought about her failing grades and the argument she had just had with her mother. She looked at him solemnly and said, "I'll go. When do we leave?"

"Right now. Just pack a few things. My parents will have everything we will need."

Crystal stared at him as if he were crazy.

"Hurry, pack!" he instructed and got to his feet to help. "I want to go right now. We will drive through the night."

Crystal looked around puzzled. "I need to call my mother."

"She will only try to get you to change your mind. You know she doesn't like me. I could see it in her eyes. You can call her tomorrow when we get there. She won't even know your aren't here going to classes," he reasoned.

Crystal found her bags and started to pack. She hurried, but Eric seemed agitated and urged her to go faster. She furiously threw things together and soon they were on their way to the car. She felt a strange rush of excitement. She had never done anything so spontaneous, and she felt a certain freedom to be able to pack up and leave. She wouldn't have the pressure of school to deal with anymore, and maybe there would be time for her to lie on the beach and enjoy the ocean. She threw her bags in the trunk. Eric had only two bags when she put hers in. She figured he probably had clothes at his parents.

CHAPTER 14

They drove through Ohio and into Kentucky before he stopped for gas. Crystal dozed as he drove. When he pulled into the gas station Crystal woke up and felt cold. When he went to pay for the gas she opened the trunk to see if he might have a blanket. She didn't see one, but there was a duffel bag. She unzipped it to look for a blanket and gasped as she saw the contents. It was filled with all types of jewelry. Even from the lights of the gas station she could tell it was expensive jewelry. She quickly zipped it back up and reached to close the trunk. A strong hand grabbed her wrist, and she turned to find herself face to face with a very angry Eric.

"Get in the car!" he demanded.

She turned, trembling, and did as he said. He didn't say a word as they continued down the road. The tiredness was gone. She frantically tried to piece things together. They were right--the police, her lawyer, her mother, Michael, and Cortney. Everyone had known the truth except her. She started to think about all the contradictions in Eric's life and realized that he had been lying to her from the start. She panicked. She knew about the jewels. He would never let her go in case she might tell the police. What if he had a gun? Would he use it on her? From the look in his eyes when he had found her looking in the trunk she wasn't sure that he wouldn't.

She thought as they drove and realized that she had made a promise to God that she had failed to keep. She wasn't any better than Eric was. She had promised God she would trust Him and start praying and reading her Bible more. Yet she had done none of it. Tears slid down her face.

I'm so sorry, Lord. Eric lied to me, and I know how it feels. I guess I'm exactly in the kind of trouble I deserve to be in. Please forgive me. I know I said it before, but I really want to follow You. I need Your help to get out of this situation. My mother says you are always with us. Please be with me now. In Jesus name, amen.

Crystal knew she was in serious trouble, but she felt a peace she hadn't felt since that night in the jail cell. She knew it would be light soon, and she noticed that Eric seemed to be having trouble keeping his eyes open. He pulled into a gas station and looked at her.

"You are coming with me. If you try to get away, I have this." He showed her a small revolver in his jacket pocket. Crystal's heart raced. "Stand beside me as I pump the gas," he said into her ear as she got out beside him.

Her eyes scanned the station for any possible escape. He took her hand and led her into the store to pay for the gas. Crystal wanted to draw her hand out of his. Not only was he holding her hostage, he was trying to act like he still liked her. The thought made her suddenly nauseated. She started to wretch, and he hurried her toward the bathroom door. She glanced at a side door as they rushed through the store. He turned as she reached the door and went to pay for the gas.

The nausea faded as soon as he dropped her hand. Her head cleared as she opened the door, turned the lock, and then without entering she crouched low and closed the door. She stayed low in the aisle below eye level and quickly went through the side door. The lights outside glared, and she ran toward the darkness. She could barely make out the outline of the woods behind the station. She ran hard and quickly entered them, and as she did she found herself climbing a steep hill. She heard Eric's voice as he called her name. *He knows I'm gone!* Her heart beat faster. She climbed faster, frantically grabbing at bushes in front of her to pull herself up the hill. His voice seemed to be moving farther away, and she breathed a sigh of relief, but her heart continued to race, partly from exertion, partly from fear. She started to move sideways on the hill instead of straight up so she could stay near the town and find a telephone when he was gone. Suddenly she realized his voice was getting closer. *He must have found where she had gone into the woods!* She dropped to the ground beside a log and covered herself with leaves. *If she kept moving he might hear her. Maybe if she stopped he would go right past her. It would be dark for at least another hour.*

Eric stopped calling her name, but she could hear his footsteps in the leaves as he got closer. She held her breath as he approached. Before he got too close he turned and went up the hill. She waited for what seemed at least twenty minutes and then brushed away the leaves. She stood up and made her way along the hillside. She saw buildings below and tried to see a telephone as she moved along. She saw one beside a Wendy's. She made her way carefully down the hillside, sliding from tree to tree, holding on to branches and tree trunks to keep from falling. She stayed in the shadows, but the telephone was under a streetlight. She looked as far as she could see. Eric, or his car was nowhere in sight. She hurried to the phone and dialed her grandmother in Ohio collect. It was answered after the second ring. Crystal could almost smell the breakfast she knew her grandmother was cooking.

"Grandma, this is Crystal," Crystal said in a shaky voice.

"Honey, what is the matter?" Grandma Liz asked.

"I need to talk to mom or Michael right away," she whispered into the phone. "I'm in a lot of danger." Crystal heard her grandmother hurry to the bedroom and get her mother.

"Crystal, what is the matter?" Britany asked in alarm.

"I am in a town in Tennessee, and Eric is after me with a gun!" She could hear Britany gasp at the other end of the phone.

"I'm at a Wendy's in the town of Cleveland. I'm not even sure if it is the only Wendy's or not. I will stay in the woods behind the store until you can come. Please park in the back of the lot when you get here and I will come to you. It will take you at least five hours to get here. If I don't show up in a half an hour after you park, see if there might be another Wendy's. Do you understand? I have to get back into hiding."

"Crystal, go to the police right now!" pleaded Britany.

"No, Mom. You know how tricky Eric is. I only feel safe with you and Michael. I'll stay in hiding until you get here. I've got to go. He may find me."

"We'll be there as soon as possible. I love you, honey!" Britany said as she hung up the phone. She turned to Michael in alarm.

"Eric is threatening Crystal with a gun. She is in the woods in a town in Tennessee. She wants us to meet her at a Wendy's," Britany said with one breath and felt as if she were about to collapse.

"No!" gasped Liz.

Britany's father Charles ran to get his rifle. Michael had an expression of sheer anger. Jonathan had Andrew on his lap and held him protectively. Amy looked up at Britany with fearful eyes, and Ben was ready to help his father fight.

Britany sat on the kitchen chair and tried to think. She looked at her mother.

"Mom, I hate to leave Andrew, but do you think you could manage? I just can't imagine what we might get into, and I don't want to worry about him." Britany said.

"I can take care of him," Jonathan said patting Andrew on the head. "He and I get along pretty well. I get frustrated having everyone help me. This is my chance to help."

Britany smiled at him. "Thanks, Jonathan."

Liz put her arms around Britany. "We will do fine here. You get your things and get going. Please call us with any news."

Charles came into the room with his gun. "Dad," said Michael. "I'm not so sure the rifle is such a good idea."

"I think it would help even the sides up a little. That guy thinks he's such hot stuff chasing my granddaughter with a gun. We'll just see what he thinks of some of his own medicine."

Liz went into the other room and came out with some money. "Take this," she said. "Something may come up, and you may need some cash."

"Mom, I have money!" Britany protested.

"Just take it," said Liz shoving it into her hand. "If you don't need it you can give it back."

Britany rose from the chair and gave her mother a warm embrace. "Jonathan knows Andrew's schedule, and you have been caring for the other two. We will be careful and be back as soon as possible," Britany said. She held Amy close and wiped the tears from her eyes. "Crystal will be all right. You pray for her while we're gone, OK?"

Amy nodded yes, and Britany held her tight. She turned to Ben. "You help Grandma and Jonathan." He looked at her with large serious eyes.

"I know how to take care of the animals Grandpa. I'll take care of them while you are gone," he said to Charles.

"I can count on you son," said Charles and patted his head. Britany gave Ben a hug with tears in her eyes.

"She'll be all right," said Jonathan quietly, looking up at Britany. "God is with her."

"Thanks,' said Britany softly and grasped his hand. She reached down, kissed his cheek, then went to get her bag.

"Let's go," she said. A vision of the long tension-filled trip loomed in front of her. She would dread every suspenseful moment until they had Crystal safe with them again. She knew it would be a long trip.

Crystal trekked deeper into the woods, trying to cover her tracks as she went. She found a cave and crawled in just far enough to be hidden from view. It was going to be a long wait, but she was so relieved to be out of Eric's sight that she didn't care. She curled up in her coat and fell asleep. She woke with a start as she heard leaves crackle. She held her breath and then laughed as she saw a squirrel scamper past the cave. The woods were bright with the rising sun, and birds sang loudly. She was glad the air was warmer in Tennessee than it had been in Ohio. Except for the hunger that was beginning to creep up, she felt quite comfortable. Each hour deepened her conviction that Eric had probably given up on searching for her and had left.

At twelve o'clock she carefully made her way down the hillside to find a hiding place where she could watch the restaurant. She found a thicket of honeysuckle as cover, and crawled into the center. From where she hid she had a clear view of the drive and parking lot. She hoped it wouldn't be too much longer.

She had been waiting a half an hour when the truck pulled into the parking lot. She saw it! Her grandfather's truck was pulling into the parking lot! She crawled from under the honeysuckle and ran down the hill. Britany looked right at Crystal as Crystal ran from her cover.

Michael was the first one to reach her, and Crystal fell into his arms sobbing with relief. Britany was quickly beside her and stroked Crystal's tangled hair. Crystal was covered with dirt and dried leaves. Her jeans were torn in several places.

"Crystal, your hands are scratched. Let's go in the store and clean you up some," said Britany.

Crystal's body trembled, "Mom, I just want to go home and get as far away from that man as I can. Hopefully he is in Florida by now!"

"If he is anywhere near here he is in big trouble!" exclaimed Charles and patted his gun. Crystal had no doubt he would use it if Eric came back. She suddenly felt safe.

"Please, let's go. I want to get as far from here as possible," Crystal pleaded.

They went down the hill and got into the truck. It was crowded with four, but to Crystal it felt secure.

"You need to stay with me and Grandma for a while," said Charles as they drove.

"But I can't miss any more classes. Eric has interrupted my schooling enough. I'm not going to let him ruin my life. I need to finish what I started," Crystal said with determination.

"You can't go back to the dorm. It would be the first place Eric would look if he is scared you would go to the police," said Michael, looking at Crystal with stern eyes. "Which is exactly what you need to do," he finished.

"No!" groaned Crystal.

"You have to, Crystal," agreed Britany.

"I'm afraid to." Crystal started to shake, and Britany put her arm around her.

Britany looked at her and said, "If you don't you will never be safe. The only way to get this behind you is for Eric to be behind bars."

Crystal cried softly, and Britany cradled her. Michael wrapped his arm around the two of them.

"Crystal could go stay with your brother, Phillip," said Charles as he drove. "He lives within fifteen to twenty minutes from the college. Eric wouldn't know where you were if you stayed with him. I'm sure you would feel safer there."

"Dad, that is an excellent idea!" exclaimed Britany. "There is probably a bus that she could take to campus."

Charles looked across Britany to Crystal with his silver blue eyes. His strong arms clenched the steering wheel tightly.

"She can use her grandmother's car. We will be all right with the truck. We always have the big truck if anything comes up. I would feel better if she had her own transportation," said Charles protectively.

Crystal was surrounded by love, and after what she had just experienced it was a very dramatic contrast. This was what true love was about. Not whatever it was she had felt for Eric. She sat in silence for a long time, thinking about how her family had came to her rescue, even after she had made a very stupid decision.

"Mom, Michael, Grandpa," she said. "I was very stupid and selfish to behave the way I did. I treated you badly and made a horrible mistake. Will you please forgive me? I will never do anything like that again," she said with emphasis and shook her head.

"Crystal, we have all made our share of mistakes, and it would be nice to say we will never do them again, but that is just part of life. Hopefully we learn from them," said Michael.

Britany nodded her head in agreement. "Of course we forgive you, Crystal," said Britany. "Don't be too hard on yourself. You are not the only one Eric deceived. He seems to be very good at it."

Britany asked her father to stop at a clothing store she saw as they exited the interstate to get gas. She bought Crystal some clean clothes. There was a Cracker Barrel restaurant on the same exit, and they stopped to eat. Michael ordered for them while Britany took Crystal into the bathroom to clean her abrasions and straighten her hair.

I know it is hard," started Britany, "but we are going straight to the police, and you are going to tell them what happened," she said as she helped Crystal with her hair.

"I don't know if I can," said Crystal feebly.

"The sooner you face it the sooner you can put it behind you. It will also give the police a chance to find Eric before he has a chance to flee the country."

Crystal gasped. "Do you think he would do that?" she asked.

"We were talking as we drove here and the three of us agreed that is exactly what he had planned when he started. I'm not sure why he wanted to involve you in this, but I think he was going to take you with him."

Crystal's knees felt weak, and Britany grabbed her to give her support. "Let's go. Our food will be ready soon. You'll feel better with some hot food in you. You still have several hours to collect yourself before we get to Columbus, but you are going to give your statement," Britany said.

Crystal nodded slightly and followed Britany out the door. The food came soon after they got to the table. Crystal was hungry, but her anxiety made it hard for her to eat much. She fell asleep soon after they were back on the road. Britany woke her as they entered Columbus. It was getting dark as they climbed the steps to the police station. Crystal trembled as she entered the door. Keith Fitzpatrick met them as soon as they entered. Phillip was close behind him. Crystal smiled and extended her hand. Keith ignored her hand and embraced her in a warm hug.

"I am so glad you are alright. I feared the worst when your parents called," he said.

"I can't believe you're not mad at me!" Crystal said. "I was very mean to you. You were right all along."

He hugged her again. "Crystal," he said, "Eric is the type of person that inspired me to become a lawyer. He's sly and took advantage of your trusting nature. Someday you will meet a terrific guy who deserves your trust. I just hope that when the time comes you will be able to trust again. Eric put you through a horrible ordeal, and for that we can put him behind bars, but don't let him haunt you the rest of your life." Crystal looked at him in confusion, but managed to nod in agreement.

They went into a crowded office. Crystal found it extremely difficult to give her statement to the police. Mr. Fitzpatrick helped by asking question after question to find the details. It sounded unbelievable even to her as she told it. When she finished she was extremely relieved and felt an unexpected peace.

It was late as they left the police station. "You are all tired, and I am exhausted," said Crystal. "I want to get to my eight-o'clock class, and so it would be much easier to go there from Uncle Phillip's." She looked at her uncle.

"She's right you know," Phillip agreed. "I can take her to class on my way to work."

Britany looked worried and grabbed Crystal's hand. Michael placed his hand on her shoulder. "Britany, Crystal will be fine with your brother. It's a fifteen-minute drive to her classes from his house. She will be more protected than if she were in the dorms. Your mother is just an hour away. I'm sure if Crystal feels threatened your mom will come and go with her to class. The sooner she gets her life back to normal the better. You have three children back at the farm that need you home. We can leave in the morning. Crystal has your parents and your brother to look out for her."

Britany nodded and held Crystal close. She knew Michael was right, but it was difficult to leave Crystal. She gave in and said goodbye and they drove back to her parents' farm. It was late when they pulled into the drive.

Amy and Ben rushed from the house as the dogs sounded their arrival. Liz ran from the house. Her face fell when she realized Crystal wasn't with them.

"Where's my Crystal? Is she all right?" she asked in concern.

Charles put his arm around her shoulder. "I'm sorry, but Crystal wanted to stay at Phillip's to be ready for class in the morning."

"I wanted to see her!" Liz exclaimed.

"We'll go first thing in the morning," Charles assured her. "We can spend the day with her and escort her to her classes."

In the morning Britany and Michael left for Tennessee. Charles and Liz drove to Phillip's to leave the car for Crystal, who was still at the house. She looked pale when Liz saw her.

"Honey, what is it?" asked Liz with concern. She put her arm around Crystal. "You look as pale as a ghost. I thought you would be in class by now."

"I just couldn't go!" said Crystal weakly. "I was determined to get to class, but when it came time for it I just couldn't." She shook her head.

"When is your next class?" asked Liz.

"In half an hour."

"Your grandpa will drive us there and wait in the car. I will go with you to class," Liz said.

"Grandma, you can't do that!" Crystal exclaimed.

"Will they throw me out?"

Crystal shrugged her shoulders. Liz looked at her with a determination that Crystal knew better than to challenge. Crystal felt secure with her grandmother beside her and they continued the rest of the day together. Crystal still felt scared the next day and Liz decided to stay with Phillip for a few days and go with Crystal to her classes until Crystal regained her confidence.

Britany rushed to the phone and called her brother as soon as they arrived home. Phillip answered the phone. "How did Crystal do today?" she asked.

"She missed her first class. Mom and Dad got here by nine and Mom went with her to her second class. It went well and gave Crystal the support she needed so Mom and Dad stayed and spent the day with her. Dad is going home to feed, but I wouldn't be surprised if Mom stays the week."

"I am so glad," said Britany into the phone with a sigh of relief. This certainly has me on edge. I can't imagine how Crystal feels. You call me if anything new develops. I'm going to try and get hold of Keith and see what has progressed with Eric. I'll call you back as soon as I find out anything."

"That sounds good, Sis. I hope it will put Crystal's mind at ease when they get him behind bars!" exclaimed Phillip.

When she finished talking to Phillip Britany checked her answering machine for messages. There was a message from the police that the Florida police had arrested Eric with the jewels and that he was on his way back to Ohio for the trial. Britany breathed a sigh of relief and called Keith to verify the message.

CHAPTER 15

Crystal looked around her at room that had been her mother's while she was growing up. It had been two months since the incident with Eric, and she was spending several days with her grandparents before she left to go home to Tennessee.

She looked out the window and sighed. Eric was in jail. They had caught him attempting to flee the country. Crystal shuddered. She still had to face the trial and seeing him face to face! To look again into those blue eyes that she once thought were so gorgeous brought a shudder to her. She pictured the gun and the angry look on his face when he had threatened her with it! She quickly turned and got dressed to go downstairs. Thinking about Eric was doing nothing except to make her upset!

Liz was making bread when she went downstairs. "Good morning!" Liz said cheerfully. I thought that maybe you could take some goodies to everyone for me."

"Sure, Grandma!" said Crystal and gave her grandmother a hug.

"Are you looking forward to getting back home?" asked Liz as Crystal sat down at the table.

Crystal said thoughtfully, "I guess so. I enjoyed being there last spring. Tennessee is beautiful in the spring. I would look forward to it more if I hadn't messed up so badly. I feel like a failure!"

"Crystal, you are alive and have a lot to live for. The only one who thinks you are a failure is yourself. To everyone else you made a mistake the same as we all have. If you beat yourself up about it you will never be able to get on with your life," said Liz. "Here, mix this while I measure." Liz handed her a bowl and a wooden spoon.

"You never give a person much room to feel sorry for herself, do you, Grandma?" asked Crystal with a smile as she stirred.

It had been two months since Eric was arrested. He was in jail following his arraignment. The trial date had not yet been set, but Keith Fitzpatrick felt it would be at least a year before the case went to court. In the meantime Jonathan had gotten his casts off and was able to walk quite well. He was getting therapy twice a month, but he drove himself, so Britany's responsibilities had eased. Crystal was going to be home for the holidays in two days, and Britany was soaring with happiness. They had talked on the telephone about Crystal taking the second semester at the local community college and Britany was thrilled at the possibility of having her close. The episode with Eric had been hard for

Crystal, and she still wasn't herself. They both thought it might be good for her to take refuge in the family who loved her. Britany was excited for Crystal to get a chance to meet Jonathan. He had become a very important part of their family, and Crystal still hadn't met him.

One morning Britany was baking pumpkin bread and cookies for the holidays. Amy was at the table decorating the cookies with frosting and sprinkles. Andrew was sitting before the cupboard with the pots and pans, making a drum out of the lids. Christmas music was playing, and everyone was in a joyous mood. Britany hurried around the kitchen talking happily with Amy. "Crystal will be here tomorrow, and I want as much of this baking finished as possible. Thank you so much for doing the cookies. You know how much she likes cookies."

"I hope they taste as good as Grandma's," said Amy in a serious tone.

Britany laughed, "You certainly do have high expectations. Your cookies will be spectacular. Crystal is sure to love them. The boys do, don't they?"

Amy shrugged. "They only like to steal them to make me mad."

"They steal them because they are good. Here they come, so watch the cookies!"

Ben burst into the house and ran to the table. He grabbed a cookie from the table.

"Ben!" cried Amy. "That was my best cookie. Take one that didn't turn out so well!" She grabbed it from him, and he took another one.

"Hurry, Jonathan!" he called. "I want Mom to see what you can do!"

Jonathan ambled through the door looking rather embarrassed. Ben ran to the radio and turned it to some music with a faster beat. Jonathan smiled, and he and Ben started to dance. Amy soon joined them, and Andrew started to walk around bobbing to the music. Britany clapped.

"Jonathan, that is wonderful!" she exclaimed. "You can't even tell anything was ever wrong with your leg!"

Jonathan laughed and did some fancy moves to show off to Ben. "I wish I could do that!" said Ben in admiration.

"Dance with me!" squealed Amy. Jonathan took her in his arms and waltzed around the kitchen. Britany watched and laughed. Jonathan put Amy down and grabbed Britany's hand.

"May I have this dance, madam?" he asked and bowed.

Britany laughed and curtsied. "I'd be honored," she said. He waltzed her around the kitchen. They both laughed while Amy and Ben clapped. Jonathan grabbed her by the waist and twirled her around. Everyone laughed. Britany laughed, but then she lost her balance and stumbled. Jonathan caught her and steadied her until she regained her balance. Britany grasped his shoulder and looked up at him with laughter. Suddenly, before she realized what was happening, she felt warm lips on hers.

"Jonathan is kissing Mom!" screamed Amy in a shrill voice.

Jonathan released Britany so fast she almost fell to the floor. The look on his face was one of horrified realization at what he had done. Amy's outburst startled Andrew, and he fell, hitting his lip on the corner of the island. He screamed, and Britany turned to see blood running down his face. Before she could turn back to Jonathan he was gone.

Britany ran to Andrew and grabbed a towel. His lip was bleeding profusely and was already starting to swell. She pressed the towel to his lip and looked around. She wanted to go to Jonathan and talk to him. She knew he hadn't meant to do what he did, and he was probably alarmed by it. She couldn't leave Andrew. Andrew cried frantically along with Amy, who was crying because of the blood pouring from Andrew's lip.

"Ben, can you get me some ice?" she asked. Ben ran to the freezer and brought it quickly.

"Ben, please go check on Jonathan," Britany said as soon as he gave her the ice.

Ben ran back into the kitchen within a minute. "He's throwing his things in a pillow case!" he exclaimed.

"Run back and tell him I want to talk to him!" Britany demanded. She wanted to run upstairs, but although Andrew's cut wasn't deep, she still had to hold the cloth to it to stop the bleeding. He and Amy were still both crying.

Britany heard footsteps run down the stairs, and the front door burst open.

"He's leaving, Mom!" Ben screamed, running after Jonathan. Britany held Andrew close and ran to the door.

"Jonathan, wait! Please let me talk to you!" Britany yelled, but the noise of the truck engine starting was louder than her voice. Jonathan didn't even look toward them as he backed up and drove out the drive.

"He wouldn't listen, Mom!" Ben said in agony. "I tried to get him to stay, but he said he had to go."

"Where?" asked Britany. "Ben, where did he say he had to go?"

"He didn't say. I don't think he is coming back." Ben started to cry and Britany pulled him close to her side as she held Andrew and stared at the truck driving into the distance. Pain tore at her heart as she realized Ben was probably right. "Dear God, go with him and keep him safe," she said softly as tears rolled down her cheeks.

Britany turned and went back to the kitchen, which moments earlier had been a very happy place. Now it was filled with despair. Amy was still crying. This time it was because Jonathan had left. Andrew's lip was no longer bleeding, but it was very large, and his face was tear-stained, mixed with blood. Blood dotted the kitchen floor and the side of the counter.

Britany started cleaning, first Andrew's face, then Amy's tear-stained face and the powdered sugar that dusted her. She wanted to comfort Ben and Amy, but she didn't know what to say.

Michael walked in to see Britany holding Andrew, cleaning Amy. Her clothes were splattered with blood, and Andrew's lip stuck out, making his face look distorted. Amy was crying, and Ben's eyes were red and puffy.

"What happened here?" Michael asked in alarm.

"Jonathan kissed Mom!" exclaimed Amy. "They were dancing and then he kissed her on the lips!"

"What!" Michael yelled angrily.

"He kissed her, and then he took his things and left!" explained Amy. Britany cringed. She wished Amy had been a little less descriptive in her explanation.

"Well, he better be gone if he knows what is good for him!" Michael yelled. Britany had never seen him so angry before. Ben glared at his dad and ran out the door to the barn.

Michael turned to Britany. "He kissed you, and you let him?" he asked angrily.

She fell into a chair. Suddenly she was very tired, and Andrew's body felt heavy in her arms.

"Michael, you don't understand. Amy was a little too dramatic in her explanation," Britany tried to sort through a reason, but even to her it sounded bad.

"Why is Andrew's lip swollen?" Michael asked. His voice, although concerned, was still filled with anger.

"He fell and hit the corner of the island,' Britany explained. "It will be all right. It just bled very badly for a while. Michael, he didn't mean to do it."

"What?" asked Michael very confused. "He didn't mean to bust his lip open?"

"No! I mean Jonathan didn't mean to kiss me. He looked horrified that it happened." Britany tried to reason.

"Well, it will never happen again, because that boy will never set foot inside this house again!" he roared.

Amy started crying again, and Britany wanted to cry herself.

"Michael," said Britany trying to calm him down, "please sit down."

He continued to stand, and Britany tried again. "Michael, there are many kinds of love: love for a brother or sister, love a mother has for her son, and the love a father has for his daughter, the love God has for us. Sometimes you just know you feel love, and it's hard to discern what kind of love you have. Jonathan has never had the kind of love he found at our house, and I think he is just very confused. He's confused now more than ever, and he needs us now more than ever!" Britany explained.

"Well, he can be confused all he wants, but not in this house!" Michael retorted.

Britany was getting angry. "Well, that is the least of your worries, because I doubt that he will ever be back!" She handed Andrew to him and turned to start supper.

Jonathan drove to the city bank and withdrew his savings. He wasn't sure where he was going or what he was going to do. He knew he couldn't stay with Britany's family anymore. He needed to go far away where he would be able to think. He seemed to be drawn back to his grandfather's house, although that was the last place he wanted to go. There were some questions in his mind as to who his father was, and he didn't know anyplace else to find answers. Being part of a family had made him want to find out anything he could about his own father.

He couldn't deny the unmistakable pull, and as he drove out of the bank he turned his truck toward Knoxville. The drive was easy, and before he understood what drew him there, he was in his grandfather's driveway. It was dark when he arrived. He entered the house to find Joe asleep on the couch. An empty bottle of Jack Daniels lay beside him, and Jonathan knew he was out for the night. Jonathan cringed as he walked across the filthy floor and heard cockroaches scurry out of his way. Some less fortunate ones crunched under his feet. He turned on a light. He didn't remember the house being so dirty when he had lived in it, but he knew it had been bad. It was the only home he had known growing up, so he didn't realize how bad it had been until he lived with Britany's family. He experienced a surge of sadness at the thought of them. He pushed the thought to the back of his mind. He didn't want to think about them now. He needed answers. There was something he needed to understand, and he didn't know what it was. He just knew it involved them, but wasn't totally about them.

He went to his old bedroom. He needed to think. He turned on the light and looked around. Memories flashed around him, and the house seemed to be alive with long-suppressed thoughts. A picture of his mother sat on the dresser. He thought about her, and the tears started to flow. She hadn't been the best mother, but she had given him all her fragile life could give. He was confused and lonely. The only family who cared about him was hundreds of miles away, and he had made it so he could never go back!

"Dear God, what do I do now?" He prayed, but he felt unworthy to call upon God after what he had done. He sat quietly and became aware of the fact that he knew very little about his grandfather. He had never ventured past the door of his room out of fear of severe punishment.

He went to stand in the doorway of his grandfather's bedroom. He glanced back to be sure his grandfather was still out. Jonathan trembled as he stared at the bedroom. Being in the house was more fearful then being alone at a strange place in his truck. It brought back the fear he had had as a little boy. Although he stood at six feet tall in the doorway his heart felt the same as when he was six and a little over three feet tall. He turned on the light and looked at the room. The bed was stripped with a wad of dirty blanket thrown across it. Clothes were tossed about the room in piles. A lone dresser sat in the corner. It looked out of place in this room. He quietly stepped over the clothes and opened the top dresser drawer. The dresser had belonged to his grandmother who had died when his mother was born. Her things still remained in them. Bed clothes were neatly arranged, and he realized that at one time the house had probably not been in such disarray. In his mind he started to sympathize with the man whose true love had been taken from him when he wasn't much older than Jonathan himself. "That didn't give him the right to treat my mother and me the way he did!" he thought angrily.

He opened the next drawer and stopped. Before him in the drawer was a pile of letters. He looked at them one by one. The first two were from his great-grandparents to his grandmother. One letter was addressed to his mother. It had never been opened! There were three letters and none of them had ever been opened! He quickly opened the first letter and blushed as he realized that the person writing the letter had been very intimate with his mother. The signature read, Your Loving Amadeo. He didn't remember any Amadeo! Perhaps it was when he was little. Jonathan looked at the envelope for a date. It was dated in May, six months before he was born! Jonathan gasped. He grabbed the other two unopened envelopes and put the three letters in his pocket. He carefully replaced the remaining letters back in the drawer. He turned off the light and left the bedroom. Looking through the room to where his grandfather was still on the couch, he left the house and ran to his truck.

Jonathan drove to a familiar park and turned into a small, secluded drive. He turned off the truck and tried to keep himself from trembling as he turned on the dome light so he could see to read the letters.

He read the first, the second and the third letter. All were written within a month of each other. The third letter implored his mother to please write and expressed concern that she hadn't. Jonathan stopped reading. His head dropped to his hands. What was he reading! Was this person writing so intimately to his mother, his father! Jonathan tried to reason out what had happened, but it just seemed to add more questions. He looked a little closer at the outside of the envelope. It was from Greece! The address in the first letter was in Greece. Was his father Greek? If so, how had they met? Why had he left and not taken his mother? Why hadn't she written back? Then he remembered that the letters were unopened when he found them, so his mother had never read the letters. His grandfather must have hidden them from her. Jonathan groaned and got out of the truck. He walked briskly, then started to run. He ran until his breath came in rasping gasps and he could run no more. Then he stopped and looked into the star-studded sky. He wanted answers, and he had no idea where to get them.

Jonathan sat on the ground and drew in the dirt with a stick. If that man was his father and he had loved his mother so much, why did he desert them and leave his mother to the lonely life she had lived? Something was very wrong.

All of his life Jonathan had wondered who his father was, but he had been afraid to find out. He was afraid that it had been just a one-night affair his mother had engaged in and that the man had cared nothing for her or himself. He had thought his father was probably as mixed up as his mother had been, and he didn't want to face that. As a little boy he had had delusions that his father was a big war hero and had gone off to battle before he was born. He had gotten lost in combat, and no one had ever found him. He had always hoped his father would someday come back. The problem was that as he got older he realized that there had been no war in those early years of his life. By then he was old enough to realize another possibility, and the fear of finding out his father was a horrible person had kept him from questioning his mother. Now he was faced with the possibility that this man, writing these tender love letters to his mother, was his father and not just a nameless person. He had a name, an address, and a face.

How was he ever going to find out? His mother was dead and she had no close friends that he knew of that would even know! Jonathan rose from the ground, gave the back of his jeans several hard swipes to remove the dirt, and stood upright. He was tired, hungry, and frustrated.

Jonathan returned to the truck and climbed into the seat. He curled up in the blankets he had kept in the truck from when he had been homeless. He would think more in the morning. Too much had already happened in one day for him to face. Too tired to worry about the hunger that gnawed at his stomach, he went to sleep.

Jonathan opened his eyes and looked around. It took him a moment to realize where he was. When he did he groaned and rolled over. The teddy bear that Andrew had given him lay on the floor looking up at him. He grabbed it and held it close to him. He wanted to go back! He wanted to go back to the Keisers' so badly that it hurt. Tears came to his eyes when he remembered throwing his things in the pillowcase and running from the house. He had thought he heard Britany call, but that couldn't have been. She should have been yelling for him to go, not to come back. Through her he had found love and warmth like he had never known. Then he took advantage of it and now he had thrown it all away. He missed her; he missed little Andrew with his downy hair and wobbly walk. He missed Ben, his little brother, and he missed Amy's laughter. Would he ever see them again? How could he possibly look any of them in the face after what he had done? He remembered Amy's scream, and the shocked look on her face. He buried his face in the pillow. He didn't deserve them anyway. *I'm just a homeless person from a broken family. No one cares for me and I don't deserve to be cared for!*

Hunger gnawed at his stomach. Slowly he uncurled himself. He sat up and looked around. He drove back down the lane and found the main entrance where the bathrooms were located. It was still early, and the building was empty, so he was able to bathe in clean water with no one around. After that he went to the store and bought some food. He would need to find a job soon so he didn't use all his college money. College! What was he thinking? How could he finish college if he didn't go back and finish high school? He needed to take one thing at a time. He had several weeks of Christmas break to decide what he was going to do, and right now he needed to find some answers about his father!

Jonathan ate bagels and drank a carton of milk as he drove to his grandfather's house. As much as he didn't want to return there, he needed some answers, and that was the only place he knew to look.

He pushed open the door. Joe still lay on the couch where he had left him the night before. He rolled over and scratched his tousled white hair. Then he sat up and stared at Jonathan.

"What are you doing here?" he grunted with disgust. "I didn't ask you to come." He reached to the floor for the empty bottle beside him and lifted it to his lips. He threw it down when nothing came out.

Jonathan stepped closer and shoved the letters in front of Joe's face.

"Where did these come from? Is the man who wrote these my father?" Jonathan demanded. He felt no sympathy toward his grandfather, who had never treated him with anything but disdain. His dark eyes glowed with anger.

His grandfather returned his look with glaring eyes. Stubby white hair covered his chin, and a strong odor emanated from him. The smell was nauseating, but Jonathan wasn't going to leave until he got some answers.

"You tell me, you bastard child! I sent Patsy to spend the summer with my sister, and she came home pregnant! I didn't want her to keep you, but she wouldn't do anything about it. I hid those letters. She wrote to him too, but I found them and burnt them, every one. Run off and gone to Greece, that's what she would have done! He ruined her life and left her with the likes of you!" He managed to get to his feet and glare up at Jonathan. "Now get out of here! I don't ever want to see the likes of you again! Don't think you will ever get anything from me. I wrote you out of my will, and you won't get anything of mine. You took Patsy away and killed her!"

Jonathan shook with rage. "You killed her. You never once treated her with anything but anger and resentment. She didn't kill Grandma, but every day of her life you made her think it was her fault. I got her away from you, yes, but it was too late. The hatred had already eaten away too far. You destroyed the one chance she had in life by hiding those letters. This man, who you admit is my father, loved her and wanted her to go to Greece and marry him. You also deprived me of knowing my father and made me think I was the result of a one-night fling. How could you have been so hateful!" Jonathan's anger raged, and he clenched his fists tightly to keep himself from striking out.

Joe reached down for the discarded bottle and hurled it at Jonathan. Jonathan ducked, but it hit his shoulder with a painful blow.

"Get out of here you*****!" yelled Joe tottering to the side, and regaining his balance before he fell to the floor.

Jonathan knew he had to leave before he let all the anger of eighteen years explode.

"Don't worry, old man," he said through clenched teeth, trying hard to keep from landing a blow to his abdomen. "I'm out of here. I didn't want anything from you but answers. Stop blaming everyone else for your problems and look to yourself!" It took all the control Jonathan had to keep from hitting Joe. He turned and ran from the house before he had a chance to swing a punch that probably wouldn't stop with one. All the pent-up anger that had burned in his heart for years threatened to spill over, and he wasn't sure what would happen if he started to let it go. He turned on the truck, threw it into gear and backed down the drive. He turned sharply into the street and squealed the tires as he shifted into first and took off. He wasn't sure where he was going, but for the present anywhere was good enough.

His mother's aunt had lived in Wilmington, North Carolina, when he was a little boy. Patsy had talked of her with fondness, but they had never ventured to go there. Ruth Anne Bodine, at least he knew her name. He flew through the streets of Knoxville, around corners and past stores, until he finally hit the intersection of interstates 40 and 75. 40 East, that was the road he wanted until he got midway through North Carolina. Then he would find a map and decide how to get the rest of the way.

Britany took the children and picked Crystal from the airport the day after Jonathan had left. It was a very quiet drive. Amy and Ben were solemn, and Britany didn't have the energy to try to cheer them up. She felt as if a great sense of loss had settled on her. She had prayed for Jonathan almost nonstop since he had left, but as she drove, she suddenly felt a strong desire to pray harder. It was almost painful in its intensity. O Lord, her heart pleaded, I don't know where Jonathan is or what is happening, but let him know he is not alone. You are right there with him providing the comfort and security that he needs. Lead him in the direction he needs to go and please hold him close. She felt comforted and even managed a smile toward Amy as she drove.

"It will be good to see Crystal again," she said as they were almost at the airport.

"Now Crystal won't be able to meet Jonathan," Amy said sadly. Britany had to swallow hard to keep from moaning at the sadness in Amy's voice.

Britany glanced at Amy. She shared the sadness Amy was feeling. It was terribly hard to explain to anyone, but it was as if one of their family had been torn away from them. Jonathan had only been with them for five months, but in that time he had definitely became one of the family. Now he was a lost member of the family in a world that is sometimes very unfriendly.

His anger made him drive much faster than he should have, and by mid-morning he was in the midst of the mountains of North Carolina. It was a warm December day, but a glaze of snow topped the highest peaks. He took a deep breath and looked at the beauty around him. He pulled over at a lookout spot on the highway. He got out and walked. There was a path leading to the highest crest, and he ventured onto it. The air was very cold and brisk. No one else was on the path. He climbed for ten minutes.

He was cold, and he thought about going back, but was drawn forward to finish his quest. He walked another fifteen minutes and started to warm up from the exertion of the climb. A fine layer of snow covered the fallen leaves on the ground and turned the world into a sparkling jewel as the sun peaked through the clouds. Suddenly the sun won, and the clouds departed. At the same time he stepped out of the trees onto an out-cropping of rock that overlooked the surrounding valley and mountains.

His breath caught in one big gasp at the view before him. He had never seen such beauty! He suddenly realized that he was part of a much larger picture surrounding him. He sat on a rock and looked in reverence at the peaks and valleys that seemed to go on forever. There was no end from where he sat. He knew God had created it. There was not even the slightest doubt that God had created the beauty spread out before and behind him. The doubt came when he though about how God, who had created the majesty he experienced, could care for him. Britany said He did. Ben agreed. But how could God care for him, alone and small in the midst of this greatness?

He sat solemnly on the rock looking out over the mountains, and slowly he began to sense God's presence. He wasn't sure how, but he knew God was there with him. He looked at the distant mountains. "That's were I am going. I have a mission now. I am going to travel far in search of my father. I have a journey in front of me that will be far and reaching like the mountains before me." His search for his father took on a purpose instead of being simply a rambling accident. He wasn't sure why, but he knew God wanted him to continue on.

Jonathan wanted to sit on the rock forever, but the cool air and the excitement of the purpose before him urged him to return to the truck. He stopped at the next rest area and got a map, looked at his destination and plotted his path. He arrived in Wilmington before dark. He was in the right city, but he didn't know where to find her house. He found a telephone booth with a telephone book. He looked through the "B's" until he came to Bodine. He couldn't remember Ruth Anne's husband's first name, but fortunately he found a Ruth Anne and Carl.

At a gas station he asked for directions to the address. They directed him through the city and up the coast. He trembled as he found a mailbox with their house number. It even had their name! Hopefully it was the right Ruth Anne. Through the darkness he could make out the silhouette of a two-story Cape Cod. Even in the dark it had a definite quaintness to it. He could hear the surf on the beach as he opened the truck door and realized the house was on the coast.

A collie dog came up to him and sniffed his leg as he stepped onto the porch. He smiled and rubbed its ears. The collie wagged his tale. Jonathan said a quick prayer and knocked on the door. A lady in her mid sixties opened the door and looked up at him. She barely reached Jonathan's shoulder and reminded him of his mother with her petite build and fragile look. Her smile had the same appearance his mother's had had, but it seemed much more alive and vibrant as she smiled up at him.

"I feel as if I should know you. You look familiar, but yet I can't seem to place you," she said, puzzled. "Please, come in."

Jonathan stepped into the warmth and light of the entry.

"Ruth Anne, who is at the door?" Jonathan heard a man's voice come from another room.

"I don't know yet, dear!" she called back. "It is a young man!"

"What is your name, dear?" she asked politely. Jonathan felt rather strange to be standing in her house. He was surprised she had opened the door and let him enter before she knew who he was. He wasn't even sure he had the right person, but surely from her appearance it must be his mother's aunt.

"I'm Jonathan, ma'am. Jonathan Quarterman." Ruth Anne gasped, and her eyes focused intently on his face. He thought for a moment she was going to stumble, and then just as quickly she threw her arms around him and held him tight. He felt her tremble and could tell she was crying. He patted her back.

"Please don't cry, Aunt Ruth Anne," he pleaded.

"Honey, who is at the door?" A man came from the adjacent room as he asked the question. He stood and looked quizzically at his wife, who was still crying with her arms around Jonathan. He waited for her to regain her composure. She released Jonathan from her hold, but grasped firmly to his arm and turned to face her husband.

"It's Patsy's baby!" she exclaimed as if he should understand what she was saying.

"Patsy's baby? He looks like a grown young man to me." The man looked at Jonathan through questioning eyes that tried to decipher what his wife had said. He was much taller than his wife and appeared to be the same age.

She laughed through the tears and said, "Carl, he is grown now, but it is still Patsy's child."

Carl shook his head as he started to understand and held out his hand to Jonathan. "Yes, of course. Now it makes sense. Come in, boy, and have a seat." He led the way through the foyer into a comfortable room with a warm fire blazing. Aromatic smells of what must have been their supper reached Jonathan, and even though he had eaten, started pangs of hunger.

He took a seat on a soft chair next to a couch. They both sat on the couch facing him. He looked around and noticed a definite nautical flare in the decor. It was a warm, inviting house. Sliding doors opening from the room to the darkness that masked the ocean. He could hear a faint pounding of the surf.

"Jonathan, I can't believe you are here!" said Ruth Anne. "We only learned of your mother's death a month ago and have been trying to find out what happened to you. My brother has not spoken to me since the summer your mother came to visit."

"My mother talked of you often with fondness," said Jonathan. He sat forward in his chair. There was so much he wanted to ask them that he found it hard to relax.

"I wrote to your mother often after that summer, but she wrote infrequently, and when she did she sounded so defeated," said Ruth Anne sadly. "I don't know what happened to my brother after his wife died, but he always seemed to blame Patsy for it."

Jonathan's eyes clouded as she spoke. He tried to hide the anger and resentment welling up in him as she spoke.

"I urged her to come live with us when you were born. I knew Joe was harsh and bitter, and I wanted her to get away and raise you in a different environment. My two boys were still little then, but we could have managed." She looked sadly into the fire. "Somehow she never felt she was good enough to get away from your grandfather. She seemed to think she deserved how he treated her." She continued and Jonathan wondered for a while if she really realized he was there. She seemed to be reviewing the past to try and figure out what had happened.

"Amadeo seemed like such a nice, respectable young man, and they were madly in love. We could never understand why he didn't respond to her letters."

"He did!" Jonathan said it so suddenly that she stared and looked at him. He took out the letters from the pocket of his jacket and reached his arm so she could see them. She slowly reached out and took them. Silently she read the envelope and opened the first one. Tears filled her eyes, and her hands dropped to her lap as she read the first page. She leaned her gray curls against her husband and cried into his shoulder. He retrieved the letter from her lap and looked at it.

"Where did you get this?" he asked incredulously with a husky voice.

Jonathan was stunned to see their reaction. He had never realized anyone had ever cared for him or his mother. It was very confusing.

"They were in my grandmother's dresser at Grandfather's house. He was drunk when I went back there, and I looked around. I needed to find some information to help me find out who my father was. I found them and left to read them. I went back the next day and asked him about them. He said he hid them from my mother. He also said he found all the letters Mom had written and burned them," he explained.

Carl shook his head. "What an awful thing to do!"

"I can't believe he would deprive his daughter of her chance for happiness," Ruth Anne said sadly.

"He didn't want her to move to Greece," said Jonathan. "I don't know if it was because of his love for my mother or his hatred toward a foreigner. My grandfather has some strange ideas."

"Whatever the reason, it was wrong!" exclaimed Carl. Ruth Anne looked at him and shook her head.

"I wish we would have driven to his house and gotten you and your mother. I can't believe my own brother would have been so deceitful!" She looked at Jonathan with compassion on her face. "You must have driven all day to get here. Would you like something to eat? I made a big meal, and there was plenty to eat."

Jonathan looked at her with eagerness in his eyes, but was afraid to admit he was hungry.

"Of course the boy wants some food!" exclaimed Carl. "You will love Ruth Anne's cooking!"

Ruth Anne rose and led the way through a door to the kitchen. Her slipper feet padded softly on the floor. Her petite body reminded him of his mother. She wore a plaid wool sweater and black slacks. She poured Jonathan a glass of juice and had him sit at the table while she warmed a plate of food.

The food was delicious, and Jonathan thanked her profusely. Carl joined them as she sat at the table.

"Could you tell me a little about Amadeo?" asked Jonathan as he finished. "Do you think he was my father?"

Ruth Anne's eyes clouded, and she looked hesitantly at Carl.

"It's all right," assured Jonathan. "You can tell me the worst. For years I was afraid to find out who my father was because I didn't want to know how bad he was. Now I just want to know." His lanky body leaned forward in anticipation. "Now that he at least has a name, even a country."

Ruth Anne sat in the chair next to him and took his hand. "It's not that he was a bad man that you read sorrow in my eyes." She evenly met his intense black eyes with her own. "He was a wonderful man. He had come here to work for two years to earn money to send back to Greece to help his father keep their lemon farm. There had been several bad years for the lemons in Greece, and he came here to save the family farm." She paused and looked at him. She reached up and touched his long black hair. "You look very much like your father, and yes, he is your father. You have his shiny dark hair and strong nose. He was very tall and slender like you too. Patsy and I wrote back and forth when she returned and found out she was pregnant."

"I'm afraid the sadness you read in my eyes a moment ago is because we wrongly misjudged your father," continued Ruth Anne. "You see Patsy returned to your grandfathers shortly before he left to go back to Greece. They wrote back and forth. Several weeks after he left she found out she was pregnant and called me. She said Jim was horrified and wanted her to get an abortion. I wanted her to come back and stay with us, but your grandfather would have nothing to do with that. At least she stood up to her father and carried you to term. I think it was because you were part of him that gave her strength. I encouraged her to write Amadeo and tell him she was expecting. They had plans to be married in

Greece as soon as he went back and made the preparations. He had wanted to get the house ready for her. She wrote to him and told him you were expected in the fall. We were hoping she could go over there soon, before she got too big. He never answered her letters. He never wrote at all. I told her to forget him. I thought he was probably bound by some tradition to not marry her since she was pregnant." She looked down at the table, and her tears started again. "Now we know he never knew about you. You, his own son who looks so much like him. He was denied the chance to raise you and provide for you."

Jonathan's jaw was hard as he listened. How could such hatred destroy two people's lives? Well his mothers might be over, but his wasn't, and it was about time someone set things right.

"I'm going to find him!" Jonathan said with determination.

Ruth Anne and Carl both looked at him with concern. "Jonathan, he doesn't even know you exist! How are you going to get him to believe you!" exclaimed Carl.

"How will you even find him?" asked Ruth Anne.

Jonathan leaned toward her, took the letters from her hand, and held them in the air. "I have an address," he said firmly.

They both looked at him. "Yes, you do," said Ruth Anne quietly. "I can understand why you feel the need to find him." She looked up at Carl. "We will do whatever we can to help. Your father was a fine young man, and I am afraid he was sorely misjudged." Carl nodded. The fire crackled, and the surf sounded in the background, but the rest of the house was quiet, and no one spoke for a long time.

The first to speak was Ruth Anne. "Jonathan, you go to your truck and get your things. It will take several days to secure airline tickets and your passport. During that time you are staying here." Jonathan started to object, but Carl stopped him.

"Son, we wanted you to come eighteen years ago. I would say it's about time you accepted our offer. We want you to stay," Carl said sincerely.

"Thank you. You are both very kind." Jonathan smiled a half-smile. Their offer was generous, and it sounded luxurious compared to his truck, but the pain of leaving Britany's family was too deep. If he weren't afraid he would hurt them he would have turned down their offer. Instead he went to the truck and got his things. Ruth Ann showed him to the spare room and then gave him a big hug.

"Good night, Jonathan," she said. "I'm glad you are finally here."

Jonathan fell asleep almost immediately. The emotional strain of the past two days was exhausting, and he slept far into the morning.

CHAPTER 16

It took almost a week before Jonathan was ready to fly to Greece. His great aunt and uncle were most gracious hosts and he was able to meet his mother's two cousins. He had enjoyed Tom and Gary very much and the three of them had enjoyed several games of basketball. His leg was still painful, and it made playing difficult, but he was determined to exercise it and make it strong. No one had commented on his limp, and he was hoping that it was no longer noticeable, although he could tell it still existed. He never told anyone about his fall from the tree. He hadn't even mentioned Britany's family. He was gone from them now and would possibly never see them again. Pain stabbed at his heart deeply.

Jonathan looked at the money that remained after he purchased the airplane ticket. Visions of the numerous yards to mow that it would take to replenish his college fund went through his head. Despite the possibility that he might not be able to start college when he had hoped to, he was certain he was doing the right thing. It was important to meet his father. He wasn't even sure if he would return by the start of second semester to finish high school. But he would face one thing at a time. It helped to have at least a small plan. He would fly into the airport at Athens and then try and find transportation to the small town north of there. He and his uncle had located it on the map. At least the town was on the map!

Jonathan looked around him at the throngs of people. There were old ladies with hard faces greeting loves ones with exaggerated emotion. Young ladies carrying babies searched the people coming from the plane. Tall, straight men looking very distinguished and speaking rapidly were everywhere. The sights were bustling as Jonathan stepped off the airplane. Voices were all around him, but he couldn't tell what they were saying. Signs hung on the walls, but they had no meaning for him. He felt as if he were lost in a mass of confusion. He stood surveying his surroundings, trying to determine which way he should go to retrieve his bag.

He walked up to the counter and asked a young lady standing there, "Do you speak English?"

She nodded in reply, "Yez, I do. Can I help you?" She had a pretty face and dark, wavy hair.

"I need to find my bags," he said.

"You're what? I do not understand." She squinted her face in a perplexed look.

"My bags," he repeated and realized he needed a different word. He held up his backpack he had taken on the plane and pointed to it. "Bag," he repeated. "Big bag," he said extending his arms to help show her what he meant.

"Oh, yez," she said. She showed him a sign above with an arrow on it.

"Follow those signs," she said and smiled politely.

"Thank you," Jonathan said. He looked at the sign again and tried to imprint in his brain what it looked like.

The crowd was hard to pass through as he made his way following the signs. He saw his one bag and lifted it from the conveyer belt. Now he wasn't sure what to do. His travel agent had gotten him a bus ticket to take him to the city he needed to go. He stepped outside to see if one could be found. He saw several buses and stepped onto the first one he came to. He showed the driver his ticket and tried to ask if he had the right bus. The elderly gentleman with gray hair and blue cap said, "No En-glesh."

Jonathan frowned and the driver looked again at the ticket. He motioned toward a bus that was several buses behind them. Jonathan smiled and said, "Thank-you." He backed from the bus and pushed his way through the crowd to the third bus down.

He showed the driver the ticket. "Is this the right bus?" he asked.

The younger driver smiled and said, "Little En-glesh, right bus."

Jonathan smiled and nodded. He found an empty seat and settled in to watch the landscape, so different than he was used to, pass by. He caught glimpses of deep blue water as they crested the tops of hills that overlooked the bay below. Low, crooked olive trees lined the hillside, along with grapevines. The road was full of curves and hills, causing Jonathan to fall into the people sitting beside him.

His heart pounded with the thought of soon seeing his father. He had practiced over and over what to say, but as he sat on the bus, surrounded by strange people in a strange land, he felt very insecure. He felt lost in a sea of people of different language and culture. The bus traveled for an hour and came to a modern looking town with relics from the past. He sat up as tall as he could and looked out to see what surrounded them. He saw a sign that read, "Khalkis". His breath caught in his chest. This was the town he had waited for. He stepped from the bus and looked around. He had a plan. He was going to go into shops and ask for directions to the address on the letter.

He walked into the first store that had loaves of bread in the window. A short man with a bald head stood at the counter Jonathan walked up to.

"Do you know this address?" he asked.

The man looked blankly at him and showed him a loaf of bread. It looked good, and Jonathan offered him some money. The man smiled and took a bill, then gave him some change. Jonathan tried again. He showed him the letter and pointed to the address.

"Yes, yes," he said. He pointed down the road. Jonathan felt helpless. He didn't know what to do. The man looked at him and came around from behind the counter. He reached out for Jonathan's hand and led him out of the store. He went to the store next door and spoke very rapidly in Greek to the people inside. A young man, shorter than Jonathan but not much older, came through the door, and the first man began to speak very excitedly.

The young man looked at Jonathan and smiled.

"Are you from America?" he asked.

Jonathan nodded. He was as excited as the old man when he heard someone speak English. "Yes, I am Jonathan," he said. "I am looking for this person."

"I am Olio," said the young man. "Maybe I can help you."

Jonathan handed him the envelope. The man looked at it and smiled.

"He lives seven kilometers from here, overlooking the Aegean Sea. He has a lemon tree farm," he said and nodded as he looked at the address. Jonathan's heart beat faster.

"How do I get there?" Jonathan asked.

The man smiled and took off the apron he wore. "I take you!" he exclaimed. Jonathan couldn't believe what he was hearing.

Olio led the way out the door to the street where a small motorbike was parked. "We ride thiz," he said. Jonathan didn't think it could hold both of them, but got on behind him. He had to hold his bag over his head as they took off down the street. It wasn't fast, but the small motorbike took them out of the city and onto a small country road. Jonathan laughed as Olio talked joyously and told him about some of the small farms they passed. They had to stop for several goats that crossed the road, and then they continued on.

Olio stopped at the bottom of a very steep hill. "I think maybe you walk up the hill? I think motor bike not take both of us."

Jonathan laughed. "I think not!" he said. He gladly got off the back and started up the hill. Olio drove to the top and waited. Jonathan was grateful to have found a ride and was not at all bothered by the fact that he had to walk. He had feared he might end up walking the entire seven kilometers. He got to the top and got back on.

Olio stopped at the bottom of another even taller hill. "Amadeo lives at the top of this hill. You can walk now?" he asked with a smile.

"Yes, I can walk," said Jonathan. He reached into his pocket and took out several bills. He handed them to Olio. Olio looked at him puzzled, but didn't take the money.

"I pay for the ride!" Jonathan explained.

"No! No!" Olio exclaimed. "You friend of Amadeo, you friend of mine. He very nice man. He help many people. Tell him Olio say hello."

"Thank you," said Jonathan and reached for his hand. "You have been very kind."

Olio accepted Jonathan's hand, and then he leaned over and brushed each of Jonathan's cheeks with a kiss the way Jonathan had seen many other Greek people do. "In Greece we say good bye like this," he said. Jonathan smiled. "You come back to store and see Olio while you visit, yes?" Olio continued.

"Yes, I will do that." Jonathan was grateful for his new friend and watched as he drove off. Then he turned and started up the hill. The sun was very hot, but a cool dry breeze kept him comfortable. Jonathan ate some of the bread as he walked and took a bottle of water from his backpack. He was glad as he walked that he had not brought many clothes. His bag was already getting heavy.

He got to the top of the hill and looked over a vast horizon of blue. He could see an island in the distance. White clouds, barely a wisp, were high in the sky. A stiff but pleasant breeze blew against his face, carrying his dark hair with it. An excitement seized him. He felt as if his surroundings were a part of him, and perhaps he really was part of something much bigger than his own small world had been so far. Directly in front of him was a pristine house built of white stone with a tile roof. It was low and sprawling. It wasn't large, but it possessed the stateliness of a mansion. Surrounding the home, as far as he could see to the right and left and trailing down to the sea, were lemon trees. Some were full of bright plump lemons, others were bare, and some had fragrant blossoms.

Jonathan's heart beat hard in his chest as he approached the house. He feared that words would not come. What are the right words at a time like this? he wondered.

Two young children ran from the house, laughing and chasing each other through the yard. They saw Jonathan and stopped. They ran to him with smiling faces and rattled off words he didn't understand.

"Do you speak English?" Jonathan asked hesitantly.

The little girl with long black hair and thick lashes giggled and said, "Yez, we speak En-glesh. Who are you?"

"I am Jonathan Quarterman, and am looking for Mr. Amadeo Vacalopoulos," said Jonathan.

"That's Papa!" said the little girl. "Come with us." She took his hand and led the way through one of the many lemon groves. Jonathan looked at the two as they walked. They were possibly his brother and sister. He wondered if there were any others. It seemed strange after being what he thought was an only child for eighteen years to find that he actually had a brother and sister.

They came to where a man stood on a tall ladder in one of the trees.

The little girl looked into the tree and said something. The man turned around. Jonathan was startled by the face he saw mirroring his own. The man also seemed to notice. He simply stared for a long time.

"Papa! He is from America! Come down!" Sisily said in English for Jonathan's benefit.

The man slowly came down and faced Jonathan. His hair was shorter, but just as black as Jonathan's. He definitely had the same nose, and they stood the same height, although Amadeo was sturdier in build. Jonathan had the smaller frame of his mother.

The man kissed Jonathan on both cheeks in Greek fashion and said, "My daughter says that you are looking for me. I am Amadeo Vacalopoulos. You are a long way from America to find me. May I ask who you are?"

"I am Jonathan, and yes, I have come a long way," Jonathan said and stopped. He searched for the words to explain his conquest. The man recognized his hesitancy and made a suggestion.

"It is a very hot day for December. Let us go to the veranda for some lemonade." He looked at the two children and said, "Sisily, go to the house and tell Mama we have a visitor and would like some lemonade." Both children ran quickly. Amadeo turned and looked at Jonathan with a searching gaze.

"You look as if you have a very important task that I am part of. I felt maybe it would be better to discuss without the children. Would you like to talk?" he asked.

"You speak very good English," said Jonathan.

"Yes, I lived in America for two years," he answered. Jonathan's heart beat faster. So He was in America!

"Sir," started Jonathan. He looked at Amadeo and suddenly felt as if he couldn't breath. He had came thousands of miles for answers, and now words seemed to elude him. Amadeo reached out and grasped his shoulder. "It's ok, boy. I not hurt you. Go on.

Jonathan took a deep breath and slowly let it out. He could see his long fingers tremble and clenched his fist to hold them steady. "For eighteen years I have wondered who my father was. Now I am close to finding out the possible answer."

"You think I can help you find your father?" he asked. "I see not how!"

"I'm under the understanding that at one time you knew Patsy Quarterman," said Jonathan.

Amadeo looked surprised and then his eyes took on a soft faraway look. "Yes, a very wonderful woman." He said softly. Then he looked at Jonathan puzzled. "What does that have to do with you?"

"Patsy was my mother."

"That cannot be!" he exclaimed angrily. "She had no baby!"

"She didn't when you were in America, but I was born six months after you left," Jonathan explained.

"That cannot be!" he bellowed and paced across the grass. "Patsy died in a car accident on her way to her father's house from North Carolina!"

So that was what his grandfather had told him to keep his father from finding out about Jonathan and coming to get Patsy. Now Jonathan was as angry as Amadeo.

"That---. How could he do that!" he blurted.

Amadeo looked at Jonathan. They were both angry, and yet Jonathan needed to control himself and explain what had happened. He took the letters from his wallet.

"My grandfather hid these from my mother. She never knew you wrote to her." He held them toward Amadeo.

Amadeo looked at them with stormy eyes. "Yes, these are from me, but Patsy died."

"No! Her father only told you that to keep her from going to Greece," Jonathan said passionately. Once again he reached into his pocket and took a picture of him and his mother, taken when he was six. He showed it to Amadeo. Amadeo looked at it and turned pale.

"It's Patsy!" he exclaimed in a husky voice. "She looks so sad and fragile. Is that you?" he asked pointing at the little boy in the picture.

Jonathan nodded his head.

"But how do I know you are not just a nephew?"

Jonathan turned the picture over and showed him the date on the back when the picture was developed. Amadeo trembled and bit his lip.

"Please sit," said Jonathan and helped him onto the grass.

"What does this mean?" asked Amadeo, slowly shaking his head. "I don't know what to think. You mean Patsy lives, and you are her son?"

Jonathan's eyes searched Amadeo's face. "She died the beginning of last summer," he said quietly. Jonathan showed Amadeo another, more recent picture of his mother taken the month before her death. He examined the picture closely, and his face showed extreme sorrow. This man in front of him had loved his mother and from his reaction still loved her. How different was the mother that he had known from the young lady that this man had fallen in love with. She must have been so full of life then. His grandfather had not only cheated him out of a father. He had cheated him out of a mother!

"But you said you don't know who your father is?" Amadeo asked, perplexed.

"She never said, but I think from putting the pieces together from these letters and what my Aunt Ruth Anne says, that it must be you. I needed to come and see for myself," said Jonathan quietly.

Amadeo buried his face in his hands. "I must think," he said. "I need time to think. It took me ten years before I could fall in love again. Now I have a wonderful wife and two lovely children with one on the way. My wife knows nothing of your mother. I can't tell her now after all these years."

"Papa!" yelled Sisily running toward them. "Lemonade waits, and you take long. Hurry!" she exclaimed.

He rose from the ground and put on a happy face. "Come," he said to Jonathan. "Rest now. We talk later." He patted Jonathan on the shoulder as they walked to the house.

Amadeo's wife Frena was a very pretty lady with almond eyes and olive skin. She looked in her late twenties. She was noticeably pregnant. Her English wasn't as clear as Amadeo's, but Jonathan could understand her well. They all had a seat on the veranda, and Jonathan enjoyed the lemonade. Jonathan turned to find Frena watching him intently. She smiled warmly.

"You remember my friends from America that I told you about," said Amadeo to his wife.

She said something in Greek. He answered, "This is their nephew, Jonathan. He is traveling and wanted to see Greece. They sent him to look me up and say hi."

She smiled a pretty smile.

"I asked him to stay with us for a while. We can show him some of Greece, and maybe he will help us with the lemon harvest," he said with a smile.

Jonathan was surprised. "Yes, sir! I would love to help, but I don't want to be a bother."

"A big strong boy like you, no bother," said Frena. "Amadeo's own children too young to help. You can help for them."

Jonathan saw a wave of sadness cross Amadeo's face. He wanted desperately to get to know this man, but he didn't want to bring him sorrow. He said no more and watched as the family interacted happily.

Jonathan went to the fields as soon as they finished the lemonade, to begin plucking the ripe lemons from the trees, filling the rows and rows of baskets and putting them onto the truck. Amadeo was pleased with the fast progress they made with Jonathan's help. It was evening, after the meal, before he had a chance to talk to Amadeo in private. They walked through the grove among the fragrance of the new blossoms. It was a full, sweet smell, as rich as honeysuckle that blossomed on warm June nights in Tennessee. They walked to the top of the hill that overlooked the bay. Jonathan could hear the waves below but couldn't see because of the darkness.

Amadeo looked off into the darkness and waved his arm to scan the emptiness. "I came to this spot after I read the letter your grandfather wrote telling of Patsy's death. I thought about jumping off the cliff to join her. It was a very hard time," Amadeo said softly as his voice was carried in the breeze. He looked at Jonathan and continued. "Now you say that Patsy died less than a year ago, and that she was your mother!" He shook his head. "It is all too confusing. I don't know if I can believe you. I need time to think. I like having you here. You are a very good worker, and I can use the help. Please stay and help finish the harvest. I promise I will consider what you say."

Jonathan's heart ached. "Then you are not ready to admit you are my father, and I cannot be sure that you are?" he asked.

Amadeo shrugged his shoulders in the darkness. "I'm sorry. I wish I could tell you for sure, but until I am certain, I cannot say."

Jonathan walked away into the darkness and listened to the surf. He couldn't push Amadeo for an answer that he was unwilling to give. He couldn't force him to say that he was his son. What if after all this Amadeo wasn't his father? His heart ached at the thought. The moment he had seen him he felt a fondness for him, and he wished with all his heart that Amadeo was his father.

What if Amadeo was his father and yet never believed the fact? What good would it do to observe his father from the distance, but never have a father-son relationship? He sat cross-legged in the sparse grass with his long legs folded easily. His hair blew away from his face in the fragrant wind, and he stared into the darkness. He was so close, yet so far away from an answer.

"Dear Lord, help me to find the truth," he prayed as the surf and the wind tried to overcome his words. The noise couldn't block his heart from God, who listened with supreme wisdom.

Amadeo watched Jonathan walk into the distance, and, although he wanted to comfort him, he could think of nothing to say. Perhaps his own pain was too deep to be able to reach out to another. He had thought the pain was gone, but old wounds still hurt when they are reopened. He watched Jonathan for a while and then walked back to the house.

Sisily and Theo were ready for bed when he returned, and he helped them under the covers. He looked into his wife's tender face when he stood from kissing Sisily. She took his arm, and they walked to the veranda.

"You came back without Jonathan," Frena commented. Amadeo looked at her without speaking. He didn't know how to begin. "Your eyes look heavy with worry," she said. "Are you afraid he may not come back?" she asked.

Amadeo didn't comment. "He looks very much like you!" Frena said with a smile.

"What!" Amadeo said in amazement.

"You think I didn't know of the lover you left in America? I may have been young when I married you, but not without wisdom," she said gently.

Amadeo took her arms and held them firmly. "How? How did you know?" he asked hoarsely.

She smiled. "It was no secret that you were very sad for many years because of her. The only thing I don't know is why you left her in America. And you have a grown boy!" she exclaimed. "Wouldn't she come back with you?" she asked.

Amadeo looked deeply into her eyes. It had been hard to not tell her about Patsy, but at the time when he had learned of Patsy's death, or supposed death, he had tried to seal off all talk of her and put an end to his pain. Now the pain was back and making his life confusing.

"We were planning on being married as soon as she could make arrangements and fly over here," he said quietly, searching her eyes for signs of pain that he might be causing her. "When I arrived, I wrote to her but she never wrote back. Then three weeks later I received a letter from her father stating that she had died."

Frena looked puzzled. "But the boy," she said. "It makes no sense."

"The boy says that Patsy didn't die eighteen years ago. Her father stole the letters I wrote. He was the one who wrote to me and told me of her death so I wouldn't write again. Apparently she thought I didn't want her anymore and never tried to contact me. I didn't try and contact her because I thought she had died. The boy says that she lived until the beginning of last summer, and that he is my son." He walked to the end of the veranda. "I just don't know what to believe," he said into the darkness.

"But the boy," said Frena. "He has to be yours. He looks so much like you!"

Amadeo walked back to her and grasped both her arms. "You really think he looks like me?" he asked with intensity. "I have to know!" He dropped her arms and ran his hand through his hair. "He says that he is looking for his father and wonders if it is I!"

Frena reached up and stroked his face. "Let your heart speak, Amadeo," she said softly. She reached out and laid her hand on his chest, over his heart. "Let your heart speak Amadeo. Listen to it. Surely you see your strong nose and jaw when you look at his face. He even walks like you. Don't you feel something when you look into those intense eyes of his that surely reflect your own?" She let her hand rest against his chest.

Amadeo looked down at her protruding abdomen. "You are a very wise, understanding woman, Frena," he said and smiled faintly. "Surely my heart did speak to me when I first saw him in the lemon groves." He looked back up into her eyes. "What do I do?" he asked.

"You go to him now," she said. "He hasn't had you for eighteen years, but he desperately needs you now." She reached up and kissed his cheek. "Perhaps having him here will help you heal."

"Frena," he said with intensity. "I loved Patsy. I'll not try and hide it from you any longer, but the love I feel for you now is so much deeper. It is like the difference between the sun and the moon. The moon simply reflects what it receives. The sun makes its own heat. You are the sun, Frena. I love you," Amadeo said and drew her close into a long embrace. Then her released her and walked back up the hill.

Jonathan heard his approach as he sat in the darkness. He didn't know where to go or who to turn to. He had been sitting trying to decide what to do when he heard Amadeo walking toward him. The elder man walked up to him and placed a hand on Jonathan's shoulder.

"I spoke with Frena," Amadeo started. "She knows you are my son. She also knows about your mother. She is a very wise woman. If she can tell, I surely have no excuse to deny it." He waited until Jonathan looked up at him.

Jonathan stared at him, unable to move. How could Frena know, when no one else did? "I don't understand. You said you never told her. How could she possibly know when you aren't even sure?"

Amadeo sat on the rock beside Jonathan. "Jonathan, you have much to learn about women. They know things without being told. She could see me in your eyes." He smiled. "I guess she knows me more than I realized. You do look like me, you know."

Jonathan stared off into the sea that was hidden by the darkness. "My aunt and uncle said I do. I guess I hadn't thought about it."

Amadeo patted him on the back. "Welcome, son," he said and embraced Jonathan.

After they resumed their previous positions and regained their composure, Jonathan spoke quietly. "I didn't know what to do after you left. I had been convinced that you are my father, but then you were so uncertain that it left me to doubt. How can I be sure you are my father?" he asked hesitantly.

Amadeo released him and stood. "Come home, son," he said and reached out his hand. "It has been a very stressful time for you, and you need some rest. You stay with us and get to know us. Then you will be sure too that I am your father." Jonathan took the offered hand and stood. Together they left the hill and walked back to the house.

Jonathan stayed with Amadeo for a month and helped with the lemons. It was hard work physically, but a restful time mentally. Amadeo and his family were strong Christians, and Jonathan learned much about God through the eyes of his father. Amadeo took Jonathan and the others on sightseeing adventures when he declared they needed a rest day from the work. Jonathan was feeling a part of the family and was glad to get to know his brother, sister and father, but something kept calling to him. He couldn't explain it, but as happy as he was he still felt as if something was missing.

Britany walked onto the deck that overlooked the woods and the flowing creek. The excitement of Christmas was over and the quietness of winter was settling in. The breeze was cool, and she tucked her hands into her pockets. She looked around at the trees below her. They were gray, and they blended into the gray sky. She sighed. Crystal was home again, attending the college she had attended her sophomore year. The turmoil she had gone through had left her feeling very insecure and Britany wished she could help her. Crystal complained of being a failure. Britany tried to get her to see that the only failure in life is to not realize when a person has done something wrong and to continuously take advantage of God's love, but Crystal still could not accept that.

She walked out to the barn and called for her horse. Misty came to the fence looking for an expected treat. Britany stroked her nose and laid her cheek against her silken mane. She reached in her pocket and pulled out a carrot for Misty. She smiled. "You always seem to comfort me when I am down," she said and went to get the brush to groom her.

She entered the tack room, and her gaze fell on the boots they had gotten for Jonathan in anticipation of the day he would be able to ride. A painful tightening grasped her chest as she pictured him in her mind. First the way he had looked when she cared for him the first day after his fall, and then the look of terror on his face as he left.

She cried out in agony. "Dear Lord, where is he!" she moaned. "Is he safe? Is he warm on these cold days, or is he living on the streets again out of his truck?

Britany dropped into the chair by the door. She longed so much to reach out to Jonathan and talk to him, to tell him she loved him and that he could have a home and not roam about searching for love and acceptance. She wrapped her arms around her waist and dropped her head. Tears filled her eyes and dropped to her cheeks. She wanted to hold him close and know that he was all right. Suddenly, through her distress a, realization dawned. The longing to hold him close and love him was the same way God felt about her the times she had turned away from Him and tried to run. God had wanted with a passion to gather her up and comfort her. She thought about the time she had turned and ran from the love that God had to offer when Jean died, much the same way Jonathan had ran. The strength of emotion that she could feel from God was overwhelming and she felt weak at the same time she felt encompassed with love.

"Thank-you Lord," she said as she sat on the chair. "I am beginning to realize in a small way how much You truly love us, your creation. If I can love a boy this strongly who was only in my life for a short time, how much more You love us whom You created. If only I can help Crystal to understand this love!"

The sky looked lighter, and the trees seemed to have a touch of green as she walked from the barn to the house. She still missed Jonathan, and she still longed to reach out to Crystal and give her self-confidence, but the knowledge of God's deep love chased away the sadness and hopelessness that had been present minutes earlier.

Jonathan spent much free time on the hill overlooking the sea. One day Amadeo found him there. He sat on the rock beside him.

"You spend much time up here. It is a very good place to think," he said.

Jonathan nodded.

Amadeo tossed a rock off the cliff. "You need to forgive your grandfather, you know."

Jonathan looked at him in surprise. "What! How can you say that?" he asked in anger. "He hurt me and my mother very badly." Jonathan's brow creased in anger. "He hurt you, too! How can you sit here and tell me to forgive him!" he exclaimed. "Do you forgive him for what he did to you?" Jonathan asked defiantly.

"Jonathan, I would lie if I told you I have no ill feeling toward your grandfather. You are right. He hurt me very badly, and it makes me angry to zee what he haz done to you and your mother. Because of thiz I ask God every day to help me forgive." Amadeo put his arm on Jonathan's shoulder. "What I ask of you iz not an easy thing. I only ask because your anger will hurt you more than it will hurt your grandfather. He haz already hurt you enough. Anger can be a deep wound that only seals on the surface. Underneath it festers and becomes poisonous."

Amadeo pointed to the sea below. "I want you to enjoy the beauty around you without the poison of anger in your heart. Jesus commands us to forgive others, and He forgives us. He also promised that He will help us."

Jonathan shook his head. "I can't do it, Amadeo. I just can't right now. I am only now finding out who I am and it is too much for me. The anger goes too deep."

Amadeo smiled. He looked wise as he sat there on the rock. Jonathan admired him, and he knew he was probably right, but he didn't want to forgive his grandfather. He wanted most of all to just forget his grandfather and live the life he was beginning to discover.

"You take your time, Jonathan, son," said Amadeo. "Someday you will be ready, then remember what I said. You are not alone. God will help you to do the impossible."

CHAPTER 17

The month in January seemed like the beginning of spring in Tennessee, and Jonathan almost forgot that he was missing school and would not be able to graduate in May. Amadeo was fast becoming a strength and encouragement to him and he dearly loved his new family. One month was left until Frena's baby was due, and Jonathan wondered if he would be around to see his new brother or sister.

Jonathan picked up a rock and threw it at a lizard that lay below the lemon tree. It hissed at him and scurried off unharmed. Jonathan laughed. "If I really wanted to hit you, I could," he promised to the lizard. "At least you know where your home is." He sat on the grass and looked up at the deep blue sky.

This is so beautiful and it belongs to my father, he thought. He has been wonderful. I guess it is more of a home than I have ever had, yet what I really miss is my home with Britany and her family. He sighed and tossed another stone. He couldn't explain the longing he had, but it wouldn't leave him. The pain and longing to go back was always there waiting to surface anytime he had a free moment to think or when a baby cried, reminding him of Andrew. He knew he couldn't go back, but he wanted to, and it hurt to think about it.

He picked up a blade of grass and grimaced hard to fight the tears that threatened to come. Why had he kissed Britany? He couldn't forgive himself for it, and he knew they never would be able to. There was no denying he loved her, but he had always thought of her as a mother. What had came over him? She had looked so beautiful and happy. There had always been something about her that made him feel loved and secure. He never had that in his life, and now he wanted that feeling back. Was it gone forever? Would he never find someone to give him that type of love and security, total acceptance? He couldn't forgive himself for what he had done. He took advantage of her when she had been so trusting. He was sure the family would never forgive him, let alone let him back into their home. Agony filled him, and it hurt.

"Jonathan!" a frightened voice called. "Jonathan, help! We need you!" Sisily called. Jonathan jumped to his feet and ran toward the voice. Her little dress blew in the wind as she ran through the rows of trees.

"Sisily, I'm right here," he said as he ran to her and knelt beside her. "What is wrong?"

"It's Momma," she said through tears. "She is hurting real bad." Jonathan grabbed Sisily into his arms and ran toward the house. Amadeo had taken a load of lemons to the next town and had left Jonathan in charge for the day. He found Frena in a chair at the table, breathing hard. He put Sisily down and quickly went to her side. He felt panicked.

As soon as she caught her breath again she tried to talk. "Jonathan, the baby. I think it is coming."

Jonathan looked at her in alarm. She grasped his arm. "I know it is a lot to ask of you, but it may be fast, and there is no one else around. I had the other two in the house, but Amadeo and the doctor were here. You can do it."

Jonathan felt his knees go weak and then prayed silently, Lord, help me! She needs me, and I don't know what to do.

Frena grasped his arm. His face was pale, and he wore a helpless expression. "You can do it, Jonathan. Nature will take-." Her sentence was stopped as another contraction gripped her, and she blew out sharply.

Jonathan watched helplessly and then grasped her to offer support. "We need to get you to the bedroom." He almost carried her in his hurry to get her there.

"Sisily, can you run to the neighbor's and send someone for the doctor?" Jonathan asked. "Tell Theo to stay in the kitchen until you get back, and you come right back! We may need you!" Sisily looked at him with frightened eyes, but ran quickly to do as he ordered. Jonathan helped Frena into the bed and hurried to get extra towels and blankets. He couldn't believe his ears when he heard a truck engine outside. Amadeo entered as Jonathan stepped through the door with an armload of towels.

"Frena is in the bedroom. It looks like she is going to have the baby!" Jonathan said quickly. Amadeo was in the bedroom before Jonathan even finished. "I sent Sisily to the neighbor's to send for a doctor, but Frena said there isn't time."

"Yez, she goes very quickly," he said as he walked to her side. Jonathan put the towels on a chair and waited. Amadeo went to Frena and grasped her hand. She was breathing hard again. Jonathan went to get a wet cloth for her forehead. Theo sat on the chair in the kitchen looking very pale. Jonathan went to him and took him in his arms.

"Your mother is going to be just fine," he said. "Soon you are going to have a little brother or sister!" He hugged him tight and then set him back on the chair. "I need to be with your mother and father for a while. You keep being such a good boy," Jonathan said. He hoped Theo understood his English. He seemed to be less anxious, and Jonathan got the cloth wet and returned.

"Get some warm water in the pan in the kitchen," said Amadeo as Jonathan returned and gave him the cloth. "It won't be long, if all goes well."

"Maybe the doctor will be quick and get here soon," said Jonathan hopefully.

Amadeo smiled. "He never made it before. I don't think he will make it this time either." Jonathan noticed Frena's breathing starting to change, and he looked at Amadeo with concern. Amadeo seemed unaware of it as he hurried to prepare the room and Frena for the delivery. "Keep cool compresses to her face," instructed Amadeo. Frena groaned, and Jonathan jumped. He grasped the cloth and wiped her face. She looked like she was in a great deal of pain, and Jonathan wished he could help her.

Sisily came running into the house, breathing hard. "They went for the doctor!" she exclaimed.

"Good!" exclaimed Amadeo. "He should be here in time to check the baby and Frena out after it is born!"

Amadeo was right. Before too long Jonathan was witnessing the miracle of birth with amazement. It was a little girl.

"Now I have two girls and two boys!" exclaimed Amadeo. A lump caught in Jonathan's throat as he realized Amadeo had included him into the family.

Jonathan helped Sisily and Theo hold their little sister while Frena slept. Theo giggled at the way Anna stuck out her tongue, but Sisily looked at her with wonder in her eyes. Jonathan smiled at them, and his black eyes sparkled.

Jonathan heard the honking of the motorbike before it appeared on the road at the top of the hill. He ran to greet Olio. He had gotten to know him well, and in the two months of his visit they had gotten to be good friends.

"You have a telegram, my friend," said Olio as Jonathan approached.

"There are only two people who know I am here!" exclaimed Jonathan. "I wonder what is wrong!" He grasped the yellow paper and read it.

"What does it say?" asked Olio impatiently.

"My grandfather is very sick, and my aunt wants me to come home," Jonathan said weakly.

"Then you must go!" said Olio.

"No!" shouted Jonathan. "I want nothing to do with my grandfather."

"But the telegram," Olio said and shook his head. "Your grandfather must want you there."

"No," said Jonathan sternly. "My aunt wants me there. My grandfather could not care less."

Amadeo had heard the motorbike and was coming in from the field. He overheard Jonathan and Olio as he approached.

He put his hand on Jonathan's shoulder and said, "Perhaps he has had a change of mind. You need to go back. I will pay for your trip. As much as I want you here, you really need to return."

"I know, so I can forgive him, right?" he asked harshly.

"It may be your last chance to tell him. You need thiz more than he does, believe me."

"Do you forgive him for what he did to you and my mother?" Jonathan exclaimed. "You didn't see the pain my mother lived with. You didn't live eighteen years of your life not knowing you had a father!"

Olio looked on with concern. He had never seen Jonathan so angry.

"Jonathan, let's go to the house and pray," Amadeo suggested.

"You pray. I don't want to pray!" Jonathan yelled and ran to the groves. Amadeo looked on but let him go.

"He needs zome time," Olio said.

"Yez," Amadeo nodded in agreement and stood watching as Jonathan disappeared through the trees. He knew where he was going, and it would do Jonathan some good to have time alone to think.

Jonathan ran to the top of the hill and stood watching the waves below. Why after eighteen years did he now have a father telling him to do something he didn't want to do?

What Jonathan didn't realize was that he also had a Heavenly Father speaking to him, and after much anger and hostility on Jonathan's part, His quiet voice reasoned with him to return to see his grandfather.

Jonathan found himself in front of the hospital looking at the vastness of it, hesitant to enter. He did enter after several minutes and found his grandfather's room. He had been in intensive care, but he was now in a regular room. Jonathan knocked and entered.

"What are you doing here!" Joe exclaimed harshly. "You should have stayed in Greece with that ****."

Jonathan wanted to strike him, but held himself back.

"I came back to tell you that I forgive you," Jonathan said, but the words were tainted with anger.

Ruth Anne entered the room and shouted with joy, "Jonathan, you came!" She hurried to him and put her arms around him. He hugged her back. He looked back at Joe to discover that he looked asleep.

"How can he be asleep when he was just wide awake?" Jonathan asked.

"Your grandfather is very sick," she said. "His kidneys and liver are both giving out from the years of drinking."

"I thought he was getting better and that is why they moved him to a regular room," said Jonathan.

Ruth Anne shook her head. "No, they can't do anymore for him and that is why they moved him to a regular room." She took his arm. "Let's go for a walk, and you can tell me about your trip."

Jonathan spent the night with Ruth Anne and Carl in a motel room they were staying in. Jonathan didn't care to go back to the hospital in the morning, but he didn't know what else to do, so he went with them. When they got to Joe's room they found that he had died just minutes before they got there. Strangely, Jonathan felt little if any emotion when the nurses told them.

The funeral was brief with only a handful in attendance. The next day the will was read, and Jonathan was surprised to find that his grandfather had left most of his belongings to him, with the exception of a few items he left to Ruth Anne. It wasn't a lot, but it would be enough to pay for his college expenses, with a small amount left over.

Jonathan was amazed. Why had his grandfather told him he left nothing to him when he had? He wondered if Jim had changed his mind and had the will redone, or if he was making an idol threat. Whatever the case, he was relieved to have his college fund replenished and whispered a prayer of thanks.

Jonathan stared at the house in front of him as he and the real estate agent ascended the porch steps. It seemed empty and harsh. It wasn't going to be hard for him to sell the house. It held very few pleasant memories that he cared to be reminded of. He showed the agent around, and they both agreed that it would need a great deal of cleaning. Jonathan worked hard for the next several weeks getting it ready to sell. It was nice to have something to do, but he knew he should be in school. He had missed so much already that he didn't want to try to fit in.

The middle of March found Jonathan with a deep desire that he couldn't understand. He continually thought of going back to Britany's, but he couldn't do it. He also thought of going back to Greece. He felt lost and insecure and wanted to get away. He bought a small tent, threw it in the truck and along with some other camping supplies drove to the Smoky Mountains. He had felt God's leading once before in the mountains, and perhaps he could find it there again.

CHAPTER 18

The sun was high in the sky when he pulled into Smoky Mountain National Park in Gatlinburg. He drove to the information center and picked up a map of backpacking trails. He drove his truck through the curvy roads to the parking spot for the highest trail he could find. The trail was frequently used, and as Jonathan looked at it he felt the desire to find a more deserted trail. He drove farther, past a rushing stream and around more curves. He came to a spot that seemed more deserted and stopped the truck. He took out his backpack and some with supplies and started to walk.

The night would come early as he was on the East side of the mountain, so he decided to put up his tent before it got too dark. In the morning he thought he would try for some fish in the stream he had passed. It felt good to be physically tired, and he slept easily despite the deep darkness and loneliness of the forest.

He woke with the sun. He shivered against the cold and zipped his coat tighter. His black hair glistened in the sun as he cast the line into the stream. His long, agile arms worked in rhythm as he cast and reeled. He smiled up into the sunrise and felt more at peace than he had felt for a long time. He heard splashing downstream and turned to see a black bear batting at a fish that she had tossed into the air from the water. Jonathan watched in amazement as she caught the fish and started to eat it. He felt at one with nature as he shared the stream with the bear. This was good to come here, he thought as he watched. When she was finished she headed downstream, her hind quarters swaying back and forth as she walked.

Jonathan's line jerked and turned his attention back to what he was doing. He had a fish! It swam back and forth as he tried to keep the line from getting tangled in the rocks. Finally he was able to bring the fish close enough to get it out of the water.

It was a nice-sized trout and made a delicious breakfast. After he had eaten he packed up his supplies and headed on up the mountain. His goal was to make camp for the night on the top. It was cool, but by noon he had worked up a sweat from climbing. He sat on a rock and took his Bible from his pack. He turned to Psalm 27 and read. "The Lord is my light and my salvation, whom shall I fear? The Lord is the stronghold of my life, of whom shall I be afraid?

He looked up and smiled. "Lord, I do feel closer to You now with no distractions around. I want to follow You, but sometimes I get so confused. You have brought me through a lot this past year, and as painful as it was, I can see how You were working. If I wouldn't have ran away from Britany, I wouldn't have found my father. If those boys wouldn't have given me the drugs, I may not have found You! Wow! That is pretty powerful to think about. Even through the difficult times You were watching over me."

The words of his father came to him as he sat in silence. "Jonathan, you need to forgive your grandfather," he could hear him say.

"Lord I can't." Jonathan moaned, but as soon as he said it he knew he had to. "OK Lord, I will try, but I can't do it without you."

Jonathan turned to the index in his Bible and looked up forgiveness. He found what he was looking for in Colossians 3:13. "Bear with each other and forgive whatever grievances you may have against one another. Forgive as the Lord forgave you."

The words spoke to him. He thought about when he had first asked God to forgive his sins. He knew at the time that God had forgiven him without requirements. The last time he had seen his grandfather, Joe was as full of hate and anger as ever, yet Jonathan needed to do what God was asking him to do. As he read and prayed he felt some of the resentment melt away. He also felt a burden lift from him that had been weighing him down without his realizing it. Full of energy and feeling very free, Jonathan grasped his pack and continued up the mountain.

He had been climbing for some time when he thought he heard a faint cry for help. Listening closely, he stopped. "Help me! Help me!" the cry sounded again. It seemed to be coming from behind him. He turned and walked back down the path, but the voice started to get softer. He called back.

"I hear you and am trying to find you. Call again!" he shouted.

Faintly he heard the voice again, and he backtracked the way he had come. He noticed a broken limb and looked through the trees. The side of the mountain dropped off sharply, and it looked as if something had dislodged some of the dirt. He looked closer and saw something move.

"I'm right here!" he heard clearly. Suddenly he could make out the form of a person.

"I see you. Are you hurt?" he called.

"My ankle is hurt, and I can't walk," the female's voice replied.

Jonathan looked through the branches and saw a beautiful but distressed face look back at him. He grabbed the tree in front of him and lowered himself down the cliff until he could safely reach the next tree for support. He descended twenty feet until he was on a level plateau and standing beside the girl.

He knelt beside her. "Hi, I'm Jonathan," he said extending his hand to her. His smile revealed a face of warmth and concern.

She returned his smile, but hers contained a look of despair.

"Hi, I'm Crystal. I am so glad you came along. I was beginning to think I was going to be out here for several days. I don't imagine you can see me from the path." She grimaced as she tried to shift her position.

"Let me take a look at your ankle," said Jonathan and reached for her foot.

"Are you a doctor or something?" she asked hopefully. She was thrilled to not be alone anymore, and she liked his smile.

He laughed. "No, I would like to be someday, but right now I'm just an ordinary high school senior." He gently felt around her ankle, and she was relieved that it didn't hurt when he touched it. She had been afraid to move it.

"It's pretty swollen," he said and gently placed her foot back on the ground. "From the looks of it I don't think you had better put any weight on it.

Did you hurt anything else? That is quite a fall you took."

"No, fortunately just my ankle. How am I supposed to get out of here!" She moaned and wiped her face with the back of her hand. It left a dirt streak that she was unaware of. Jonathan smiled.

"So you think it's funny, huh? Do you think you can take advantage of me since we are alone down here?" she asked fiercely.

"No, you just wiped dirt on your face," he said mildly with a smirk on his face.

"Oh," she said with an embarrassed giggle and tried to wipe at the smudge, putting more dirt on her face.

He grasped her hand and pulled it away from her face. "Let me help," he said. He took a towel from his backpack and wet it with some water from his water bottle. Then he gently cleansed her face, removing the smudge and some other dirt that had gotten there from the fall.

"Thank you," she said. "I'm really sorry for saying that."

He smiled again and sat down beside her. "That's all right. I know it's hard being in a bad situation and having to trust a stranger. It's not easy, but really I'll try to help, and, believe me, I won't hurt you."

Crystal laughed and nodded, then looked up. "How in the world am I going to get up there?"

Jonathan followed her gaze and thought for a while. He looked around and surveyed the situation. "I think it would be best if you stayed here for the night. You need to rest your ankle. Then we can try it tomorrow and see if it's better to walk on. If not, then we will go from there."

"That's easy for you to say!" she exclaimed. "You're not the one stuck on this hillside with nothing to eat and the wild animals around!"

"I have a tent in my backpack and enough food for tonight and tomorrow. I'll go get some more water so you have enough to clean some of the other scrapes and bruises you got from the fall. I'll also keep guard against the wild animals."

"How do I know that you aren't one of the wild animals I'm talking about!" she exclaimed.

He looked at the ground and shook his head. His black hair was held by a bandana across his forehead, keeping it from falling in his face. When he looked up he was smiling.

"Crystal, you don't have much choice but to trust me. I'm sorry. I know I'm rather rustic, but I'm afraid I'm all you have right now, and you really do need some help."

She reached out and touched his arm. "I'm sorry. You have been very kind and I guess you are right. It will be dark before too long, and even if I make it up the hillside, it's not safe to walk on the trail in the dark. I ended up here walking in daylight. Imagine what I could do in the dark!"

"How did you end up here?" Jonathan asked, looking up to the spot where he had started his descent.

"A snake went right in front of me, and when I jumped out of the way I fell off the side there," she said pointing to the place he was looking at. "I don't even think it was a poisonous snake," she finished, shaking her head. Her long blonde hair was caught up in a ponytail, and it tossed as she talked. She wore a ball cap, khaki shorts and a tank top. She looked fairly tall and her long legs were well-shaped. Fortunately she had on hiking boots, or her injury might have been worse.

Jonathan was tempted to reach out and touch her hair, but he was afraid she would misunderstand his intentions. It just looked so soft and silky. He realized he was staring and diverted his attention to the forest floor around them.

"It's really fairly level here for being on the side of a mountain. You picked a good place to land," he said.

"Gee, thanks," she replied. "You said you have some food. I hate to ask, but I am really very hungry. I haven't eaten since breakfast."

Jonathan took his pack off and started to go through it. He got out some bagels and carrots. "I had some fresh fish for lunch, but I don't know where there is a stream close by, so I guess it is from a can for supper. If you want to munch on some of this I'll build a fire and warm up a can of stew. I brought them along just in case I wasn't successful in fishing and hunting," he said, handing the pack to her.

"This is wonderful!" she exclaimed. "Don't apologize. At least you came prepared. All I brought was a water bottle. I was rather upset when I left camp this morning."

Jonathan was already busy building a fire. As he waited for it to get going well he put up the tent. It was starting to get dark already, and he hurried to beat the coming darkness.

"I'm going to go up the trail a little way to see if I can find some water before it gets dark," he said, standing up after putting the pot over the fire. "Try to stir this a little if you can. If it gets too hot just set it off the fire until I get back."

She looked up at him anxiously. "Do you have to go? The prospect of staying dirty sounds better than being alone in the dark."

He smiled and said, "Don't worry. If I don't find something soon I'll be right back." He reached down and patted her back. Her hair did feel silky. He smiled and started up the embankment. Fortunately there was a stream just up the trail several hundred feet, and he returned with daylight still left.

He wet the rag, and she washed the dirt from her arms and legs. She handed the rag back. He took it and soaked it in the remaining water.

"This water is really cold. It will be good for the swelling." He took the soaking rag and wrapped it around her ankle. "In a few hours I'll go back and get some more to soak it again."

"But it'll be dark!" she protested.

"It's not far, and I know the way now. Let's have some of that stew," he said as he dished out some and handed it to her.

She looked at the dish, but didn't take it. She looked up at him. "Aren't you going to have some, too?" she asked.

"I didn't plan on two for supper. I only packed one dish," he said simply and pushed it toward her. She took it and smiled. He reached over and took a bagel to eat while she ate the stew. When she finished he dished some up for himself.

"I think it's one of the best meals I have ever had. Thank you," she said as they finished.

"That's because you were really hungry," he laughed.

"Maybe so, but it doesn't change the fact that it tasted wonderful. I would have liked to have some of those fish you were telling me about," she said.

He tossed a rock into the trees. "Maybe we can stop at a stream on the way back tomorrow. We will need to take rest stops anyway." He stopped and looked at Crystal. Crystal began to get uncomfortable by the directness of his gaze. Eventually he asked solemnly, "How did you get here? I don't mean the fall. I mean, what were you doing walking in these mountains by yourself?"

She looked up toward the darkening sky. "I've kind of had a rough year." She paused and thought. She wasn't sure how much she wanted to tell him. The real reason was because she had been seeking God's guidance in her life and had felt drawn to go up toward the top of the mountain to be alone to think. She didn't know if this young stranger knew God or believed in Jesus. It would be very hard to explain to someone who didn't. She decided she could tell him part of the story without all the details.

"Some friends and I decided to go camping," she began. "I started the year at Ohio State University and am now in a college in Tennessee so I can stay with my parents. I still have some dear friends at Ohio State. It is spring break for all of us, and we decided hiking in the Smokey's would be a great way to spend it. I thought coming out here would help me get away from things, but seeing my friends only made the memories come rushing back. I just needed to get away from everything, including them. I only planned on being gone for an hour or so, and they were all asleep. I planned on being back before they got up. I just kept climbing higher and higher. I had been walking for a long time before the snake crossed the path above."

"So no one knows you're up here?" he asked, retaining his serious look.

"No," she responded. "What about you? It looks to me that you are up here by yourself, too. Does anyone know where you are?"

He looked down and gave a half chuckle. "No, I guess no one ever knows where I might be, especially me."

"Don't you have a family?" she exclaimed.

"I have a father and half brother and two half sisters in Greece, plus and aunt and uncle and some cousins in North Carolina, but I've been pretty much on my own for some time."

"Oh, I'm sorry!" she exclaimed and laid her hand on his shoulder.

He smiled and said, "It's not so bad." He reached over and stirred the fire then got up to put another log on.

"So where do you go to college at?" she asked.

He grimaced and looked a little embarrassed. "Actually I'm not in school right now."

"Are you taking a year off from college?"

He sat back from putting the log on and said, "No, I haven't finished high school yet." He looked at her. "Could we go somewhere else with this conversation?"

Crystal realized she had touched on a sensitive subject and was immediately sorry she had brought it up. "Sure," she said and continued. "I've heard Greece is a beautiful country. Is it?"

He smiled and nodded. "Yes, it is very beautiful. My father has a lemon tree farm and he and his wife just had a new baby girl. I was there for the delivery."

"Wow," she said. "That must have been exciting!"

"Yes, very," he replied. "I thought for a while I was going to deliver it by myself."

"Were you frightened?" asked Crystal, her eyes large.

He thought about telling her his plans of being a doctor, but didn't. It seemed impossible now to be able to go back and be accepted to college for medicine when he had dropped out of high school.

He nodded, "Yes, I was very scared, but Frena wasn't. She told me what to do until my father arrived." He looked at her and continued, "I think it is about time you get some sleep. It's getting rather late. You crawl into the tent there," he said, pointing at the opening behind them. "I rolled out the sleeping bag."

"What are you going to do?" she asked with concern.

"I'll stay here and keep the fire going while I keep the wild animals away."

"But it's going to get cold!" she exclaimed.

"That's why I'm going to keep the fire going!" he responded.

She looked at the tent and hesitated. She didn't want him to stay out by the fire all night while she slept in his tent, but she knew it would be a very bad situation for them to share the tent and sleeping bag. She took off the jacket he had given her.

"At least keep this," she said.

He smiled and took it. "Thanks," he said. He helped her up and supported her as she walked to the tent.

She gingerly made her way into the tent. She crawled into the sleeping bag and tried to sleep. She was very tired and her ankle hurt, but all she could think of was Jonathan. She had never felt this way about Eric. She was troubled by the fact that he apparently had dropped out of school. He seemed too strong and knowledgeable to have flunked out or been too lazy to finish. It troubled her. Maybe she was misjudging him and she had better be more careful in her assessment of him, because she was definitely feeling attracted to him. His face was continually on her mind as she fell asleep.

Jonathan shivered as it got late into the night. It was getting cold, and he was very uncomfortable. Sometimes it was very hard being a gentleman and doing the right thing.

Crystal woke during the night and realized the temperature had dropped sharply. She was even feeling a little cold in the sleeping bag. Jonathan must be freezing! That was enough. It was more important that he get warm than they keep up appearances for the animals! No one else would see them. For some strange reason she trusted him even though caution told her to be careful. She sat up and unzipped the tent. He was awake and looked at her. He looked very cold.

"Jonathan, you come in here right now and warm up. I trust you to not try anything. It is just crazy for you to freeze. You have to stay well to help me get off this mountain!" she exclaimed with authority in her voice.

"Are you sure?" he asked.

"Can you behave yourself?" she asked.

He smiled and nodded, "I'm too cold to take advantage of you! Do you promise to not take advantage of me and ruin my spotless reputation?"

She giggled and nodded. He crawled through the opening. It felt warmer just to get inside the small enclosure. She unzipped the bag so they could lay it over the both of them. Jonathan sighed as he curled beneath the warmth.

"Thank you so much!" he exclaimed through clattering teeth. He had turned so his back was toward her when he got in. She rubbed his shoulders, trying to help him warm up.

"Why didn't you say something when it got so cold?" she asked.

"I didn't want to wake you. From your breathing you sounded like you were sleeping very peacefully," he said in short bursts as he trembled from the cold.

She giggled. "People tell me I breathe very loudly when I sleep. Well you shouldn't have been so valiant."

Jonathan wasn't sure how long he had slept or when he had gone to sleep. All he knew was that he was no longer cold. He looked over his shoulder to see Crystal sleeping deeply beside him. He carefully rolled over and lifted up onto his elbow. He looked down on her as she slept. Something about her reminded him of Britany, but the feelings he was having for Crystal were much different than those he had felt for Britany. Could he be falling in love in less than twenty-four hours? He wasn't sure, but for now he just wanted to paint a picture of her beauty in his mind to cherish forever. Presently she looked up at him and smiled. He felt embarrassed to be caught staring at her.

"Good morning," she said through sleepy eyes. "Did you warm up?"

"Yes," he said. "Thank you very much for letting me come inside."

She laughed. "It's your tent! Thank you for giving me a place to stay. Besides, I was getting cold, too."

"Are you hungry?" Jonathan asked.

"Mmm, very! But it is too cold to get out from the covers!"

"I'll go see if there are any fish in the stream I found yesterday. You go ahead and rest some more." He slipped out from the blanket and tucked it securely beside her to keep out the cold.

"You are sweet," she said. She was glad to have some time alone to take care of her morning routine. He returned much sooner than she expected. She had just snuggled back under the cover.

"Crystal, I'm sorry," he said as he unzipped the tent and looked in. "The stream is too small. I guess we'll have to eat some more bagels for breakfast. Maybe we can find another stream on the way down the mountain."

"I just hope I can get up the side of this cliff!" she moaned.

He looked at her sympathetically. "Look, I've been up the cliff three times now and it's really not that bad."

"Not if you can use both feet!" she exclaimed.

He shook his head. "What I mean is that there are a lot of small trees, and they are spaced so that you can pull yourself up the side. If you reach for the one in front of you and pull yourself up until you can reach the next one," he said, demonstrating with his arms, "I think you can make it to the top without putting too much pressure on your ankle. I'll follow below you and push you as you climb."

She looked at him with doubt. "I hope you are right."

"Let's eat and get your strength up." He took food from his pack and offered her some. When they were finished he efficiently packed the tent and supplies into his pack.

He stood in front of her looking like an expert mountain climber she had seen on television. "Well, let's give it a try." He said with enthusiasm.

Crystal looked up and grimaced. "Let's stay here another night," she pleaded.

He chuckled, "To be quite truthful I would like that, but I am sure there are others who are very worried about you."

She let out a quick breath. "Yes, I suppose so. You have to be so practical!" She got to her feet and gingerly put weight on her leg. To her surprise it held and the pain wasn't intense. She took a few steps and turned to look at Jonathan.

"Look!" she exclaimed. "I can walk again!"

"Great! But let's go ahead with my plan. We have a long way to go and I don't want you to stress it too much."

Crystal reached for the first tree and pulled herself putting all her weight on her good foot. She could feel herself being easily lifted as she pulled. Jonathan stayed close behind her and gave her support as she climbed. She realized she was going to make it as they crested the top. She stopped and looked back to the place below where they had made the fire and pitched the tent. A wave of sadness passed as she realized she was leaving something she would always remember. Jonathan's eyes followed her gaze and he looked back at her. His eyes bore into her with such intensity she had to look away.

She looked back and took the last thrust to the top. She sat at the edge of the cliff and laughed. Jonathan easily hoisted himself over the ledge and sat beside her. "You made it!" he exclaimed and patted her back. "How is your ankle?"

She shook her head. "It's fine, but I must have been quite a clumsy sight!"

He smiled. "I was just thinking how graceful you were."

"Yeah, sure," Crystal scoffed. "You were behind me, secretly laughing. Thanks anyway." She took a deep breath and let it out. "Whew! I am so glad that is done. Now we only have five to ten miles back to camp. At least it's downhill!"

"Do you need a rest before we continue?" Jonathan asked with concern, looking at her ankle.

Crystal reached for the tree next to her and pulled herself to her feet. "No," she said. "I think I would like to continue. I feel a boost of adrenaline now that we've reached the top."

Jonathan nodded and stood up beside her. They started down the path. They had walked for over an hour when Jonathan noticed they were going slower. Crystal tried hard not to grimace, but her ankle was getting very sore again.

"It's time to rest on this log," said Jonathan, and taking her arm he helped her to sit.

Crystal sighed as she lowered herself down. Jonathan bent down to examine her ankle. He cupped his hand gingerly around it. "It's swollen again as much as last night," he said as he looked up at her. "This is not going to work. We are going to have to try something else. I'll see if I can find a branch to use as a crutch." He took off his pack and set it beside her and then went off into the thicket. He returned soon with a long branch.

He took his pocketknife and stripped off the branches. Then he began to fashion a handle. When he was finished he took a towel from his pack and wrapped the handle for a cushion. Crystal watched as he worked steadily. When he was finished he held it up for her to see. She smiled.

"You are very creative!"

"Are you ready to give it a try?" he asked as he handed it to her.

She nodded. He helped her to her feet.

"That's much better," Crystal said as she tried the crutch. Her ankle was still very painful, but she smiled and continued on the path.

"I hear rushing water!" said Jonathan.

Crystal stopped and listened. "I hear it too! Does that mean I get some of those delicious fish? I sure could use some right now."

Jonathan looked at her. "You can also use a rest. I think the stream is just around the bend. Do you think you can go that far?" he asked with concern.

"Of course!" said Crystal, but as she took a step the pain was unbearable.

Jonathan reached for her elbow to steady her. Then he reached down and lifted her off her feet into his arms.

Crystal was surprised and gasped, "What are you doing?" She threw her arms around his neck to help support herself.

"I'm taking you to the stream," he said simply as he started walking down the path.

"But I'm too heavy! You will hurt yourself."

He laughed. "So now you don't think I'm very strong?" he asked as he continued to walk.

"No! I...I...I mean yes, I think you are strong enough, but, no, that is not the reason I don't want you to carry me!" she said in exasperation.

"Then don't worry and relax. You would be much easier to carry if you weren't so tense."

Crystal sighed, "Oh, all right. But don't hurt yourself or we will never get back."

"I kind of like that thought," Jonathan said softly.

Crystal looked at him and smiled. The idea sounded nice to her, too, but she didn't say anything. She relaxed and rested her head on his shoulder. His strength and confidence made her feel secure, and the release of pain from her ankle felt soothing. He smelled of outside and woods as her cheek rested on his denim shirt.

He had only walked several hundred feet when the sound of water became very loud. She looked up to see a large stream cascading down the rocks directly in front of them. He carried her to a large rock and gently set her on it. Then he reached down to remove her shoe. She looked at him in question.

"If you put your foot in the water the coolness of it will help the swelling," he said. When she was comfortable with her feet in the cold water he took the pack from his back and searched through it. Soon he pulled out a fishing rod and some lures. He sat beside her on the rock and cast it among the other rocks in a shaded spot.

"I certainly hope this works!" she exclaimed as she watched.

"Shhh, you'll scare the fish away!" he said, putting a finger to his lips.

Crystal laughed and said, "The water is to loud for any fish to hear me talk. Look!" she exclaimed pointing to the water. A fish was hiding close to a rock several feet from them. Jonathan expertly cast the line toward the spot, and the fish jumped for the bait as soon as it hit the water.

"Wow, it sure is a nice one," he said as he brought the fish toward them. The fish splashed and jumped in protest, but Jonathan reeled it in. "One more like this, and we will have our meal!"

Jonathan jumped from rock to rock down the stream. Crystal looked at the trees hanging over the water. A few of them had green leaves. Green undergrowth dotted the shore. Birds called to each other through the branches. She breathed deeply of the fresh spring air. Suddenly she heard a splash and she looked to see that Jonathan had another fish on his line.

"Ready for lunch?" he asked, holding the two fish on the stringer. He stood on a rock in the middle of the stream. His enthusiasm warmed Crystal's heart as she watched.

"I've been ready for lunch ever since you told me about the meal of fish you had yesterday!" she yelled above the rush of the water.

Jonathan jumped from rock to rock as he made his way toward her. "Do you think your ankle has gone down any?" he asked as he reached down to run his fingers across the swollen tissues. He looked up at her. "It looks better."

She smiled. "I'm sure it will feel much better after I have some of those fish. The protein should help it mend."

Jonathan stood and reached for her hand. He helped her across the rocks to a soft spot where he put a blanket down for her to sit on. He then went to gather some wood. When he brought it back Crystal got on her knees and arranged the sticks to start a fire.

"It looks like you have this under control. I'll start cleaning the fish," said Jonathan when he saw her work.

"I like that idea very much," Crystal answered. She found some matches in his pack and soon had a nice fire going.

"There are a few potatoes in the pack if you would get them, along with a carrot. I will wash them off in the stream as soon as I am finished," Jonathan said.

"There is an onion and lemon, too!" exclaimed Crystal as she searched.

"Yeah," said Jonathan as he walked to her and reached down for the potatoes. "I came prepared to eat fish!"

"I certainly did pick the right person to come to my rescue!" laughed Crystal.

"I think it's more like I found the right person to rescue," said Jonathan, looking at her with a serious expression in his black eyes.

Crystal felt herself blush. He turned and walked to the stream, and Crystal looked down to start slicing the onion. He seemed to confuse her. She didn't want to be attracted to anyone right now. She was young and needed more time. She had been very hurt from Eric and she didn't want a serious relationship. She had thought Eric was a Christian and a trustworthy person. She had thought wrong! She no longer trusted herself to make accurate judgments.

Jonathan seemed trustworthy, admirable, and a Christian, but she could be wrong again. He wasn't in school, and he hadn't graduated yet. Did that mean he had dropped out of school? Did he plan on going back? She wasn't sure she wanted to know. She couldn't bear to think of going through a situation like the one with Eric again. She groaned as she worked. The problem was she liked him whether she wanted to or not.

Why am I always attracted to the wrong person? Help me, Lord, to know what to do, she prayed as she worked.

Jonathan sighed when he got to the water's edge. He couldn't believe how intense his feelings for Crystal were becoming in such a short time. It seemed a little ironic. He had come to the mountains to search for God. Instead he found a beautiful blonde! A very nice, intriguing blonde. He felt more confused than he had before he came. How could he possibly become involved with a girl like Crystal? He had nothing to offer, especially since he wasn't even going to be graduating. She was a magnificent girl. Too good for a guy like him. Life could be very confusing. He came to find answers, not complications. Jonathan washed the potatoes and carrots.

When he returned Crystal had a steady fire going. She watched as he skillfully arranged the fish and vegetables in a pan and cooked them over the fire.

"Where did you learn to cook like that?" asked Crystal. "Did your father take you camping a lot?"

Jonathan thought to himself, I wish that were the case. "Something like that."

Crystal didn't hear his response because she was thinking about her childhood. "I didn't have a father around while I was growing up. I always wanted one. I finally got one when I was eighteen." Jonathan looked at her in surprise as Crystal continued.

"Imagine getting a father when you are eighteen! My mother finally got married the fall I went to college. He is a good man, and I really like him. He treats me with respect and love. I appreciate that." Crystal thought about Michael as she talked.

Jonathan looked back at the fish. Crystal was a very surprising person.

"I think maybe there was one good thing about not having a father when I was young," Crystal said, "I never compared my Heavenly Father to my earthly father. What is your father like?" she asked, looking at him as he was bent over the fish. His hair tried to fall forward, but was kept back with the red bandana he used as a headband. He had on regular jeans and a blue T-shirt.

Jonathan thought about his father. It was the first time that anyone had asked him about his dad that he actually could tell them something.

Jonathan stirred once more and then stood to walk beside her. She liked his closeness as he approached. He sat on the rock beside her.

"My father is tall and very proud, with many years of wisdom. He looks like me, people say, but I'm not so sure. My mother died, and now he has a new wife and a new life in Greece. I have an eight-year-old sister, a little brother and a tiny baby sister that I told you about earlier."

Crystal looked at him. "If they are in Greece, what are you doing here?" she asked.

Jonathan hesitated. He wanted to tell her the entire story, but he needed to reason things out before he shared them, so he proceeded with, "I have some things in my life I need to sort through. I came back to the place where I grew up." Abruptly he stood up.

"I think the fish is done," said Jonathan and bent down to test it. He put half on the plate and handed it to Crystal.

"It's delicious!" Crystal exclaimed as she took a bite.

Jonathan used his knife and scooped a piece from the pan. He smiled. "I think this is my best fish ever! It must be because of the good help I had."

Jonathan reached for Crystal's plate as she finished. Suddenly they heard voices, faintly at first, and then they became louder. Crystal heard her name called. She started to jump up but fell as she forgot about her ankle. Jonathan quickly grabbed her to keep her from falling but he didn't release her as she regained her balance. He held her tight.

"My friends," she said softly.

"I know," he said and bent down to kiss her. Crystal had never felt such gentleness and warmth. She held him close and for a moment forgot about her friends.

CHAPTER 19

Crystal heard her name again and withdrew from Jonathan's embrace.

"Cortney!" she called. She looked back at Jonathan. He continued to hold her elbow to support her. His eyes looked sad. "I need to let them know I am all right," she said.

"It's OK. I just don't want to let you go," he said and then smiled. Moments later Britany saw Terry and Cortney run up the path. Cortney ran faster when she saw Crystal, and threw her arms around her. If Jonathan hadn't been holding her elbow it would have knocked Crystal to the ground. Terry was close behind her.

"Cortney, be careful!" he warned. "Crystal's been hurt."

Cortney stepped back and looked at her in alarm. "Crystal, oh, my goodness! Terry's right. You have been hurt. What happened?"

"I fell and twisted my ankle," Crystal explained. She looked up at Jonathan. "Fortunately Jonathan came to my rescue.

"It looks like he came to your rescue in a big way. What was this you had for dinner?" asked Terry, looking at the campfire.

"Jonathan caught fish and fixed them. They were wonderful!" exclaimed Crystal.

Terry whistled through his teeth. "Do you think you could fix some for us?" he asked.

"Terry!" exclaimed Cortney. We have been searching for Crystal since yesterday and all you can think about is your stomach!"

"Crystal is safe, and I'm hungry," he replied.

Crystal laughed. "How far are we from camp? I kind of lost track of how far I went."

Cortney pointed down the path. "It's only about an hour. Do you think you can walk that far?"

"I think so," Crystal answered. "We walked most of the morning, and it got very sore. But Jonathan had me soak my ankle in the cold water, and it feels much better now."

Terry looked around. "Let me help you gather your gear, and then we'll get started. The rest of the group is still out looking. At least if we are at camp they will know you are safe when they check in."

Terry helped Jonathan, and Crystal told Cortney how she had fallen down the cliff and how Jonathan found her.

"We thought you had gone another direction. That's why we didn't find you sooner. Terry and I decided to take this path on the chance you may have gone this way," said Cortney. "Why didn't you at least tell someone where you were going?"

"I didn't think I would walk very far, and you were all asleep. I just planned on a short walk, but I kept walking and walking. I didn't realize I had gone so far until this morning trying to walk back," explained Crystal.

"God was watching over you, Crystal," said Terry, swinging Jonathan's pack over his shoulder.

Jonathan looked at him. "Why are you carrying my pack?" he asked.

Terry patted him on the shoulder. "I think you could use a break for awhile. You are going with us, aren't you? We need to introduce Crystal's hero to the rest of the group."

Cortney took Crystal's arm and helped her start down the trail. Terry and Jonathan followed.

Jonathan shook his head. "I'm no hero. I just happened to come along and heard her call."

Terry smiled a full smile that revealed dimples. "You were in the right place at the right time. You did the right thing. You were also God's answer to our prayer for Crystal's safety."

Jonathan stood taller than Terry, and his long legs covered the ground easily. He shook his head. "You don't really think God led me to find Crystal, do you, Terry?"

"Don't you believe in God?" asked Terry.

"Actually I just came to know Jesus about six months ago, but I don't see how He could have led me to help Crystal," Jonathan said with a frown. He glanced at Crystal as they walked. She seemed to be doing fine. She and Cortney were talking animatedly.

"Look! A deer!" exclaimed Cortney. Her pink cheeks glowed with excitement as she pointed toward a thicket.

Jonathan could barely see the doe as she stood looking at them not more than a hundred feet away.

"Oh, look!" exclaimed Crystal. "She has a little fawn beside her. She's trying to hide it."

The doe looked at them for several minutes and then bounded off into the trees with the fawn at her side. The four stood watching and then continued on.

"We could have walked right past that doe with her fawn if Cortney hadn't seen it. I'm sure that there are a lot of deer in these trees that we have walked beside and never seen," said Terry as they walked. His hiking boots crunched on some dry leaves as he walked.

"You asked me if I thought God really led you to find Crystal." He looked over at Jonathan. "God is working all around us. Sometimes we have to keep a special look out to see it, and when we do I like to call it a God sighting, just like a deer sighting. I do think God put you in the position to find Crystal. She is searching in life, and she needed someone to help her out and learn to trust again. You helped her. You didn't take advantage of her. She needed that."

"That seems strange," said Jonathan thoughtfully. "I came out here because I'm the one who needed to sort things out. How can I be of help to someone else?"

"God works in mysterious ways. Maybe you needed to find her as much as she needed you."

Jonathan's eyes were dark and solemn. He appreciated Terry's thoughts, but they were too bizarre for him to accept.

Jonathan was at Crystal's side quickly when she stumbled, and he picked her off her feet into his arms. Her face grimaced in pain, and she didn't protest. She laid her head on his shoulder and tried not to let the tears flow from the pain.

"Oh, Crystal, you can't go on like this!" exclaimed Cortney in concern. Her red hair shone in the sun that filtered through the trees.

"It's not far. Just ten minutes more," said Terry.

"Jonathan," said Crystal, "You can't carry me that far!" She held tightly to his neck.

"I think we had this conversation before," said Jonathan with finality.

"Don't worry, Crystal," said Terry. "If he gets tired I'll carry you for awhile. It's just around the bend. You did very well to make it this far. Just relax."

Jonathan didn't want to but he had to let Terry carry Crystal for a while before they arrived at camp. The camp was empty. It was on the edge of a large stream. He placed Crystal on a rock and made her put her ankle in the water again. It wasn't long before two more people arrived. There were two tents set up in the clearing with a campfire in the middle.

Jonathan fished, and Terry joined him on the rocks, casting toward shore.

"Fish for dinner!" Terry announced as he caught one.

"It's going to take more than one fish to feed all of us!" exclaimed Cortney.

"You don't have enough faith in us!" answered Jonathan.

"So, Jonathan," said Terry, "we would like to get to know you a little more. Do you think you could stay with us while we camp here?"

Jonathan's arm stopped in mid-air as he started to cast his line. The line drifted in the air and fell limply onto a rock. He looked at Terry. "You want me to join you guys?" he asked in disbelief.

"Sure," said Terry. "Why not?"

"Well," said Jonathan, "you don't know me. I could be a thief or something."

Terry laughed. "If you weren't trustworthy, you could have taken advantage of Crystal."

Jonathan paused. He couldn't even think of hurting Crystal. With all his strength he wanted to protect her.

"Someone would have to be a low-life to take advantage of Crystal!" he exclaimed angrily.

Terry looked at him and said seriously, "Some low-life did. That is why it was so important that you treated her the way she needed to be treated, with warmth and respect."

Jonathan shook his head sadly and said quietly, "I just wish I were good enough for her."

"What do you mean?" asked Terry.

Jonathan looked at the water. The thrill of fishing was suddenly gone. He felt empty. "I'm not even in school. My father is in Greece, and my mother died. I have no future. How can I possibly be good for her?"

"Stay with us for these few days, Jonathan. You need some friends in your life. Just let us be here for you while you are searching. God will guide you. Just trust Him and take it one day at a time."

Jonathan cast his line and looked up. "I'll stay tonight and make you a meal of fish and then see about tomorrow."

"That's the way. One day at a time!" exclaimed Terry with encouragement.

Jonathan felt a little jealous to have everyone else take care of Crystal. She was talking constantly to whoever was around. He enjoyed being there, but he missed being alone with her.

They caught enough fish to make a meal, and everyone loved the fish he cooked. Later they sat around the fire, and Terry played his guitar, and they all sang. Jonathan didn't know the songs, but he enjoyed them. Crystal looked at him during the music and motioned for him to come.

He went and sat beside her.

"Do you not like my company anymore?" she asked.

He looked at her in surprise. "Oh, no! I have been wanting to be with you all afternoon, but everyone else was busy talking to you. I didn't think you needed me around to get in the way."

She reached for his hand. "Don't ever think that again. I love to talk and am always talking to someone, but I wanted it to be you. Please don't think I don't want you around."

Jonathan felt helpless as he looked into her eyes. She was beautiful, and she wanted to be with him! He couldn't believe what he was hearing. He smiled. "You are a very amazing person, Crystal. Has anyone ever told you that?"

She laughed. "My mother, but I don't think she counts. Mothers always think their children are wonderful."

"Not all mothers are able to express it," Jonathan said and was surprised that he had once the words were out.

Crystal looked at him questioningly. "Didn't your mother ever tell you how wonderful you were?" she asked. Her head was tilted to the side, and her gray eyes shone with concern in the flicker of the firelight.

"Let's just say things were not exactly easy when I was growing up, but she tried."

"I'm sorry. The way you talked about your father I figured you had a good childhood with caring parents."

Jonathan squeezed her hand. "I don't suppose you'll feel sorry for me tonight and share my tent with me?" he said with a smirk on his face.

"You can't fool me, Jonathan," said Crystal laughing. He loved the sound of her laughter. Fortunately she used it often. "You are just trying to change the subject. But that's all right. If you aren't ready to share with me, I can wait until you are. I think we both need some time to learn to trust."

Crystal waved at Terry. "Hey, Terry!" she called across the campfire. "Jonathan wants to know what is happening tomorrow!"

Terry stood and walked across to where they sat. "We're going to look for more damsels in distress to rescue since he is so good at it."

"No, you don't!" exclaimed Crystal. "He's my prince, and I don't plan on sharing him with any other damsels!"

Terry laughed. "In that case I think we will tackle that mountain up there," he said, pointing in the darkness. "Are you up for it in the morning?" he asked Jonathan.

Jonathan looked at Crystal. "You go on the hike with the guys," she said. "The girls are staying here anyway, and there will be things I can do around the camp," said Crystal.

He didn't want to leave her, but since there was no need for him to stay he looked at Terry and said, "It sounds like quite a challenge. What time do we leave?"

"As soon as the sun comes up," said Terry.

Jonathan was more tired than he realized when they retired for the evening. Morning came quickly, and he rolled over to hear a stir as the sun came up. He dressed quickly and found Terry and Bill stirring the embers left from the fire the night before. They fried some eggs and then started up the mountain. Jonathan was disappointed when Crystal didn't rise before they left. He thought of her often as they climbed. The morning air was cool, and their progress was vigorous. He liked Terry and Bill. They treated him as if they had known him for a long time. Soon he found himself enjoying their company.

"My father lives near a mountain that over looks the Mediterranean," said Jonathan as they stopped for a break.

"Wow!" said Bill. "Did you grow up there?"

"No," answered Jonathan. "I just went to visit for several months. I grew up several miles from here, although I didn't come to the mountains often."

Terry looked at Jonathan. "You are a very mysterious person, Jonathan. Do you have an adventuresome past?"

Jonathan's eyes clouded. "It wasn't adventuresome, just rough."

Bill noticed his hesitancy to continue. "So was Greece nice?" he asked.

Jonathan smiled. "Yes, it is very beautiful. I liked it very much. My father is a lemon farmer, and I helped with the harvest."

"I think we need to continue on," said Terry, standing up.

The walking had been fast, but the grade became steeper, and they had to slow their pace. The air became cooler, and Jonathan put his jacket back on. They came to a cliff that overlooked the other mountains. Buzzards flew overhead in the quiet sky. Jonathan grasped the branch in front of him to help himself climb. His breath came hard and fast, but it felt good to be alive and enjoy the spectacular view.

He marveled at the beauty around him. He looked behind him at Terry as he ascended the mountainside. "Do you ever wonder how God can make all this beauty and still care for us?" Jonathan asked.

Terry took the last step to stand beside him. "All the time. When did you first become a Christian?" he asked.

"Last fall. I met a wonderful family who took me in and treated me like I was their own. The showed me God by the way they lived. I had never known love like what they showed me. I ran away, and when I did I tried to run away from God, but fortunately He wouldn't let me." Jonathan shook his head as he talked.

"God works in mysterious ways. I told you that you had a mysterious air to you. I'm glad God didn't leave you alone," said Terry. Bill was still a hundred yards below them, breathing hard as he reached for the next tree.

"If the family was so wonderful, why did you run away?" Terry asked with a puzzled look.

"I did something horribly offensive." Jonathan looked toward the next tree. "I can't go back. I wish I could take it back and undo what I did. I miss them terribly, but I can't," he sighed and started to climb again. He was starting to feel the pain again as the wound was reopened. He wasn't sure why these people were having such an effect on him.

"Hey, wait up," called Terry. A rock slid out from his foot as he hurried. He grasped Jonathan's arm as soon as he reached him. "Man, what did you do, make a pass at the guy's daughter or something?"

Jonathan stared cold and hard at Terry. "It's OK," said Terry, throwing up his hands as if he were surrendering. "I'm not trying to be nosey." He put his hands back down and continued, "It seems to me that you are carrying a heavy burden that you need to share with someone. I promise I just want to help. God tells us to share one another's burdens."

"What can you do?" Jonathan challenged.

Terry waved his hand in the air. "Probably nothing, but you might be amazed at how much having someone to listen can help." Bill appeared behind him as Terry waited.

"According to this map we should reach the waterfall in another ten to twenty minutes," said Bill with a smile and pointed at the map.

Jonathan turned and climbed vigorously. Bill thought he was inspired by the news of the nearness of the waterfall and hurried to keep pace.

Jonathan burned with anger as he climbed. He didn't want to tell anyone what had happened. He didn't want anyone finding out about his past. He had come on the trip to get away from his past, not be confronted. He shed his jacket and was sweating as he reached the next plateau. He looked to see Terry and Bill far below. He felt a satisfaction in climbing harder and faster than they did. He turned and continued on.

The waterfall caught Jonathan by surprise as he climbed over a rock. It was beautiful. He pulled himself up on a big rock and sat between two large rhododendrons. Their waxy green leaves were dotted with moisture. The water cascaded down a two-hundred-foot drop and bounced off protruding rocks and tree branches. The roaring of the water was so loud the call of birds could no longer be heard. All was silent except for the thunder of the water. The power and might of the water captivated Jonathan's attention.

He sat on a rock and watched. All other thoughts fled his mind, and the anger he had felt earlier flowed away as quickly as the water he watched. He didn't know how long he sat before Terry stood beside him. He was vaguely aware that Bill was there, too. The three of them watched, mesmerized by the power displayed before them.

Bill took his camera and snapped a picture. "There is no way you are going to capture that on film!" Terry yelled to be heard above the roar.

"I know," answered Bill. "But just a portion of it makes a great picture. At least we will have something to show Cortney, Crystal and Tammy."

"I wish they would have come. If I knew it was like this I would have encouraged them to come, but they were so relieved to have Crystal back in camp that they didn't want to leave her," yelled Terry.

"Maybe we can come back and bring the girls one of the days we have left," suggested Bill.

Terry looked at Bill with a wide, dimpled grin. "I'd like that!" he said.

Jonathan knew Crystal would never be able to make the hike. He longed for her to see the beauty with him, but his heart sank as he realized that after the few days of spring break he might never see her again. He would at least encourage her to go on her own someday.

Jonathan felt inspired as they descended the mountain. God was very close, and he could actually feel His presence. He had seen God's work in a real way in the power of the waterfall. His heart was at peace, and his step was light. It was still a welcome break when they stopped for a snack.

"Jonathan," said Terry as they were eating trail mix, "I think you need to trust us enough to share what is going on in your life. I can tell it is bothering you a great deal. Maybe we can help."

Jonathan stiffened. Why was Terry doing this to him?

"Whatever it was that happened I think you need to go back and apologize. You are certainly repentant. I can tell that from what little you have told me."

"You don't understand," said Jonathan. "They don't ever want to see me again."

Terry looked at him with concern. "Did they tell you that?"

Jonathan shook his head and bit hard on his lip.

"I didn't think so," said Terry. "If this family is as strong in Christ as you said they were, then you at least owe them a chance to forgive you."

Jonathan looked at him. "Terry, if I told you the entire story of my life you would never believe me."

"Try me," Terry challenged.

Jonathan looked at Bill. "Terry is right," said Bill. "You can trust us. We want what is best for you. I know it's hard to believe that in a world like ours today people really want to help each other, but that is what being a Christian is all about. Christ commands us to love one another."

Jonathan sighed and looked at the ground. "My mother died last summer. I was living on my own, but it wasn't much different than my earlier life had been. I grew up thinking I had no father. My mother and I lived with my grandfather, who constantly told my mother how horrible she was. Her mother had died in childbirth, and my grandfather blamed it on my mother. For some stupid reason she believed him, and she lived her life thinking she was worth nothing.

When I was little she found comfort in alcohol. Many times I would go to bed after my mother and grandfather had both passed out from drinking. When I was in my teen years she started on drugs. I finally persuaded her to move away from my grandfather, and we moved across state. I could work and support her is the only reason we were able to move. When she died I just lived in my truck so the authorities wouldn't find out I was under eighteen and send me back to my grandfather. She had already signed me up for my senior year of school.

I went on the first day of school, but some boys slipped me some drugs in a candy bar. I had a bad trip and climbed a tree and jumped out. I ended up in traction at the local hospital. I was unconscious, and when I woke up a beautiful face was looking at me. I thought she was an angel. She wasn't really an angel, but a nurse, although to me she is still an angel. I fell in love with her.

"She brought her family to meet me, and they were wonderful! She was married and had a little boy a year old, a little girl eight and another son who is ten. You'll never believe this, but when I was able to leave the hospital they asked me to live with them! For the first time in my life I had a family." Jonathan leaned against a tree. Once he had started talking the words just seemed to flow, and it brought him some comfort to be sharing his story with someone else.

"I was with them for several months, during which time I had my casts removed and was learning to walk again. It was a wonderful time. One day we were getting ready for the holidays and she was baking with her daughter in the kitchen. The oldest boy wanted me to show him how well I could dance. We turned on the music and everybody laughed and sang. I took her arm and started twirling her around the table. She was so happy and beautiful," he leaned his head on his fist that was resting on the tree trunk. "I kissed her. It happened so suddenly that I didn't realize what I was doing. Her little girl started screaming. I ran out of the house with my things and never looked back."

Jonathan looked at Terry. "So now you see why I can't go back."

Bill, who had been listening intently, said, "Are you still in love with the lady?"

"Yes, well, no." Jonathan stuck his hand in his jeans pocket and leaned on one leg. "What I mean is, I still love her, but now I realize that I love her as the very special person that she is, not in a romantic way."

"I still feel the same way," said Terry, breaking a twig. "You need to go back and explain. I'll bet she is worried about you."

"Her husband might kill me!" exclaimed Jonathan.

Terry laughed. "Maybe you need to take that chance. He might be really angry, but I doubt that he will kill you. If that family gave you that much love, they must be worried sick about you."

Jonathan tossed a rock across the path. "I never thought of them being worried about me. I just always thought about how mad they would be."

Bill walked up and slapped Jonathan's back in a friendly manner. "Terry is right. You have plenty of time to think about it. We're not asking you to return this minute. Take your time and pray about it. God will help you do the right thing." He looked down the path. "Let's get back. I'm getting ready for supper, and we may need to catch it before we eat it!"

Jonathan thought hard as they walked. It seemed that lately he always had something serious to think about, and the answer always seemed to elude him.

His concerns vanished as soon as Jonathan saw Crystal's smiling face. The ladies had prepared supper, and Terry, Jonathan and Bill were eager to eat it. They were hungry after the long hike.

CHAPTER 20

Following the meal they took a drive to Cade's Cove. It was a restored settlement in the middle of the national park. The six of them got into Terry's old Grand Prix. Jonathan sat behind the driver and Crystal sat beside him. He put his arm around her shoulders to give the rest of them more room. She looked at him and smiled.

The road curved to the right and then to the left as they went up and down the mountains.

"How did your hike go?" Crystal asked Jonathan as they drove. A bump in the road threw her against his chest. "I'm sorry," she said and started to move over.

"I'm not," said Jonathan, and pulled her back close.

"Terry and Bill were pretty rough on me," Jonathan said in response to her question.

"Who was the one who went way ahead and made us catch up?" asked Terry from the front as he looked at Jonathan in the rearview mirror.

"Yeah," added Bill. "Next time I'm wearing running shoes instead of hiking boots. Seriously, though, we want to go back and take you girls with us. It was indescribable. You just have to see it to appreciate it."

"I thought it was a long, strenuous climb!" exclaimed Cortney.

"Well, it is, but the difficulty of getting there makes the view that much more spectacular," answered Terry.

"But Crystal can't handle a hike like that," responded Cortney.

"I'll stay with Crystal," said Jonathan protectively and held firmly onto her shoulder. "I saw the falls today."

"Man, what a sacrifice," said Bill. They laughed.

"Why are all the cars stopped?" asked Terry as he brought the car to a halt behind them.

"Oh, look, there are three deer beside the road!" exclaimed Tammy. They watched as the deer looked around. The deer seemed unafraid of the cars and continued to eat until someone called out to them. Then they turned ran off. Terry turned off the main road and traveled down a small path. A cloud of dirt trailed up behind them.

"The cars are stopped again," said Bill. "Pull over. I want to get a picture this time."

"I don't have to," said Terry. "We aren't going anywhere right away. The cars are lined up bumper to bumper for the next twenty cars."

"But I don't see any deer," said Cortney.

"It's a bear!" screamed Tammy, pointing toward a grass field.

Terry turned off the car, and they got out. Jonathan offered his hand to help

Crystal. She smiled. Bill stood on the bumper of the car to see better. Suddenly the bear stood on his hind feet to look around, and they could all see him. Then he turned and bounded into the woods. His bulky hindquarters shook with each jump he took.

"Wow, that was great!" exclaimed Terry. "Let's travel on and see what else we can see!" The traffic was moving again, and they followed slowly behind.

It was dark when they left the cove. They stopped in the town and bought their supper, then returned to the camp. They soon got a fire going and finished the evening singing to the music of Bill's guitar. Jonathan had never heard the songs before, but they repeated enough that he was soon singing along.

"I like to hear you sing," Crystal said to him.

"I'm enjoying singing songs to Jesus. We're not even in church," he replied.

The fire was burning low, and the singing slowed down.

"I guess that means it's time to retire for the night," said Crystal as she leaned against Jonathan's shoulder. Jonathan stroked her long, flowing hair. He wished he didn't have to say goodnight. He brought his other hand around to hold her chin in his hand. Softly he kissed her cheek. She reached up and grasped his hand to caress it and kiss his palm. Jonathan's chest tightened, and his breathing felt restricted. She smiled, and he kissed her. Then he gently released her and rose to his feet.

He reached down to take her hand and helped her to her feet. "How does your ankle feel?" he asked as she gingerly stood on it.

"It's a little tight again from not using it for awhile, but it is much better than yesterday," she said.

He helped her to the tent. "Goodnight, Crystal," he said.

"I was disappointed to not see you this morning before you left," she said softly.

"So was I," said Jonathan. "I won't leave you tomorrow." He held her and kissed her cheek again. "Goodnight, Crystal."

"Goodnight, Jonathan," she whispered and then went into her tent. The night air grew cool and the stars shone brightly through out the night. Terry was the first to awake.

"Rise and Shine!" Terry called as he came out of the tent. Jonathan rolled over and pulled on his jeans.

"Not everyone needs to get up this early!" said Jonathan as he unzipped his tent.

Terry laughed. "But you need to get a early start on the fishing. They bite the best early in the morning."

Jonathan slapped Terry's back. "I knew you had something in mind."

Crystal was up before the group left for the hike. She looked at Jonathan and smiled. He smiled back, and she felt a warm glow. She made some instant hot chocolate with the hot water that was heating over the fire. The prospect of spending the day alone again with Jonathan was exciting. The more she was with him the more she wanted to be with him.

Cortney opened her Bible and read Psalm 103 to the rest as they ate breakfast. As high as the heavens are above the sky is how high my love is for those who love me. I will forgive their transgressions and cover their sin. As

Cortney read, Crystal looked at everyone sitting around. This was where she needed to be. Praising God with friends. How foolish she had been to think expensive jewelry and eating in fancy restaurants could make her happy. God had a plan for her life, and she needed to stay close to Him. She had made a wrong choice, but as Cortney read she knew that God was there to forgive and love her through it.

When breakfast ended, Terry, Cortney, Tammy and Bill left on the hike. Jonathan looked at Crystal. "What now?" he asked.

"I guess we need to start catching those fish for supper," she said with a smile. Crystal used Terry's fishing equipment. The sun was warm on her back as she cast her line into a quiet pool where water had collected between the rocks. The warmth felt good in the chill of the morning.

"You have fished before," commented Jonathan from a nearby rock where he was standing jigging his line across the water.

"A little. I like to but don't get the opportunity very often," she answered. Her attention was shifted suddenly when she felt a strong tug on her line. She pulled back quickly and felt resistance. She could see the fish glisten in the sunlight as it jumped from the water.

"Don't jerk too hard or you will lose it," called Jonathan as he scrambled across the rocks to reach her.

"I'm trying not to!" she laughed. "The fish seems to be doing that for me!" She carefully reeled in the line and tried to guide the fish around the rocks. Then she pulled, and the fish was suspended in the air, dangling from the line. It squirmed and fought in the air. She reached for the line and drew the fish to her side.

"It's a nice one!" exclaimed Jonathan with a smile.

"Not too bad for the first ten minutes of fishing!" she said proudly. "Now it's your turn."

The fish continued to bite, and the air warmed up enough that Crystal took off her sweatshirt.

"I'm getting hungry. How about we take a break from fishing and eat," Crystal suggested, as the sun was high in the sky.

Jonathan smiled and reeled in his line. With his pole in hand he jumped from rock to rock to where Crystal was. He grasped her hand and helped her to the shore. "Be careful on these rocks. They are slippery, and your ankle is still healing."

Crystal reached up and gave him a kiss on the cheek. "You are always watching out for me," she said. Jonathan felt a lump in his chest from her tender gesture. He held her arm securely as she moved across the rocks.

Crystal finished her juice and looked at Jonathan. "I think we have enough fish to feed everyone tonight. How about going for a walk?" she asked.

Jonathan reached out to clean up from the lunch. "I would like that, but you have to promise not to go so far that your ankle gets sore again."

Crystal picked up the bread and cheese. "I promise. I don't want to make you carry me again. You are going to end up with a sore back if you keep carrying me!" she laughed.

They walked slowly along the path, and Crystal reached for Jonathan's hand. She clasped it, and he looked at her and smiled. "So what do you plan on doing next year when school starts back?" she asked.

A shadow crossed his face. "I had planned on going to college to be a doctor, but now I won't even be graduating in the spring. A high school dropout will never make it to medical school."

The resignation in his voice tore at Crystal's heart. "Jonathan, this is America, the land of opportunity! Surely there is a way for you to go be a doctor if that is what you want to be. You certainly have the heart for it."

His dark eyes were very serious. "It is also a land of reality, and I need to face the reality that I will never have a better life than the one I came from."

Crystal stopped and faced him. "What is it that is in your past that you won't share with me? How can it be that bad?" She took both his hands. "I've had some bad things in my past, too," she said. "Trust me and let me help you like you've helped me with my ankle."

Jonathan backed up and turned to walk back toward the camp. Crystal hurried to keep up. "Jonathan, what is it!" she exclaimed in exasperation walking beside him.

"Please, Crystal, don't ask me anymore. I need to get some things in my life straightened out," he shook his head and kept walking. Crystal tried hard to stay beside him. He was shutting her out, and she didn't know why.

He crossed the stream that ran beside their camp, and she followed. She jumped from the rock she was on to the next one. Suddenly her ankle buckled, and she screamed in pain. The next thing she knew she had plunged headfirst into the icy mountain water.

Jonathan turned as he heard her scream, just in time to see her fall into the water. He jumped into the waist deep water and helped her to stand. She was flailing because of the pain in her ankle and the shock of the cold water had disoriented her.

Jonathan grasped her to him as soon as he lifted her from the water. Her long hair dripped with water, and her teeth were chattering from the cold.

"I am so sorry, Crystal! Please forgive me!" he pleaded, holding her close.

"It's OK, Jonathan. I'm all right, just cold," she said, grasping his shoulder.

"But if I wouldn't have been going so fast you wouldn't have been trying to keep up and fallen into the water," he moaned, looking distressed. He laid his cheek on her wet hair and continued to hold her. Crystal felt him shake, too. He released her and looked at her.

"You are soaking wet and cold," he said and ran to get a towel out of the tent. He ran back and placed it around her shoulders. Crystal realized as he put the towel around her that she was wearing a white T-shirt. Her cheeks turned red as she blushed. He held her close again and she warmed in his arms. She felt desperation in his embrace, and she looked up to see a tear fall from his cheek.

She reached up and brushed it from his face. "What is wrong, Jonathan?" she asked gently.

He shook his head, and she thought more tears were going to fall, but they didn't. "I'm just not good enough for you, Crystal," he said hoarsely.

"Would you please let me be the judge of that!" she pleaded.

"I think you had better get some dry clothes on," he said and helped her to her tent so she could change.

"You had better dry off, too," she said through chattering teeth. He nodded solemnly.

Jonathan groaned and dropped to his knees as he entered his tent. Why did he have to care for her so much? He loved her, he knew he did, but how could he ever expect her to love him back? Even if she did, he had nothing to offer. He wasn't good enough for her.

Slowly he found dry clothes and changed. He lifted the flap to his tent and went out. Crystal was still in her tent. He took the fish from the stringer in the stream and started to clean them.

"You're busy already, I see," said Crystal as she came out. She was worried about what had happened and was afraid that if she said the wrong thing he would be upset again. She went to the campfire and started building it up again to cook the meal. They both worked quietly, Jonathan cleaning the fish and Crystal gathering wood.

Crystal was relieved when she heard Cortney's cheerful voice in the distance.

"I guess they are back!" she said.

Jonathan nodded. "Just in time, too. It looks like you have a nice fire going." He came near with the cleaned fish in a bowl. She looked at him, but he refrained from making eye contact. She looked away, feeling hurt.

"Crystal!" called Cortney as she ran up to her. "The waterfall was so beautiful. We will have to come back when your ankle is better so you can hike up there."

Terry collapsed in a chair by the fire. "I am so tired! We must have walked twenty miles!"

"Actually it was close to it," sighed Bill. "I think we will try to find a shorter hike tomorrow."

"I know one thing," said Terry as he joined the others. "I sure am looking forward to some more of Jonathan's fish." Then he looked at Crystal. "So how is your ankle doing?" he asked.

"She hurt it again," said Jonathan before Crystal could answer.

"I didn't really hurt it again. It gave out while I was crossing the stream and I fell into the water. My ankle is fine," she said shrugging her shoulders.

"Oh, Crystal, the water must have been freezing!" exclaimed Cortney. "I hope you don't catch a cold or pneumonia."

Crystal looked at her. "I'm fine really," she said. "The water was cold, but the air was warm so it wasn't so bad. I just got a bath. I needed one anyway." She shrugged her shoulders. She wished Cortney wouldn't have been so worried about the incident. Jonathan already felt as if he caused her to fall and she didn't want him to feel any worse than he did. She looked up to see him watching her, but again he quickly looked away. He took the fish and placed them in the pan. Terry got up to help him.

Crystal went into the tent to get some supplies for the meal and Cortney followed her. "What happened while we were gone?" asked Cortney as she came close.

Crystal shook her head. "I'm not sure," she said. "He was quiet today. We went for a walk and when I tried to find out what was bothering him he got mad. He turned and walked away. I tried to follow him and that's when I fell. He said he was the reason I fell and he felt terrible about it. Cortney, he actually cried. Since then he hasn't said much. He won't even look at me.

"Wow," she said softly. "I knew he looked withdrawn and you looked distressed." She shrugged her shoulders. "Maybe he said something to the guys yesterday and they know what is bothering him. We really don't know him. There is an honesty about him that just makes you like him." She patted Crystal's shoulder. "Don't worry. Give him some time. Maybe he will be open up more tomorrow and things will be OK."

"I sure hope so," she said and finished gathering supplies. Her arms were full as she prepared to leave the tent. "I really like him, Cortney!"

"I know you do, Crystal," said Cortney and squeezed her arm. "He's a special person. Maybe he just needs time to realize that."

Crystal smiled and took the supplies to the table.

Jonathan remained quiet the rest of the evening and retired early to his tent. Crystal felt hurt when he left. He said goodnight to everyone as a group, but didn't say anything to her. He didn't even look at her. Terry glanced her way when Jonathan left and saw the pain in her eyes.

Jonathan entered his tent and crawled into his sleeping bag. He had decided he was going to leave before anyone woke in the morning. The longer he stayed the harder it was going to be to leave. He slept fitfully and was awake long before dawn. He silently packed his tent and belongings and headed back up the trail he had brought Crystal back on. The coming of dawn brought enough dim light to be able to find his way across the rocks in the stream.

A cry caught in Crystal's throat when she opened the flap of her tent. Her eyes that immediately searched for Jonathan found the empty space where his tent had been. She looked at Terry who was sitting by the fire.

"He was gone when we got up," said Terry holding a cup of coffee. "As far as I know he didn't say anything to anyone."

She looked at Terry stunned. "But where would he go?" she gasped.

Terry put his coffee down and went to stand beside Crystal. "Crystal, he was alone when he found you. He probably went back to where he came from."

"I need to follow him," she said starting toward he path.

Terry grabbed her arm. "Crystal, you can't make that long of a hike and he knows it. If he wanted you to follow he wouldn't have left like he did."

"What did I do to cause him to run away?" Crystal felt frantic. "I didn't mean to make him angry. I just wanted to help him," she moaned.

Terry took Crystal by the shoulders and made her face him. "Crystal, on the hike to the waterfall we had a talk. Jonathan is very confused right now and I think he needs some time to search for answers. He has something in his life he needs to correct. I'm thinking that his feelings for you were getting too strong for him to face right now. Give him some time to think for awhile."

Crystal looked at Terry with tears. "He doesn't know where I live. He doesn't have my address or telephone number or even know my last name. I don't know his either. How will I ever find him again if I don't go after him now?"

"He knows we go to school at Ohio State. It's not totally hopeless," said Terry. "I told him about our Campus Life meetings. He can always find us through there and we can tell him how to find you."

Crystal went to the stream and looked down the path. She felt helpless and lost. How could he just leave me without even saying good-bye! She searched the path for signs of him. As her eyes scanned the empty path she began to get angry. How could he leave her like he did? He seemed so perceptive and tender. She thought there was something endearing between them. She had thought he cared for her, but someone who cared would have considered her feelings, and not simply his own. He was just week and shallow, afraid to face her, and afraid to face life. He had deceived her in the same way Eric had only worse. He had stolen her heart, not jewelry.

She folded her arms in front of her and clenched her jaw. She braced herself and determined to be strong. If he was going to walk out of her life she would just think of him as never being in her life!

Jonathan covered ground quickly and by the time the others discovered he was gone he had reached the place where he first found Crystal. He descended the cliff to where they had pitched the tent. He looked around. He remembered the way Crystal looked the morning when he woke and a smile crossed his face. He remembered with a stab in his chest the way he felt when he saw her lovely face. He looked back up the cliff. He needed to keep going. The desire to go back was too strong. If he didn't keep going he would talk himself into returning.

"She was better without him." He thought as he looked up. He didn't know if he would ever be in the position to come back after Crystal or not, but for now he wasn't worthy of her and he didn't need to let things get more involved that they already were. He grasped the closest tree to him and started his ascent up the cliff. When he reached the top he looked where he had came from. Then he turned to where he needed to go. His heart was torn, but with determination he took the path that led back to the time without Crystal, not toward her.

"Crystal, you surprise me. I thought you would be more upset about Jonathan leaving than you are," commented Cortney in the evening when they were cleaning up after the meal.

Crystal shook her head with her chin in the air. "I decided it was for the best. If he is going to run away that easily, then what would happen further in the future? I think he probably did me a favor," Crystal said defiantly.

"That is exactly how he looked at it," said Terry. "Don't you see, he is just trying to protect you from what he feels is a mess in his life."

"Protect me!" exclaimed Crystal. "From what! Don't try and stand up for him. You didn't try to protect Eric."

Terry looked her in the eye. "Crystal, don't even start to compare Jonathan to Eric. Jonathan is a good kid with some issues in his life he needs to deal with.

You need to be supportive and help him."

Crystal's eyes glared, and her fists clenched tightly on her hips. "Support him! He didn't trust me enough to let me know how to support him. He just ran out with no explanation!" Crystal's eyes glared with anger, but her heart filled with despair.

"You can be supportive by being patient and giving him the benefit of the doubt that he did what he had to do when he comes back for you," said Terry.

"Thanks for the words of wisdom, but I was taken advantage of once before. Jonathan is from now on out of my life!" she yelled and walked away from the others. She would have run if it weren't for her ankle.

Cortney ran after her and put her arms around her shoulder. "Terry can be abrupt. He likes to tell things as he sees them," said Cortney. "Do think about what he said, though. Terry is very perceptive, and I've come to appreciate his insights into people. Take some time. Nothing needs to happen immediately. We don't know where he is or where he is going. All we can do is wait for him to contact us."

"I can't, Cortney," whispered Crystal hoarsely. "I can't wait to see if he contacts me, because I can't bear to think that he may never contact me. I need to wipe him from my life."

The next two days lost their adventuresome spirit, and the group was quiet as they packed the tents and supplies.

"Goodbye, Crystal," said Tammy and Bill as they got into Bill's Blazer. Crystal smiled and waved.

"School will be out for the summer soon," said Cortney as she stood beside Crystal's car. "I'll be back to Tennessee and spend a week or two with you and your family. I'm looking forward to seeing your mother again." She reached up and gave Crystal a hug.

Terry reached out and grasped Crystal's hand. "Remember what I said. When Jonathan returns, give him time and trust him. Not all people will abuse your trust."

Crystal simply nodded and got into her car. She looked up and waved as she pulled onto the road. Before she knew it the trip was over, and instead of finding peace she was terribly confused. The ride had gone quickly, and she was glad to be turning into the drive to her family's house.

Amy ran from the house and threw her arms around Crystal as soon as the car door opened.

"I'm so glad you are home!" Amy said as she hugged her tightly.

Crystal laughed. "Me, too!" she answered and looked up to see her mother coming out the door carrying Andrew. Andrew squealed when he saw Crystal.

Crystal and Britany both laughed. Crystal took Andrew from Britany's arms and held him close. "Is it possible that you have grown in the short time I was gone?" asked Crystal.

"Possible and quite probable," assured Britany as she took a sleeping bag and pillow from the back seat of her car that Crystal had driven.

"Crystal, you are limping!" Britany exclaimed as they started to walk to the house. She quickly put the sleeping bag down and reached for Andrew. "Here! Give him to me. You don't need to put any more strain on it."

Crystal handed Andrew to Britany and said, "Mom, it's not bad. I sprained it the first day of our trip, but it is doing really well now."

Britany looked at her. A little crease appeared between her eyebrows. "Crystal, I had hoped you would have a good time. I'm so sorry," she reached out to put her arm around her and realized she was still holding the pillow. She laid it beside the sleeping bag and then hugged her.

Crystal was close to tears. If her mother only knew how much more her heart hurt than her ankle. She wished she could have told her that she had met the most wonderful guy, but instead she would have to tell her that she had once again met a gut who had deceived her. She didn't want to deal with that acknowledgment yet.

She gave a half smile. "It wasn't so bad, and it was good to see my friends again. Terry and Cortney are growing very close. I wouldn't be surprised if they get engaged soon, although Cortney doesn't want to get married until she graduates."

Britany looked at Crystal with concern. She sensed that something was wrong and that Crystal was avoiding talking about it. She took her arm and led her to the house. "Come on," she said. "Ben and I will get your things later. Right now I want to get you off your ankle."

"Mom, I've been walking on it for the entire week. It is healing up just fine."

"Crystal," said Amy, "listen to Mom. She's a nurse, remember?"

Crystal smiled at her. "Yes, I remember. I will be a good patient."

They started walking back toward the house. Amy ran up the stairs and held the door. She talked as she stood by the door. "Mom took care of Jonathan when his leg was broken."

A stab of pain tore at Crystal's heart when Amy mentioned the name Jonathan. Britany also felt a twinge. Her mind pictured Jonathan entering the house for the first time when he came home from the hospital. She wondered where he was now. She continued to pray that someday he would come back. The empty feeling that one of her children had strayed away never ceased to be with her.

Crystal realized that Amy was talking about the person who had lived with their family for a short time. He ran off too, she realized. "Do all Jonathan's run away?" she thought to herself.

CHAPTER 21

Jonathan returned to his grandfather's house from the mountains. He had never felt much fondness for the place, and now it seemed even more empty and desolate. He was relieved when he talked to the realtor and found the closing was scheduled in five days. He was looking forward to having the house gone, although he didn't know where he would live. He entertained thoughts of going back to the town where he had spent the summer. The warm weather meant the grass would be growing, and he could possibly get his yard jobs back. The big problem with that was the very real possibility of running into Britany. He couldn't face her or her family, although he longed with all his heart to see them. She had been like a mother to him, and he loved her very much. It was good to realize how he loved her, as a mother, and not as his mixed emotions had tried to lead him.

He glanced at the pile of letters he had in his hand. Advertisement! Advertisement! Advertisement! Why did they waste the paper and postage? He tossed them on a pile in the kitchen and started the burner to cook some eggs. When they were finished he sat at the table and shuffled through the advertisements as he ate. He uncovered a letter that was postmarked Greece.

He stopped eating and tore open the letter.

Dear Jonathan,

I would never write and ask you this if the situation wasn't desperate, but I am very worried about your father. He fell from a lemon tree and broke his leg. He is to stay off of it for several weeks. He is so worried that he cannot relax. I am afraid he will go ahead and do something he shouldn't. I cannot help because the baby is so little and the other two children are too young. He is too proud to ask you for help, but I'm not. It was wonderful to have you with us. If things are all right with you grandfather I hope you can come. We will gladly pay for your expense to get here.

Sincerely,

Frena

Jonathan reread the letter. His life seemed to be moving too fast in different directions. First he was in Greece finding the father he never knew. Then he flew home to make amends with his dying grandfather. While he was searching for answers in his life he met Crystal, which complicated his life more than ever. Now his father needed his help! It seemed too much to comprehend, but he knew he needed to go. He loved his father and newfound family. He finished his eggs and reached for the telephone to call airlines. He found a flight that left the afternoon of the closing on his house.

He put down the phone and looked out the window. The idea of having a place to go to where he was needed as soon as the place he was staying closed seemed comforting. He crossed his arms and leaned back. The idea was becoming more and more appealing. A smile crossed his face. He leaned forward again and picked up the phone. He wanted to assure Frena that he would be there and tell her to prepare Olio for his arrival so he would have a ride to the farm.

Excitement built as the plane was nearing the landing strip. Jonathan stared at the blue-green ocean below. They circled hard, and then the plane descended sharply to land smoothly on the runway. Two young bodies ran toward him as he went through the door at the bottom of the ramp. "Jonathan!" they screamed and threw themselves on him. In amazement Jonathan dropped the case he was carrying and reached out to hold them close. He kissed the tops of their silky black hair. He quickly looked up and scanned the crowd. There stood his father smiling deeply.

He released his hold on the children and stood. He retrieved his bag and walked toward his father. Amadeo was leaning on crutches. Jonathan carefully grasped his father's shoulders and brushed each cheek with his own. Amadeo readjusted his weight and grasped Jonathan's shoulder with his free hand.

"I'm so glad you are here, son," he said huskily.

"Me, too," said Jonathan and impulsively embraced him. He saw Frena out of the corner of his eye. He released the hold on his father and turned toward her. She smiled warmly and reached up to kiss his cheeks. He bent to oblige her and grinned widely.

She was holding his little sister. Jonathan stared at her wide-eyed. He reached for her, and Frena gladly handed the baby to his waiting arms.

"She has grown so much!" exclaimed Jonathan, shaking his head in wonder.

Amadeo laughed. "She eats all the time, so it is no wonder she is growing!" He adjusted the crutches again and looked uncomfortable.

Jonathan handed the baby back to Frena and looked at his father. "We need to get you to the car!" he said sternly, grasping his father's arm.

His father looked at him with a dimple showing. "So now you are going to give me orders also!" He nodded toward Frena, his handsome face trying to look stern. "Frena is constantly telling me what to do. I will never have a moment peace now!"

Jonathan laughed. "You are in no condition to complain. I know how you feel, and that is why I am here. The more you listen to us and let us help the quicker you will be up and around like your old self!" He looked around to be sure the children were following as they walked through the airport.

"I can't believe you came to the airport," said Jonathan, shaking his head. His silky hair waved over his shoulders. He had to slow his pace to match his father's.

"You don't think we would let you fly all the way here and not come to get you, do you?" asked his father as he swung one crutch and followed it with his leg. The progress was slow, and Jonathan was afraid Amadeo would tire too much before he reached the car. Jonathan ran ahead and retrieved his bag from the conveyor belt.

The ride to the farm was filled with excitement as Sisily and Theo each tried to tell Jonathan about their father's fall. Jonathan was glad to be back. He looked at Frena and his father. They had the same kind of love for each other that he had seen between Britany and Michael. He suddenly realized that more than coming to help his father he had needed to come and learn how to be a good father and husband. His mood began to lighten more than it had been since he left Crystal. Maybe this would be a start to help him be worthy of her!

Jonathan jumped from the car as soon as it stopped and opened the door for his father. "Jonathan!" exclaimed Amadeo. "I know you came to help with the farm, for which I am entirely grateful. I can help myself, though!" he continued with frustration.

Frena smiled gently at Jonathan from the driver's seat.

"Father, my leg was broken last summer," said Jonathan. Amadeo looked at him with bewilderment. "Oh?" he questioned.

Jonathan nodded. "Yes, and my arm also. I received an abundance of care from a loving family, and I am more than ready to give some back." Jonathan reached for the crutches and leaned them against the side of the car. He brushed back some hair that had fallen. His eyes shone as he spoke, partly from fond memories and partly from the pleasure of being able to share with someone else who was having the same frustrations he had faced.

"They helped me with every aspect of my personal care, but I soon healed and was able to do things on my own again. You will heal quickly. You won't be dependent for the rest of your life. Let us help you now for this short time."

Amadeo smiled and placed a strong hand on Jonathan's shoulder. "You are a very smart boy. I am proud to call you my son." He took Jonathan's offered arm and rose from the car. Jonathan reached for the crutch and helped place it under Amadeo's arm. They stood eye to eye as Amadeo steadied himself. Jonathan smiled and turned to see if Frena needed any help with the baby. He saw that she was watching them with a smile on her face.

"It's good that you are here," she said softly as he met her gaze. He smiled shyly at the compliment.

Amadeo took Jonathan for a walk as soon as the children were settled. He was concerned that many things had been left undone since the fall.

"These young trees will never make it without some water, but the irrigation line broke, and I have been unable to dig," said Amadeo, waving his arm over an acre of waist-high trees with deep green leaves. "Every day I pray for rain," said Amadeo, raising his face to the sky, "but maybe I was praying for the wrong thing." He looked directly at Jonathan. Lines edged his face that hadn't been present at Jonathan's previous visit. His raven-black hair was edged with a few more gray strands. "Now you are here and can fix the pipes. I never thought that I should pray for you to return." He patted Jonathan on the shoulder, and Jonathan felt a surge of pride and belonging.

Amadeo continued the tour to the next field. Jonathan turned toward him. "Father, you look very tired. I know you have many more things to show me, but I can only work on one project at a time, and you need some rest. Let's go back, and I will put on some clothes and start digging to fix the pipes."

Amadeo shook his head and waved his hands. "No! No! You have traveled many miles, and you need to rest. You can start tomorrow."

Jonathan laughed. "Because I have traveled many miles I need to exercise my body for awhile."

Amadeo looked at the ground and shook his head again. "You are a very determined boy!" he exclaimed.

Jonathan reached out and laid his hand across Amadeo's shoulder. "I guess it must be inherited from my father." They both laughed as they walked toward the house.

The ground was hard, but fortunately the pipe was buried shallow. Jonathan was able to expose the broken end quickly. He cut the pipe and fitted a new splice. He tried the water and was thrilled when water filled the air above the trees. When he was assured the pipe was no longer leaking, he covered it with dirt.

Theo ran ahead of him as Jonathan walked to the house. He ran through the open screen door shouting, "Jonathan fixed the pipe! Water is in the air!"

Amadeo was sitting with his leg propped up. "How did you do that? I thought you would come and get me when you finished digging so I could give you instructions on how to fix the leak."

Jonathan shrugged, "I use to do yard work in the summer, and many people have sprinkler systems. It came in real handy to learn how to make minor repairs."

Frena laughed. It was a lovely laugh like a small brass bell. Amadeo looked at her and smiled. "I have you to take care of me in the house and a skillful son caring for the farm. I am a very blessed man!" Frena laughed again and hugged him tightly.

Jonathan awoke with a start. He opened his eyes. Darkness surrounded him and confusion raced through his head. Where was he? He sat up and reached for he light as he slowly remembered that he was still in his father's house and not back in the upstairs bedroom with Ben at Britany's house as in his dream. His heart pounded as he remembered Britany's agonizing voice calling for him as she searched through the house. He could see Amy crying at the door. In his dream he was standing there, watching them look for him, trying to talk, but they couldn't see or hear him. Britany looked scared and worried. He tried to tell her he was all right, but she wouldn't respond to him. She walked past him as if he wasn't there and continued her search.

His head dropped to his hands. He ached to see them again. To see Britany and Amy in such distress was agony, even though it was a dream. Maybe Terry had been right and he needed to go to them and apologize. He got up and paced the room. He ran his fingers through his black hair. He sat on the edge of his bed. He did need to go back. He knew in his heart that God was urging him to return. The agony of Britany's face in his dream was too real to deny, and he paled to think he could be causing it. His long legs folded as he dropped to his knees beside the bed. "Dear Lord, please be with Britany and Amy and assure them I am all right until I can return. I would leave tomorrow, but Father needs me still. I will return as soon as he is able to care for things on his own. Thank you for showing me the direction I need to go."

CHAPTER 22

Crystal tore open her French book. She was determined not to think about Jonathan again today. School had started back after spring break just two days ago, and every day she focused on Jonathan. It left her feeling helpless and lost. She had fallen short of her expectations of schooling in the fall. She had gotten into a bad situation with Eric that she had been warned against. Then she met Jonathan, and for several days things were wonderful! But that had failed. Crystal was determined to succeed in one thing.

"Crystal, do you have time to run to town with us?" Britany asked, opening the bedroom door and peering in.

"Please!" begged Amy running in and jumping on the bed beside her. Her dark eyes were big with excitement. "Mom promised me some summer clothes, and I want you to help me pick them out."

Crystal looked at her and held her close. "I guess if we won't be gone for too long."

"We won't, I promise," assured Amy.

Britany left Andrew with Michael for the evening. It was a short drive to the store, and soon Amy was thoroughly looking at each piece of clothing.

"You planned this little shopping trip to get me out, didn't you, Mom?" asked Crystal as they stood nearby.

"I hope you don't mind," said Britany with a guilty expression on her face. "You hurt your ankle on that trip, but that has healed fine. There is another part of you that seems a lot more hurt." Britany wiped a stray strand of hair from Crystal's troubled cheek.

Crystal looked away and said, "I forget that you know when things are wrong five hundred miles away. I guess you would notice when I'm here."

Britany nodded silently.

"I just don't feel ready to talk about it yet, Mom."

Britany frowned, and her heart hurt with Crystal, but she didn't ask her any more. She knew that in time Crystal would tell her.

"When you are ready to talk, I will be here," said Britany.

Crystal smiled with her lips, but not with her eyes. "I know, Mom. Someday I'll be ready."

Amy brought a pair of shorts and a blouse for Crystal to examine. "What do you think?" she asked.

"It looks great on the hanger. Why don't you try it on?" suggested Crystal.

"Amy, you look lovely!" exclaimed Britany as Amy tried on the clothes.

"Mom, you always think I'm beautiful. What do you think, Crystal?" Amy asked, looking at Crystal.

"She's right," Crystal said in agreement. "You do look lovely."

"I think we've accomplished our task here. Let's head for home!" exclaimed Britany.

Crystal was in a lighter mood on the way home. It was a relief to think of something else and get her mind off of Jonathan. She was laughing with Amy as they entered the door. Her laughter stopped as she saw Michael's face.

"What's wrong?" gasped Britany. "Is Andrew all right? Where is he?" She panicked and started to look around for him. He was sitting quietly on the floor playing with Ben. Britany looked back at Michael questioningly.

"It's your father, Britany," said Michael quietly.

"What's happened?" Britany managed to get out.

"There was an accident with the tractor. Your brother called. They are at the hospital right now. The tractor flipped with your father on it. It threw him clear, but he is unconscious and broken up. Your mother is with him, and so is your brother."

Britany looked around trying to decide what to do first. "We need to go to him and Mother."

"I've already packed items for the boys and me. I'll help Amy. You go get some things for yourself," said Michael, taking Britany by the arm to give her direction. Britany looked into his warm eyes.

"Thank you," she said. "He is going to be all right. He just has to," she finished in a whisper. "I don't know what my mother would do without him."

They drove through the night and arrived as the sun rose. The hospital was quiet as they walked through the front door. Andrew looked around bright-eyed, but Amy and Ben were subdued and quiet. Britany looked down at Amy's pale face as they took the elevator to the second floor. Her cheeks were pale and her breathing shallow. She grasped Britany's hand tightly. Crystal noticed and started to take Amy's hand. Britany looked at her and shook her head.

"No," she said quietly. "You take Andrew. Amy needs me more now than Andrew does. I know how she feels." She patted Amy on the head. She wished she could tell her that Grandpa Charlie would be all right, but Amy had been through too much to be given false sentiments, no matter how well meant.

Britany took a deep breath as they stepped from the elevator. They walked to the waiting room. Her mother was asleep on a chair with her head resting on a pillow. Britany's brother Phillip rose to greet her. "Hi, Sis," he said and wrapped his arms around her. Liz stirred and looked up.

"Britany!" she exclaimed and got quickly to her feet. "And look! Amy! Ben! Crystal! Andrew! Oh, my goodness, Michael. You must be crazy to drive your family through the night to get here!" she exclaimed.

Michael crossed the room, and taking her in his arms, he kissed her gently on the cheek. "We are all family now, and we needed to be here," he said quietly and firmly. Liz looked as though she was going to cry, but she smiled.

Britany grasped her mother's hand. "How is he, Mom?" she asked.

"He regained consciousness, but he is still in intensive care. His hip is broken, and they are considering a hip replacement. He is scheduled for surgery tomorrow if he remains stable. He told us to go home, but I just couldn't go home yet," Liz said. Britany had never seen her mother so worn and pale. It frightened her.

"Mom, please come sit back down. Have you eaten?" Britany asked with concern, grasping Liz's elbow and leading her to the chair. Liz shook her head no.

Michael looked at Britany, then down at Liz. "I'm going to go downstairs and see if they have some soup. You need to eat something. How about you, Phillip?" he asked.

"Actually, I will go with you. Now that you guys are home Mom won't be alone, and I could use a walk," commented Phillip, and he went with Michael.

Britany sat beside her mother with Amy on her lap. She had many questions she wanted to ask, but her mother looked pale, and she wanted to wait,   so   they   sat   quietly. "Thank you, Michael," said Liz when they returned, and he handed her the soup.

"I'm going to go see if the nurses will tell me how Dad is doing," said Britany.

"I'll go with you," said Phillip. "They know me and I'll introduce you."

Britany smiled. "So, what can you tell me?" she asked as they walked.

"It was pretty bad. Mom noticed the noise of the tractor seemed to be in one spot for a long time and went out to check on it." He stopped and looked at her. "Dad was unconscious when she got there. She yelled, but no one was around. She had to run back to the house to call 911. She did everything she could, but it was very traumatic. The little nap and the soup seemed to help her some. I'm glad you came. She can use all of us for support. She always tries to be strong, but it's not good to do it on your own."

"Are the kids and Lori at the farm?" asked Britany.

He shook his head. "Actually they are home. I sent them home around eight when Dad woke up. It isn't that far, and it's easier on the kids."

Britany nodded and walked to the nurse's station. "Hi! I'm Britany. My father is Charles Becker."

The young nurse looked at her and smiled. "Yes, of course," she said politely. "I see the family resemblance." She stood and walked around from the desk. "Come with me," she said, looking at them. "He is awake, and I'm sure he would like to see you. We are preparing him for surgery." She walked toward the room directly across from the desk.

Britany looked at Phillip with a puzzled look. He shrugged his shoulders. "I guess they decided he was stable enough," he said.

Britany wasn't ready to see her father lying in the hospital bed with tubing and machines around him. She stopped. Phillip grasped her shoulders and steadied her.

"Come on, Sis," he whispered.

He smiled and went to their father's bedside.

"You have a visitor, Mr. Becker," the young nurse said as they stood beside him.

He looked up, and his eyes brightened. "Britany!" he exclaimed. He tried to raise himself up and suddenly cringed.

"Dad! Don't move!" Britany pleaded. He reached out this hand and Britany took it. She gently kissed his cheek. "You gave us quite a scare," she said softly.

Despite his full smile he looked pale.

"From what I hear your mom did real good," he said. Britany nodded. "You must have driven the entire night to get here!" Charles said.

"Michael drove most of the way." Britany grasped his hand hard. Images of her friend Jeanne passed through her mind. The similarities were too close to push away the doubt that was crowding her mind. Jeanne had been full of life when she ended up in the hospital facing surgery the next morning, surgery from which she never woke up. Now her father was bravely facing the same situation. Britany felt a compulsion to run from the room to a faraway place that didn't exist, where pain and sadness didn't exist. The desire to stay with her father held her steadfast to his bedside. She studied the bags of fluid hanging above his bed, flowing into his veins.

"The nurse said they are getting you ready for surgery," said Phillip as he stepped forward.

"Ten o'clock, if all the blood work comes back. They still need to test for blood clotting to be sure I won't bleed too much. It seems they've put enough needles into my veins to know that by now," Charles said and lifted his arm off the bed to show the IV attached to his hand.

"Isn't it too soon?" asked Britany with concern in her voice. Her forehead wrinkled, and her green eyes were pleading.

"I don't like having to be strapped to this wedge. The sooner they fix it the sooner it will heal, and I will get back on my feet again," said Charles. His eyes closed slightly, and he looked as if he were going back to sleep.

Britany looked at Phillip. Her eyes looked close to panic. "It's too soon," she said softly so she wouldn't wake her father.

"They wouldn't do the surgery if they thought he wasn't strong enough," Phillip tried to assure her.

Britany shook her head. "But he was unconscious for ten hours. I think they need to wait!"

"Britany." Britany turned to see her father looking at her. He reached for her hand again. "I'm not Jeanne."

"Dad," she stammered, "I know you're not Jeanne. I just think they should wait!"

Charles spoke strongly despite the medicine he was on for pain. "Britany, I'm not Jeanne. I can see the panic in your eyes. I need to do this, and you need to trust God to see me through."

"Dad, it's just happening too fast," said Britany and looked down at the sheets.

"Britany, look at me. I can't promise you I will make it through the surgery. You aren't a little girl anymore, and you know that I can't promise you that. God didn't make a mistake when He took Jeanne to be with Him. If He decides to take me He won't be making a mistake either. He could have taken me when I was lying on the ground, but He didn't. He still has plans for me, and I truly feel my time is not up yet. If it is, then you will be all right. You are stronger than you think you are."

Britany shook her head and started to protest, but her father's eyes were closed, and she realized how much energy he had used to talk to her. She leaned down and kissed his cheek again. "We will bring Mom back in a little while. You sleep now," she said quietly.

Phillip walked to the door and held it open for Britany. They turned and walked down the hall. The hospital was alive with energy as the day shift was coming on and morning activities were beginning.

"I'm scared, too, Sis, if it makes any difference," Phillip said as they walked.

"Dad's right," said Britany. "God's in control. Sometimes it's just hard to accept what He has in store." She shook her head. It had been a long night, and she was suddenly feeling very tired.

Amy was awake when they came to the lounge. "How's Grandpa Charlie?" she asked.

Britany smiled. "He's doing very well. He's pleased as can be that we came."

"How could we not come!" exclaimed Amy. Britany smiled and gave her a big hug.

"Mom," Phillip stepped up to where Liz was seated, "they are doing surgery at ten."

"That's good," she said evenly. "He needs to get that hip set as soon as possible. I'm going to go stay with him now as long as they will let me."

"I'll go call Lori," said Phillip. "She will want to know what is happening."

Britany looked at Michael. Andrew was trying to squirm off of his lap. "Maybe we should go get some breakfast," she suggested. Michael nodded.

When they returned the nurses allowed each of them to visit Charles for a short time, and then they took him down to surgery. Britany tried hard to relax during the long wait, but visions of what had happened to Jeanne kept coming to her mind. Amy was also very restless.

"It's hard to not think about your mother, isn't it?" Britany asked Amy as they stood looking out the window.

Amy nodded her head. "Sometimes it's hard for me to remember everything that happened that day, but I'll never forget the last time my mother held me."

Britany squeezed her tightly. "Hold on to those memories, Amy. Your mother was a wonderful person, and she loved you very much."

Amy looked up at her. "I hope God doesn't decide to take Grandpa to live with Him now, too. We still need him here on earth," she said.

Britany looked into her misty eyes. "Well, I can tell you that Grandpa Charlie doesn't feel his job on earth is done! I think that is a good sign, but I must tell you that I am very worried, too."

Amy seemed to relax as she talked about her fears. She soon joined Ben in a game of checkers. Time seemed to pass slowly. Crystal and Liz went for a walk.

"Let's go outside," Liz suggested. Crystal held the door as Liz led the way. They walked down the sidewalk through the flower gardens on the front lawn. Liz looked up and sighed. "Grandpa loves large trees. Somehow these trees seem to give me peace as I look up at them." Crystal followed her gaze toward the tops of the trees as Liz continued. "Life is so short. It's good to see something whose life span surpasses ours."

"Grandma," said Crystal, watching the white clouds float above the branches. "You always seem so confident about life. How can you be so sure of things?"

Liz looked at Crystal. "It seems to me that you have some things on your mind that you need to talk about."

Crystal shrugged her shoulders and studied the budding rose in front of her. "Life seems very confusing to me right now. A lot of things don't seem to make sense."

"Crystal, life can be very confusing." She waited for Crystal to continue.

Crystal sighed. "I've let my mother down."

Liz took Crystal's elbow. "Crystal, your mother has put her entire life into raising you. She loves you very much!"

"That's what I mean. I know she loves me. She has given me anything I ever needed. It's just that I seem to keep messing up. I was so naive to believe in Eric. My foolishness caused Mom a lot of pain."

Liz shook her head. "Crystal, Eric was a pro at deceiving people. You can't blame yourself for that mess he got you into."

"Well, a lot of it was my own fault, and I am not going to try and deny it," said Crystal firmly. "The worst thing is that I thought I had my life back together and was following God, but I still messed up."

"And you will continue to mess up the rest of your life. None of us are perfect. God doesn't expect perfection. That is why he offers forgiveness. Neither does your mother expect perfection."

Crystal walked some more. She wanted to tell her grandmother about Jonathan, but she felt so foolish that she wasn't sure she wanted even her to know. Liz walked quietly beside her.

"I asked for God's insight," Crystal decided to confide in her grandmother. "And I still misjudged someone. I guess I just don't understand men. They seem to have a way of deceiving me about who they really are." Crystal shook her head sadly and walked further. "It's just that even though I was angry with him and tried to forget him I can't get him off my mind."

"Crystal, what are you talking about?" Liz asked, looking at her quizzically.

Crystal sighed and looked at her grandmother. "When I went camping with my friends for spring break, I met a guy. He was alone, and he joined us for several days. I could talk to him like I've never been able to talk to anyone else. I thought we shared something special. He was caring and sensitive. Then he left without even saying goodbye. I don't even know where he lives or anything!" Tears were in Crystal's eyes, and Liz put her arm across Crystal's shoulders.

"I don't ever think I will trust any guy again. I guess I just don't understand men. Do you think it's because I grew up without a father?"

Liz squeezed Crystal's arms and shook her head. "Crystal, you have always had your Heavenly Father, and He can help you through this. Let Him guide you. The right man is out there for you. You are still young."

Crystal walked forward. "But I did ask God. That is what is so confusing."

Liz took Crystal's hand and walked back toward the hospital door. "I still think you need to give it more time." Crystal smiled and followed her. She watched Amy and Ben play a game of checkers and then the door to the waiting room opened.

"The surgery was a success, and he is doing very well," announced the doctor as he came into the room.

"Praise God," Britany said with a sigh of relief.

"Can we see him now?" asked Liz.

The doctor looked at her. "You can come with me, Mrs. Becker. The rest of you will need to wait several hours, and then you can see him."

Amy ran to Liz and gave her a big hug. Liz smiled and looked very relieved. She followed the doctor and found Charles resting peacefully. A nurse was by his side. He opened his eyes when Liz took his hand. "I told you God isn't finished with me yet!" he said and drifted back to sleep.

Britany and her family stayed with Liz for several days and then traveled back to Tennessee.

CHAPTER 23

Britany measured five cups of granulated sugar to stir into the jam as she watched the pan of pureed strawberries heat on the stove. The barking dog diverted her attention, and she looked through the blowing curtain to see why the dog was barking. A familiar truck was coming up the drive. The smell of strawberry jam floated around her as she ran to open the door. She hurried to wipe the granules of sugar from her hands. She yelled back over her shoulder, "Amy, turn the burner off!"

Britany ran to the drive as the truck came to a stop. Her heart pounded as Jonathan opened the door and stepped out. "Jonathan!" she cried, and threw her arms around him to pull him close. Tears streamed down her cheeks as she looked up into his smiling face. "You came back!" He held her close, unable to believe her warm welcome.

Jonathan's smile disappeared, and he stumbled slightly as he stared toward the house. Britany grabbed his arm to steady him. His face turned pale, and she turned to see what he was looking at. Crystal had come around the house from the deck and was staring at Jonathan with anger in her eyes. He wore a look of disbelief, and his breath was shallow and quick.

Crystal walked up with her eyes glaring, "So that's why you left! You are in love with my mother!"

"Your mother?" Jonathan looked from Crystal to Britany. Crystal was tall with blonde hair and gray eyes. Britany was much smaller with brown hair and green eyes. There wasn't much resemblance between them.

Britany stared at Crystal. Confusion filled her mind as she tried to figure out what was happening. "You know Jonathan?"

"Let's say we met once! Apparently I don't know him as well as you do!" she exclaimed in anger as she glared at her mother.

Britany glared back at her. "Crystal, don't you ever talk to me with that tone of voice! You are totally mistaken, and you owe us both an apology."

Jonathan felt his knees shake and couldn't believe what he was witnessing. He was still in awe trying to comprehend that Crystal was Britany's daughter. He watched in silence as Crystal turned angrily and stormed back into the house. He reached for the door of his truck. Britany grabbed his arm.

"Oh, no, you don't," she said. "You left once over a misunderstanding. This time you need to stay and clear up the matter. Come in and sit down."

He stood and looked at her. Memories of warmth and acceptance flooded back. He wanted to do as she said, but it seemed like an impossible situation. He had worked hard to get the courage to face her. Suddenly he was also facing Crystal. He wasn't ready for that, and fear filled him. He hesitated. She took his hand and held it firmly.

"Come on, Jonathan. Come into the house with me." He listened and followed obediently.

"Jonathan!" shrieked Amy as Britany led him into the kitchen. Jonathan looked to see Amy's brown eyes light with excitement. Warmth flooded his senses at the sight of her loving smile. The familiar sights of the house filled his being. Tears came to his eyes as Amy threw her arms around his neck.

Britany pulled out a chair and motioned for him to sit down. She got a glass of orange juice and placed it in front of him. He sat quietly staring at all the familiar sights in the kitchen. The few months he had spent in this house had been the happiest of his life. Britany pulled out a chair and sat beside him. He looked at her with troubled eyes.

"I came back to apologize," he said weakly. "I was wrong to do what I did. Honestly, Britany, I didn't mean to do that." He shook his head sadly. "You offered me the best life I had ever had, and I blew it."

Jonathan's dark hair was straight and reached his shoulders. He was tan, and his shoulders and arms were filled out from the work on his father's farm. He had definitely grown up and matured.

"You look older, Jonathan," Britany said as she observed him. "Where have you been?"

"I went back to my grandfather's. I found some answers, Britany. When I left here I was so confused. I loved you, and you were so beautiful. It was very impulsive of me. Please forgive me."

Britany grimaced, and her heart beat faster. How was she going to get him to understand? Jonathan covered her hand with his.

"It's all right Britany. I know now the love I have for you is as a mother, not a lover."

Britany let out an audible sigh. "Oh, Jonathan, I am so glad. I wasn't sure how to explain the difference to you." Suddenly Britany had a glimpse of what had happened and what Crystal was so upset about. "Did Crystal have anything to do with you finding the difference?"

Jonathan paled. "Who is she Britany? Why is she here?" he asked in a whisper.

Britany's eyes lit up. "She's my daughter! Crystal! Remember? The one I flew to see while you were here. You never met her. You left the day before she came home for Christmas."

"What!" he exclaimed and got to his feet. "But her last name is Becker! I don't understand!"

Amy laughed. "Mom's name changed when she married Dad!"

He leaned over the table with his hands resting on it. He looked from Amy to Britany. He laughed a small, shallow laugh. "Wow, I don't understand how in the middle of the mountains I meet this most wonderful girl, and she's your daughter."

"Jonathan, suppose you sit down and tell us what happened. Crystal hasn't told us a thing," Britany said.

His eyes looked troubled. "I guess she wouldn't. I left her without any word of explanation. She probably thinks I am the most horrible person on the face of the earth."

Instead of sitting, Jonathan walked across the kitchen floor and looked out the French doors to the hill in the distance. He looked back at Britany with pleading eyes. "She's too good for me, Britany. She has a future. She's in college. You've done a wonderful job raising her. She's the most wonderful, caring, witty, and gentle person I have ever met. I don't deserve someone like that. I left her because I needed to get my life in order. I had a lot of things to make right. Coming here to apologize was one of them. Her friend told me to come back and talk to you, but I just couldn't at the time. He told me you would welcome me back because of God, but I couldn't believe you ever would." He looked back to the door. "I had to leave. I don't think she will understand that." He looked back at Britany. "Besides, right now I am a high school drop out. What do I have to offer her?"

Britany walked up beside him. She put her hand on his shoulder. "Don't use that as an excuse. You are young and still have time for a good education. You have ambition and determination. Go talk to her. She's upstairs."

He looked at her. "I can't. I love her too much. If she doesn't understand, I don't know what I will do!" he moaned. The look on his face was heartbreaking.

Amy came up beside him and took his hand. "I'll tell her how terrific you are."

Jonathan smiled and caught her up in his arms. "Maybe I'm after the wrong sister. I really missed you, little Amy." He held her close.

Amy laughed and hugged him back. Jonathan placed her back on the floor and looked at Britany. "Well, here goes. If I'm going to do this I have to do it now before I think about it too much."

Jonathan walked to the stairs and hesitated at the bottom. If I don't go now I never will be able to. God, please be with me! He grasped the rail and pulled himself up. He knocked on the door to her room. Crystal opened it and stood glaring at him.

"May I come in?" he asked. She looked beautiful. Her skin was golden brown from the sun. Her flowing golden hair accented her eyes as she stared at him.

Crystal looked at Jonathan's sorrowful face and thought of the careful way he had looked after her when she was injured. She remembered the joy he had stirred in her heart and her resolve started to weaken. Then she remembered how he had left without an excuse. She had been hurt too badly. The pain still remained and caused her to build a wall of protection and self-defense.

"No, I'd rather you not. Anything you have to say you can say in the hall," Crystal said coldly.

His dark eyes looked hurt. He reached for her hand, and she jerked it away. "I'm sorry, Crystal," he began. "There were things in my life I needed to resolve, and I didn't want to hurt you."

Crystal interrupted. "You don't owe me an apology. There were no commitments made between us. You didn't want me in your life, and now I don't want you. You can leave now."

"Crystal, please!" he moaned. He reached for her hand again. This time she didn't notice him move, and he grasped it. Her stiff exterior was shaken for a second before she could recover and pull her hand away. He saw for just a second the change in her countenance.

"Please, Crystal," he pleaded.

"No!" she shook her head and shut the door, leaving him standing by himself in the hall. "What happened?" asked Amy as he got to the bottom of the stairs.

He shook his head. "She won't talk to me."

"Let me talk to her," said Britany, heading toward the stairs.

"No," said Jonathan. "She's right. I was wrong, and I have no right to come back and expect her to trust me."

He reached down and gave Britany a hug. "Goodbye, Britany," he said. "Thanks for taking me in as one of your own. I will never forget that. It was the best thing that ever happened in my life."

He bent over and kissed Amy on the cheek, and a tear escaped and traveled down his cheek.

Britany stood in front of him, blocking the door. She raised her arm and placed her hand against his chest. "Jonathan, you are making quite a habit of running away from your problems."

"I don't know what else to do. It seems to have served me well in the past," he said defiantly and started to walk past her. She blocked him again and stood firm.

"Then why are you back? The past doesn't just stop. You need to work through your problems so you can continue on, not run away from them."

Jonathan stared at her, his dark eyes stern and unwavering. Britany stared back. Suddenly his shoulders sagged, and he shuddered. "Then what do you suggest?" he asked with his palms uplifted.

"Give her some time," said Britany. "Stay around, check into schooling, and see what you need to graduate. Show her that you can be dependable instead of telling her."

"We want you to be our brother, Jonathan," said Amy and took his hand. "Mom's right, you know. She's always right."

Jonathan smiled. "Ok, I'll try it."

The back door opened, and Ben's voice was heard throughout the house. "Where is Jonathan!" he yelled. "I saw his truck." His footsteps could be heard running through the kitchen, and soon he was in the room running toward Jonathan.

"Jonathan!" yelled Ben. "You are finally home!" Jonathan stood, and Ben almost tackled him as he threw his arms around him.

"Yeah, and now Jonathan likes Crystal, but Crystal doesn't like him!" added Amy with emphasis.

"What?" asked Ben in confusion.

Britany looked at Amy disapprovingly. "Amy, sometimes you don't have to tell everything you know. That is something you need to let Crystal and Jonathan tell people. "

"Jonathan doesn't even know Crystal. They have never met!" said Ben.

"We met while we were hiking in the mountains," said Jonathan, looking at Ben and sitting down in the chair at the table. "I didn't know she was your sister. It is very complicated, but your mother is right. Once again I ran away from my problems instead of facing them. Now Crystal is very mad at me, and she has every right to be." He reached out and rubbed the top of Ben's puzzled head.

"I've been contemplating trying to get my mowing jobs back and staying in town here."

"That would be great!" said Ben. "He can stay here, Mom, can't he?"

Jonathan shook his head and looked toward the floor. "Ben, I'm afraid that would be very complicated."

"But then Crystal could see what a great guy you are!" added Amy. "Can he stay Mom?"

"Please, Mom!" added Ben.

Britany put up her hands. "You will have to address that question to your dad. I'm afraid he is the one who will need convincing."

Jonathan's countenance fell as he realized he still needed to face Michael. "Was he really angry?" he asked. Britany gave his shoulder a squeeze. "Yes, very, but I think he has also done some thinking. I'm just not sure what his thinking has discovered. Hang in there. God will help us get though this." Jonathan shrugged his shoulders. He was thinking how much easier it would be to leave.

Jonathan didn't have too long to contemplate what to say to Michael. The dog announced his arrival as they sat at the table. Michael came through the door with a curious look on his face. He came to the table with his hand outstretched. "Good to see you, Jonathan," he said jovially as he grasped his hand and shook it firmly.

"Hi, sir," said Jonathan as he rose from the table to acknowledge the greeting.

"I can see everyone is excited to see you. It's about time you came back," he said warmly.

"I came back to apologize, sir," he said meekly. "I was out of line. I didn't realize what I was doing, but I have discovered a lot about myself since then. I had a lot of mixed-up emotions that I have sorted through. I felt I needed to apologize to you and Britany before I could straighten some things out in my life."

Britany held her breath. She and Michael had discussed the situation many times, but she wasn't sure how he felt. She prayed silently as they talked.

Michael looked at Jonathan with a serious expression and the air was still with the ominous silence.

"It takes a lot of courage to apologize," Michael said sternly. "I accept your apology. I'm sure we have all learned a lot from this and can continue to learn from our mistakes. You are welcome to stay here if you need a place. We all enjoyed having you around and would like you to be part of our family again."

Jonathan appeared very solemn. Slowly a tear came to his eye, and then another one. He dropped to the chair and laid his head on the table. His body started to tremble. Britany put her arm across his shoulders. "It's all right, Jonathan. You are loved."

He shook his head and the tears continued to fall. "I just can't imagine how you can care for me the way you do and give me a second chance. I need to learn to love like that."

Michael sat beside him and waited until he regained his composure and looked up. "I must admit," he said in a soothing voice, "I was angry when you left and vowed you would never come back in this house again. God worked with me and helped me to see past my gut reaction to your confusion. We serve a great and wonderful God, and any love you find here comes from Him." Jonathan nodded.

Michael stood and said, "Let's go get your things. We may as well get you settled while Britany makes supper. I guess you will need to stay with Ben. Crystal is home and I'm sure she won't be too happy to give up her room." Then he looked around as if he were discovering something new. "I just thought about the fact that you haven't met Crystal yet," he said happily.

"Actually I have, sir," Jonathan said slowly.

Britany put her arm on Michael's shoulder and pointed to a chair. "I think you had better sit down, honey," she said as she started to explain the camping trip and how they had met, and Crystal's anger.

Michael laughed, "Who would have ever thought of something like that happening! I guess things might get a little uncomfortable around here for a while. Life should be interesting, that's all I can say!"

Britany went with Jonathan to the school on Monday to see what they needed to do before he could graduate. He was thrilled to find that he only had government and English to finish before he could get his diploma. Both were offered over the summer, and before they left he was signed up to start classes the following Tuesday.

He wanted to sing and shout as they left the building. "I can't believe it, Britany. This is just too good to be true! I can start school in the fall just as I had planned. I will have to apply and hope they accept me, but I have the money that my grandfather left me."

Jonathan ran into the house as soon as they arrived and lifted Ben off the ground. "I can graduate little brother!" he shouted. He turned to see Crystal standing at the bottom of the steps. She froze and gave him an icy glare. Then she turned and walked back up the steps.

Crystal had heard the commotion and left her studies to see what was going on. At the bottom of the steps she heard what Jonathan said. Her first impulse was to be thrilled with him, but the anger caught her and she quickly masked her enthusiasm. "He may be fooling the rest of the family, but he isn't going to hurt me again!" she thought.

"Don't let her ruin your enthusiasm. She's just being an ornery big sister," said Ben. She can get moody sometimes."

Jonathan shook his head sadly. "I really don't think of Crystal as my big sister!" he said. He looked to where she had disappeared behind closed doors. "I've been here four days so far, and she won't even talk to me. She won't look at me when we have our meals, and I'm sure she would spend more time with all of you if I weren't here. I don't know how much of this I can take. It hurts too much. I may need to find a place in town," he said with a faraway voice as he gazed up the steps.

"No," said Ben and grabbed his hand. "Come with me and we will tell Dad about your graduation. He should be home any minute. This is really exciting news!" Ben tugged on him until Jonathan finally gave up and followed.

Several days passed in which Crystal tried to avoid Jonathan, but he seemed too close as she sat in church. Amy sat between them, but she definitely felt his presence. She turned her attention to her mother setting beside her. Michael and Ben sat beside them.

The congregation sang a medley of praise choruses. Crystal's heart lifted with gladness as she relaxed and sang. During the song she turned to smile at Amy who was singing loudly beside her. When she turned her gaze fell on Jonathan. He was looking at her with his intense black eyes, and she felt as if they would bore right through her. She quickly looked away and tried to concentrate on the music again. The choruses slowed and the sermon began. During the sermon the pastor spoke of love and forgiveness and how they only come from God. Tears filled Crystal's eyes as she listened. Jonathan reached an arm around Amy and patted her on the back. She looked into his concerned eyes, and the tears fell even harder.

"Crystal, are you all right?" Amy asked. Britany looked up as she heard Amy. Tears were running down Crystal's cheeks.

Crystal wanted to speak and tell them she was all right, but the words wouldn't come, The pastor's words were touching her heart and she suddenly realized how hard she had been on Jonathan. She had been trying to protect herself; only she wasn't protecting herself. She was hurting herself and Jonathan by letting the anger and resentment crowd out any other feelings. She tried to take a deep breath as the last song was starting, but the air didn't seem to want to come.

Jonathan was worried. Tears were running down Crystal's face, and he didn't know why or what to do! She started to cry worse as she looked at him. Maybe it was too much for her to handle having to look at him every day and in church also. He couldn't help himself and reached out his hand to touch her. He wanted so badly to comfort her as he had done on the mountain!

He expected her to freeze as he touched her shoulder, but instead he felt her shudder. They stood as the rest of the congregation rose for the last song. Amy looked up at Jonathan and moved forward so he could be closer to Crystal. He slipped closer and put his arm around her shoulder. She looked up at him with tears running down her face.

"I've been so mean to you!" she said through the tears and in the midst of the singing. He drew her closer. "Please forgive me. Do you think we could start over and get to know each other again?" she asked.

Jonathan put both arms around her, and in the middle of the church, with singing all around them, he kissed her. Amy hugged them both as they stood there, and Britany and Michael smiled as they watched.

Jonathan felt as if he could fly on his own without the singing tree. He held Crystal close and thought of all the events that had led him to this moment! He realized down to the finest detail of Crystal's fall and him finding her that God had been leading the entire time. He looked up to see Britany smiling at him.

"I'm flying and the tree isn't singing!" he whispered to her. She winked back in understanding.

Britany looked at Michael, Ben, Amy, Andrew, Crystal and Jonathan, and thanked God for bringing them all together!

Printed in the United States
25529LVS00005B/28-81

9 781932 701586